I0736164

Love Matched

A SMARTYPANTS ROMANCE OUT OF THIS WORLD TITLE

LONDON LADIES EMBROIDERY

BOOK THREE

LANEY HATCHER

WWW.SMARTYPANTSROMANCE.COM

# Copyright

One

My dance partner was choking on a lemon rind.

Truthfully, I was unsure how these things kept happening to me. Despite being a well-liked young lady of two and twenty who hailed from a wealthy and respected family, I was perhaps the most hapless woman in London.

Eyes widening, I patted the viscount's back rather forcefully. It felt necessary. If news circulated that a gentleman succumbed after having recently danced with me, it would be most unfortunate. My reputation and sparkling personality could handle the goose attack on Charles last year and the mud puddle incident with Patrick Morley the previous spring, and even the champagne disaster with Lord Grant.

However, an association with Viscount Bunsen's death by citrus fruit—no matter how unintended—would undoubtedly lower my odds of finding a proper match this season.

And, of course, I did not want the man to choke to death. He seemed like a good sort.

With his brown eyes watering and my solid thwacks between his shoulder blades, Carlton Barrington—Lord Bunsen—finally managed to expel the lemon peel into his glass.

"Are you all right, my lord? Would you like some water?" My tone was earnest. I was truly concerned for his health. The viscount was a pleasant man. Twelve years my senior, Lord Bunsen was said to be on the hunt for a wife. I'd hoped our dance, subsequent conversation, and agreeable acquaintance this evening would lead to an eventual courtship before an eventual betrothal and then an even more eventual marriage.

I had a feeling, however, that the unfortunate drink garnish would seal my fate where Carlton Barrington was concerned.

He coughed once more before attempting to speak, and when that did not take, he cleared his throat. "No, my lady." Another forceful *ahem*. "I am quite well, I assure you."

"I'm so happy to hear that," I said with a smile, watching as Lord Bunsen pressed a hand awkwardly to his green patterned waistcoat, just above his sternum. "I was hoping we could continue our conversation and take a turn about the—"

"Apologies, Lady Cassandra," he interrupted without meeting my eyes. "I find I must take my leave."

"Oh," was the only reply I managed before the Viscount Bunsen was well on his way and out of earshot.

Sighing from my place on the edge of the dance floor, I smiled awkwardly and met the eyes of several curious attendees. Tonight's ball was at my family home, Dameron Hall. My birthday celebration was being hosted by my parents, George and Caroline Fields, the Earl and Countess of Crait.

Being the guest of honor at my own event might afford me some goodwill in terms of gossip, but it was unlikely. I could already see Belinda Whitmoore's lips flapping as she waved her fan and glanced my way in the stuffy ballroom. By tomorrow morning, news of Lord Bunsen's misfortune in my presence would be discussed and relayed as members of the *ton* broke their fast.

I pasted on a winning smile—directed pointedly at Miss Whitmoore—and turned to find my circle of friends. *Actual* friends. Ladies who would be more concerned over another lost prospect than my reign as the unluckiest lady in England. I knew where my friends would be. I'd drawn their attention earlier to the table along the back wall that would display the lemon tarts I was so fond of. And, sure enough, tucked away behind the pillars of candles and extravagant floral arrangements were my ladies and several of their husbands in attendance.

Before I could entirely push away my disappointment from the encounter with Lord Bunsen, I was approached by a tall gentleman.

"Lady Cassandra! Felicitations on your happy day," remarked Charles Langeford, Marquess Windthorpe.

"Thank you, my lord. I'm so pleased you were able to attend," I said. And I meant my words. Despite how things ended between Charles and myself—numerous goose bites in the middle of a proposal in Hyde Park—I had enjoyed our courtship and near engagement last season.

Charles beamed before happily indicating the woman at his side. "I wanted to introduce you to Lady Amelia Hampton. We're to be married next month. I do hope you'll attend the celebration. I feel as if I owe you so much."

I frowned inwardly at his phrasing. I was not sure what I had done to contribute to his betrothal to Lady Amelia—besides incite an animal attack that ended any hope of our own engagement. But outwardly I smiled and extended a delicate hand to the dark-haired woman on Windthorpe's arm. She smiled shyly and returned my greeting.

"Well, I look forward to the invitation. Congratulations on your betrothal. Please, enjoy yourself this evening. I am so happy you are both here." I held my smile firmly in place as we bowed and curtsied our farewells and parted ways.

I had every intention of continuing my progress across the ballroom toward Ashleigh and Eliza and the lemon tarts. But before I resumed my path through the crowd, I noticed Patrick Morley nearby, accompanied by Sophia Wells. She was a kind young lady from a wonderful family and I was pleased to see Morley in her company. I hadn't yet heard of their association through *ton* gossip, but it was early in the season. They would make a fine match, I was certain, and smiled at the thought.

During our brief and disastrous attempt at an outing this spring, Patrick had misstepped while descending his carriage. He'd landed in an enormous puddle, drenching us both in mud and other liquids too horrific to contemplate. The incident had ended our courtship before it had even begun. Morley had been too embarrassed to even make eye contact with me following his fall. I'd shrugged off the blunder and attempted levity, as I was wont to do. And when that hadn't done the trick, I'd said "Good day" and gone inside to change my skirts.

Seeing Morley here with Miss Wells sent an odd pang through my sternum. I wasn't jealous. Not really. I'd enjoyed my brief acquaintance with Patrick, but it was certainly no love match. I was glad he'd found happiness, even with someone else.

I did not begrudge others their futures simply because I had not wrangled my own as of yet. But I was growing weary of my misfortune. All these missed opportunities were starting to weigh upon me. I wanted all of the things respectable young ladies longed for—a husband, a family, and a household of my own. Currently, my future was a hazy, nondescript approximation lacking any defining details.

While at two and twenty I was not quite a spinster, I was starting my fifth season in London. I hadn't thought it would take quite so long. Nor could I understand the odd occurrences that seemed to plague my every encounter with the opposite gender.

Pushing aside any lingering inhospitable feelings, I started moving once more toward my friends before stopping altogether as something…or rather *someone* caught my attention.

There, at the edge of the ballroom, was that man! Impossibly tall with dark hair peeking out from beneath his wig, the liveried footman was unmistakable. It was the very same servant I'd recognized many times over in ballrooms and events all across Mayfair in the last year.

My eyes narrowed and I resumed my stride, only now with far more expediency and determination.

Why was that man here, in my family's home? He was not a servant of my father's. And as far as I knew, additional staff had not been hired for tonight's event. So, why did this antagonistic footman keep turning up like a bad halfpenny?

He hadn't yet seen my approach and continued serving a group of gentlemen from the tray held easily in his large hands.

I could not wait to confront him.

In our earliest encounters, he'd done nothing more than irritate me. Speaking beneath his breath, rolling his eyes at my over-the-top antics while in the company of my friends. Those actions from anyone, much less a hired footman, wouldn't have been notable in my day-to-day life. But this servant had made himself painfully memorable after serving a tray of champagne all over my companion at Lady Helm's soiree earlier in the year. I'd known it was him. And I'd known that those spilled drinks had been meant for me.

I could not say what I had done to antagonize this young man. He seemed perfectly capable of interacting with members of the *ton* and serving them refreshments. And yet when tasked with serving me, he could not muster up a polite word nor expression.

I'd never had anyone treat me thus. Men adored me, and I was friendly with young ladies my age. Matrons found me amusing and refreshing. But this sad excuse for a servant was unaccountably rude to me. Anyone else would have demanded the man be sacked for his behavior. But that simply was not my style.

I preferred to get even.

My maniacal glee must have been a noticeable beacon because the footman looked up, startled by my impending presence. But he recovered quickly and straightened before glancing hurriedly around. My smile widened. He had nowhere to go. This was my home. I would hunt him down if I had to.

I lengthened my stride, closing in on his location and registering a very tiny self-satisfied smirk turn up the corners of his lips.

But before I could do what I'd dreamed about when faced with this scenario —get my hands on him in order to strangle him—my father stepped directly into my path with my mother on his arm.

"Oof." My breath expelled as I made contact and rebounded off my father's wide chest.

"Cassandra, darling, are you all right? Where are you off to in such a hurry?" My father grasped my upper arms and steadied me, lest I stumble back and fall on the floor.

"Sorry, Papa. I saw someone I wished to speak with and was entirely distracted. Determination over good sense, I always say." I stood on tiptoes and risked a glance over my father's broad shoulders, knowing what I'd find.

No blasted footman.

He'd used the disruption to scurry away.

"Well, are you enjoying the ball, Cassandra?" My mother's kind voice brought my attention back to the Earl and Countess of Crait.

They were staring at me in concern. I was behaving oddly—even for me. "Yes, Mama," I assured her. "It has been a lovely event. Thank you for hosting such a wonderful celebration."

She and my father smiled, pleased with my words. I was indeed appreciative. I had a supportive and kind family. In all honesty, they were probably too indulgent. I got away with quite a lot.

And now I needed to escape and find this footman.

"Why don't you and Papa take to the dance floor? I find myself needing the ladies' retiring room," I said sweetly, glancing quickly beyond for any sign of his large form.

"That is a lovely idea, darling. George, lead the way." My mother placed her hand upon my father's arm as he smiled down at her with vivid green eyes—so much like my own—and led her toward the musicians and happily dancing couples.

I bustled over to the closest hallway leading from this side of the ballroom for I did not see the footman anywhere in the vicinity. He could not have gone far.

Undoubtedly blinded by foolhardy determination, I made my way as quietly as possible down the corridor, passing the ladies' retiring room. I turned the corner and moved in the direction of the kitchens. If he was retrieving more drinks, he would be going there. Before I could take off at a gallop, movement to my right caught my attention and had me pulling back suddenly. Edging carefully around the corner, I peered down the long corridor that would lead back to the front of the house.

Why would a supplementary servant for the ball tonight need to access our main living quarters? What was this stranger up to? And why did I feel the fierce need to follow him?

With my dress mostly hidden behind the wall, I peeked my head slowly around the corner once more and watched a flash of white wig pause briefly at the door to my father's study before going inside.

Keeping my movements as swift and as soundless as these ridiculous underskirts would allow, I followed the path the footman had taken and paused briefly to ascertain that the door to the study was locked with the stranger inside.

I smiled then.

What this interloper likely did not know was that I had been born and raised in this household. I'd played and explored and hidden from my nurses like any rambunctious child was wont to do.

Quietly moving to the library next door, I cast a quick glance over my shoulder making sure I hadn't been seen. Slipping easily into the dark room, I moved by feel to the heavy drapery in the corner. I removed my shoes and pressed forward on stocking feet. Shifting the fabric aside, I entered the cool darkness of the hidden passageway. With the light whispering around the edges of the curtains on the opposite end of the short corridor, I moved toward my target.

Generations ago, this hidden hallway had connected a nursery to a small bedchamber. As was typical of the time, the passage between rooms was convenient for a nurse or nanny. Somewhere along the way, one of my father's family members had seen fit to redecorate. And while the two rooms no longer resembled the originals, the connection between them had never been boarded up. As a child, I'd loved sneaking from the library to my father's study, the secret passage covered only by heavy draperies. And I was grateful for the design choice now.

Displacing just enough of the fabric to take in the room, I could not help but smile to myself once more. The study was lit with several candles upon my father's desktop. The fire in the grate gave off a fair amount of light as well. Papa had likely been in here before his presence had been required in the ballroom.

The remaining light made it easy enough to see the figure lying on his back beneath the desk. The chair had been pushed out of the way and a pair of exceedingly long—and firm-looking—legs were visible, thighs straining the seams of his dark velvet breeches. White stockings to the knee completed the look. His wig had been cast aside on the patterned rug along with his black jacket and white waistcoat.

I froze in my perusal as the man heaved a frustrated sigh. He repositioned slightly and shifted more of his upper body beneath the desk. The movement raised the disheveled hem of his shirt and brought into view a sliver of toned midsection and a rather intriguing line of hair just above the waistband of his breeches.

Shifting out of innocent curiosity, I nudged the drapery aside in order to lean forward. The stranger cursed softly from his hidden position and the sound was a reminder. He was not a statue in a museum to be admired. He was a liar and a potential thief.

Shaking myself out of my distraction, I focused on the facts.

This footman had abandoned his post in the ballroom and entered our private quarters without permission. And now the intruder was in his shirtsleeves beneath the desk fiddling with something. I could hear wood or perhaps metal scraping occasionally as his feet planted themselves and his knees bent slightly, as if bracing.

Well, I'd give him something to brace for.

"What do you think you are doing in here?" Whipping the deep red curtain aside, I stepped boldly into the study from my sneaky secret passageway.

The legs beneath the desk jolted. A loud crack echoed through the study followed by a muffled "Fuck" before the footman maneuvered his large frame from beneath the furniture.

I stepped smoothly around to the front of the desk and palmed the letter opener that lay upon the surface. While I was behaving recklessly and allowing my preoccupation with this mysterious man to drive me to make an undoubtedly rash decision, I could still be realistic. I'd placed myself in an unknown situation. It was better to be prepared and armed. So I held tight to the blade in my hand and kept distance between myself and the duplicitous servant.

He stared at me first in recognition and then in astonishment, glancing between the still-locked door and the interior corridor half hidden by the drapery. "How?" he questioned, voice trailing off.

"You should really be more careful when breaking and entering. And you probably should have left that wig on." I indicated the red lump quickly forming on his forehead above rather intense dark eyebrows. "It would have likely absorbed some of the blow."

The man's eyes narrowed.

Mine narrowed right back.

He didn't lunge for me or attempt escape. He simply watched me, as if I were a worthy opponent or a confusing new adversary.

"Are you going to tell me why you are in this room, uninvited? I'm fairly certain you are meant to be in the ballroom tonight."

The reminder of his position, and the inherent duties of serving myself and my guests, seemed to jar him out of his surprise at being caught. His expression hardened and, if I wasn't mistaken, regarded me with a fair amount of disgust.

Huh, that was different.

"Do you know who I am?" I asked, appraising his reaction. I wanted to confirm if he did indeed recognize me from all of our previous encounters. Did he recall the time he ignored me completely and served everyone else their drinks while I stood there like an idiot with an outstretched hand? Had he forgotten the time he'd "accidentally" upended an entire bottle's worth of champagne onto my dance partner, soaking my shoes and hem in the process? Or would he remember snorting a discreet laugh in my direction when I'd been conversing with my friends?

Did he single me out for his antics? Perhaps he antagonized many ladies across many ballrooms in Mayfair. I couldn't imagine he'd keep a position very long with those sorts of interactions. But when one was employed temporarily for special events that required additional service—as he so often seemed to be —perhaps he did not care about being sacked frequently for bad behavior.

I also could not say why the thought of this nefarious footman engaging in similar acts to annoy and provoke other young ladies made my eyes narrow, but they did.

However, the tall stranger misunderstood my question and seemed to interpret it in a haughty and self-important manner, for he rolled his dark blue eyes at me and said, "Yes, Your Highness. I know who you are."

I frowned at his tone. "That is not what I—"

"You are the belle of every ball." His voice changed and his accent became mockingly highborn. "A diamond of the first water. The most eligible and sought-after young lady in London."

"All right. That's enough," I said flatly.

His dark brows quirked. "You don't want me to go on? Sing your praises, Princess?"

I scowled. "That was not what I meant by that question." Lowering my voice to conspiratorial levels, I said, "I wanted to know if you recognized me from… all the other times…before."

He appeared puzzled. His brow furrowed and his rather distractingly full lips opened in confusion. "While I did hit my head on that rather solidly constructed desk, I did not suffer brain damage. Of course I recognize you. I just saw you in the ballroom. Honestly, Your Highness, you should be getting on back to your subjects. It is your celebration, after all."

I took in this infuriating man before me. His nearly black hair was disheveled, likely from being poorly concealed under a wig all evening. Standing loosely behind the desk, he hadn't made to approach me or escape through the open passageway nor the closed door. He held himself still. Perfectly poised and in control of this situation. One in which—by all accounts—I held every playing card. I could scream right now and have this man arrested and imprisoned. He'd clearly used his position tonight to attempt to steal valuables from our study. I didn't know what my father kept in his locked desk drawers nor whether they contained false bottoms for jewelry or money, but clearly this young footman assumed some sort of treasure awaited him.

And here we were, in a standoff. I didn't really know where we went from here. Of course, I wanted answers for his behavior. Not just tonight but in all our previous encounters. I was painfully curious, and as a person who generally got her way, I was seldom swayed when I put my mind to something. I'd followed an unknown person and was now locked away with him. At the risk of my safety and reputation, I'd pursued this blackguard all because he'd wounded my pride and proved to be a difficult puzzle to solve.

Ah, well. In for a penny, in for a pound.

"Why did you spill champagne on me and behave so rudely at all those other events? Why provoke me specifically?" I demanded.

He smiled then, and I took a step away as a result. For it wasn't until this moment that I felt the danger in the room. His unrepentant grin transformed his entire face. The hardness fell away and he looked impossibly young and so handsome that I nearly lost my breath. My heart beat a warning in my chest and warmth flooded my cheeks. But the danger lurked as this footman, this man—whoever he was—bit his bottom lip gently before replying, "I have no idea what in the hell you're talking about."

Frowning, I had to think back to the question I'd asked. So distracted I'd been by his wide smile and full lips, the even white teeth revealing themselves. But when I registered his continued denial of our shared history, I found my lost breath and glared at his smug expression. "You should not curse in front of a lady," I challenged. "That's twice now."

His features hardened at my words. Whether at the rebuke in my tone or the reminder of my station—there was no way to tell with this unreadable male.

Sweeping low, he reached for the discarded items on the floor. "Apologies, my lady. I find I am doubly improper this evening. For I should definitely not be so attired in front of a young woman such as yourself."

My eyes meandered from his white cravat, high on his neck, down to his aforementioned improper shirtsleeves. The firm planes of his chest stretched the fine lawn of the fabric before tapering to a slender waist and hips.

My eyes snapped up to his as he cleared his throat pointedly. "Could you turn so that I might re-dress?"

"Of course." My reaction and agreement were instinctual. Decades of well-bred manners and ladylike acquiescence fought for dominance and won. I turned quickly to afford the man privacy so he could don his waistcoat and jacket and presumably his wig, so that we might converse when he was more appropriately attired.

Speaking to the closed door of the study, I fingered the letter opener in my hand. "You know, I don't believe my father keeps any valuables in this room, if you are in need of... If you are in need. The desk likely only houses reports from his land agent and solicitor. Nothing of means. And nothing that would improve your wealth."

"I see," came the quiet reply amid the sounds of fabric brushing and perfunctory movement.

I glanced down at the pale green fabric of my gown while my stockinged feet peeked beneath the beaded hem. "I don't condone your efforts to steal from my family. But if you need help..." I took a deep breath while my gaze moved to the jewelry encircling my wrist. The gems caught the candlelight easily where they rested against my evening gloves. I wasn't actually going to reward this potential thief, was I? What was I thinking? Perhaps he had a sick family member in need of medical care. I could ask Eliza for help. Or maybe he had a father with gambling debts. Clearing my throat, I hedged, "Do you? Need help, that is?"

He didn't answer.

Actually, I could discern no sound from behind me.

Hand tightening on the letter opener, I spun quickly. A hurried glance showed I was alone. *Dammit.*

Lunging toward the open passage, I stopped abruptly when I noted a sudden chill in the room. The fire still burned merrily but the candles wavered from a strong breeze from the open window. The second-floor window that had not been open when I'd entered this room.

I rushed back, crossing the carpets and approaching the far side of the space. I stuck my head out in time to see the bright white of the wig atop his infuriating head reflect the full moon shining in the night sky. The once-again uniformed footman loped easily across our empty back garden while I watched.

He'd likely climbed the trellis and then dropped down the few feet into the hedges before making his escape.

After a frustrated exhale, I hissed loudly, "I could have had you arrested. You owe me, you know!"

The man slowed and turned to grin at me. Even from the distance, some yards away, I could see his wide smile. "And what could I possibly owe you, Your Highness?" He held his arms out wide as if to imply he simply had nothing of worth to offer in exchange for my silence.

"I don't know," I said, voice rough. "I haven't decided yet."

Grin still in place, he began walking backward, away from me and this unbelievable evening. "Well, you be sure to let me know once you've made your decision. But for now I think you should go back to your party, Princess."

Then he was gone, the darkness swallowing him and taking my answers along with him.

Two

Thomas Burke, the Viscount Blake, stirred his tea carefully.

Three rotations counterclockwise. And then one final swish in the opposite direction before finally placing his spoon on the saucer.

I observed my companion's ritualistic drink preparation despite having witnessed the display many times.

Thomas and I were having our monthly light luncheon and planning session for the Home for Incurable Children. We acted as our own self-appointed board of representatives for the volunteer and philanthropic work we were passionate about.

Several years ago, I'd asked my dear friend Eliza for advice on the best way to support the poor and destitute in London. My pervasive privilege and plentiful circumstances necessitated giving back to the community in some way. Despite my success and popularity among the *ton*, I'd never been a very good debutante. I felt compelled to do more with my abundant lifestyle than simply enjoy it. Eliza, a respected physician and valued member of society, had recommended focusing my efforts on children. Hospitals, orphanages, foundling homes, and private care facilities required more support than ever due to the government's reduction in funding for the impoverished.

So it was with a naïveté that I wasn't proud of that I set out to volunteer my time and energy for the Home for Incurable Children in Maida Vale two seasons ago. The establishment in Northwest London offered care to children for conditions requiring long-term assistance. Those children with epilepsy, rickets, and spina bifida were often difficult to treat in hospitals. The Home for Incurable Children took over until the children grew to be around sixteen years of age, at which time they returned to their families.

I'd met Thomas early on in my philanthropic efforts—when I hadn't known what I was getting into—and over the past few years a comfortable friendship was born. His younger brother, Paul, was a resident patient in the Home. Thomas was dedicated to Paul despite the rest of his family having written off the adolescent as something embarrassing and other. My friend had been desperate to raise awareness and funds for his brother's caregivers, having seen the continuous hardships these children faced.

While I enjoyed visiting the children once a week in Maida Vale, it was a constant battle within my heart. I had to fortify my emotions and present a friendly and jovial facade in order to lift their spirits and provide a brief respite from the unfairness of their conditions. Being faced with children in pain—children who would never be well—was overwhelming some days. But I swore to myself I would never let them see anything beyond the joy I felt to be in their lives.

I was quite sure the Home appreciated my efforts—the time I spent during visitation, the knitted caps and toys I brought for the children, and the monetary support my family offered. However, my strengths lay in utilizing my popularity, organizing donations, and raising awareness among my peers.

Thomas and I had combined our efforts to form our charitable organization of two. Over the years, we'd arranged many functions to bring support to the Home, and quite successfully. This was more than a pet project for the both of us. Our goals were aligned and we enjoyed each other's company. Where I was loud and opinionated, Thomas was quiet and thoughtful. We balanced each other nicely, and we made a fine team—facts we'd discussed in some detail.

It was enjoyable to have a male friend. While I had my circle of ladies and our regular meetings on Tuesday afternoons for embroidery and biscuits—mostly biscuits—it was fascinating to have Thomas in my life. I knew he valued my commitment to the Home and our efforts there. His friendship felt anchored in respect and our shared determination. He took me seriously in a world where I was often brushed aside. While my peers often saw a sparkling and engaging debutante, Thomas regarded me for more than just my accomplishments on the dance floor.

"Are you hosting the garden party next spring or shall I?" Thomas asked without looking up from his notes. His meticulously prepared tea sat half full on the low table before his slender frame, and only his brown hair was visible as he scratched along the parchment.

"I'll host the garden party. You're arranging the musicians for the upcoming musicale. My family will be happy to welcome attendees in the spring," I replied to the top of Thomas's head.

He nodded absently, before saying offhand, "And your friend, Miss Winstead, is still planning to volunteer her time regularly?"

After a quick sip of my own tea—stirred whichever direction I felt like—I confirmed, "Yes, Ashleigh decided after she accompanied me last month that she wanted to visit once per week on Thursday mornings."

"Good." Thomas made another jerky notation on his parchment before placing his pencil on the table and finally meeting my gaze. "Do you have any other business to discuss?"

I shook my head in the negative.

Thomas was organized and predictable. Although he was less than five years my senior, Thomas possessed an innate sense of responsibility and an extremely dry wit. One would assume the viscount was nearing eighty instead of seven and twenty.

"And are you betrothed yet?" he asked easily. Thomas inquired monthly about my marital status. His dedication to asking stemmed from the belief that I would certainly become affianced any day now. With the regular frequency at which I acquired suitors, he was convinced it was just a matter of time. But we had a plan in place should the seasons grow too long and myself along with them.

I appreciated his optimism, but my own was starting to wane.

I thought back momentarily to my birthday celebration less than a week ago and the unfortunate incident with Lord Bunsen and the lemon rind. I fought a sigh and smiled brightly instead. "No, Thomas. Not yet."

"What happened this time?" His straightforward question and the general air of expectation surrounding it proved that my efforts to find a husband were fairly cursed.

"Lord Bunsen nearly choked on a piece of fruit after we danced," I admitted. My maid, acting as a chaperone for the viscount's visit, made a surprised sound on the opposite side of the room before clearing her throat.

Thomas paused with his teacup partway to his thin mouth. "I see." His eyebrows didn't move, but I could tell they wanted to.

I fidgeted with the lace at my sleeve before tucking an errant red curl behind my ear. "And once he recovered, he bolted so quickly from my presence that he could have given Papa's thoroughbreds a challenging race."

After finally managing a sip from his cup, Thomas returned it to the saucer and regarded me. "Did you want him to stay? Did you truly have your heart set on a match with Bunsen?"

I frowned, considering. "No, not particularly."

Thomas nodded, as if he'd expected that answer. I wasn't sure how that made me feel. "Then it should be no great loss."

Ah, Thomas. Pragmatic as ever.

I swallowed, but said nothing. Despite having no particular affinity for Lord Bunsen, it still felt wrong to think of him so dismissively.

Perhaps to reassure me, Thomas's calm voice eventually said into the suddenly awkward silence, "It's only September. Still very early in the season, Cassandra. There is plenty of time."

"I know that," I replied automatically, voice overly loud.

Thomas flinched, and I fought to moderate my volume and my reaction. I wasn't worried about my chances per se. Rather, I was responsibly concerned. The years and the gentlemen filtered through my mind, and it had never been more obvious that quantity did not indicate quality. Because none of these men found anything of substance in me—nothing worth staying for. Outings with me had proved to be a trial. According to gossip, I was messy, dramatic, and attracted all the wrong sorts of unfortunate attention. And when you lived in London, gossip was enough. Gentlemen didn't see my desire for a family. They were overwhelmed by the spectacle and my reputation.

Men noticed my appearance. My very eager heart often went ignored.

An image of the dastardly footman appeared in my mind quite unexpectedly. He had seen nothing of substance in me either. The mysterious interloper didn't even appreciate my face or my figure. But to my mortal embarrassment, I'd noticed his. The wide smile that transformed his countenance. The fabric straining across his muscled chest and rounded shoulders. That intriguing expanse of firm midsection.

Forcing away the image of the thief—*the thief, Cassandra!*—I focused on my friend. Thomas didn't need to concern himself with my crisis.

"And there is, of course, our contingency plan should you grow weary of the spectacle of the season." Thomas's voice was soft, concerned. He'd made a concerted effort for me and I felt nothing but weak as a result.

I knew the plan he was referring to. In the beginning, I'd hardly considered it. After all, what woman wanted to rely on her male friend to facilitate a marriage of convenience should she reach spinster status and fail to find a husband on her own? It was something we'd discussed in great detail, and as was Thomas's way, in the manner of a business transaction. Detached and emotionless. A marriage, of all things!

Thomas had a complicated relationship with his family. He resented that his father, the marquess, had shoved Paul and his condition under the rug. Thomas wasn't even permitted to speak of his brother lest his mother become hysterical and his father irate. Then there was my friend's distaste for society functions and interacting with people in general. Thomas preferred to live his life in privacy and unencumbered by "ridiculous aristocratic demands." And there was also the simple fact that a traditional marriage to a woman would never make my friend happy. His proclivities were not permissible nor accepted, and were downright dangerous for him. If Thomas could not marry the gender he preferred, he'd decided that perhaps there was an alternative future that included us both.

He knew of the challenges I'd faced since my debut, and as one of my closest confidants, he felt that our circumstances could benefit one another. For quite a time the offer of marriage from Thomas had seemed like a distant and unlikely possibility. But with every failed courtship and every mishap came a tiny voice within that wondered if I might be better off settling down in companionship with my friend. He'd promised a family, as was expected for an heir. We could be content with one another, I was sure.

But amid the whispers and wonderings, some distant part of me questioned if there was not more to my future than settling for any suitable match or as a convenient bride for my friend.

Unlacing my anxious fingers, I pasted on what I hoped was a convincing smile and finally responded. "It is still very early in the season, indeed. You're absolutely right." With as much enthusiasm as I could muster, I concluded, "These bachelors are not yet ready for Lady Cassandra Fields."

Thomas's brows lowered in concern—the opposite of my intent. "Cassandra, I'm worried about you."

"Whatever for?" I laughed. "I assure you, I am not yet on the shelf. Perhaps when you inquire after a betrothal next month, I shall have happy news to share."

Swallowing away the tightness in my throat, I brought my lukewarm tea to my lips. There had been so many times when I'd thought my happiness was right there, waiting for me. Just within my grasp. I'd been prepared for all of my past courtships to come to fruition. I would have been happy to marry any one of those gentlemen. *They* had never been the problem.

It had always been me. I was the common factor—the troublesome woman, the unlucky victim of circumstances so far out of my control.

I was ready to meet my future, but I was losing faith in what it might look like.

❧

THOMAS TOOK his leave after confirming my upcoming visit to the Home for Incurable Children.

I needed a moment to gather myself after our oddly introspective luncheon, but my ladies were due for our Tuesday embroidery salon in under an hour. Despite my excitement to see and spend time with my friends, I felt rushed and off-balance.

Our cook, Mrs. Chapman, had been warned of the upcoming meeting here at Dameron Hall and had thoughtfully prepared all manner of delicious treats for our gathering.

Each of my guests were shown to the parlor on the main floor and I greeted them warmly. Eliza and I were seated together on the velvet settee.

"Where is Nicolas? Will he not be joining us this week?" I asked. Eliza's husband had happily joined our ranks last spring while attempting to woo my staid and practical friend. His charming determination to win Eliza and also learn to embroider had easily garnered our collective support. Eliza and Nicolas had finally found their way together and married earlier in the year. We were all happy for our friend. And Nicolas even continued to attend our weekly meetings as he was able.

"There is an extra rehearsal today. He replaced an actor unexpectedly, so they're getting the new performer settled," Eliza replied while carefully selecting sandwiches from the tray before her.

Mr. Nicolas Morgan had been a stage performer for years but had decided to try his hand as a playwright. His first show would be opening soon on the Strand, and we could hardly wait to attend the theater and support him in his efforts.

"Is Nicolas performing in the play as well as managing it?" my friend Ashleigh asked from her seated position on the adjacent armchair, embroidery already in hand. My Scottish friend was extremely talented with a needle and thread, and often more serious in her craft. The rest of us were mainly here for tea and treats.

"He was," Eliza confirmed after a sip from her teacup. "But the actor he discovered is more suited for the role, he decided. So Nicolas is stepping back and will simply be directing the production."

"That's admirable," Jane said decisively. She was pragmatic in nearly everything, but the tiniest bit starstruck when it came to Nicolas. It was actually quite adorable to witness. The nearly unflappable Jane, logical friend to all, found it exciting that one of our circle was married to a famous stage performer, soon-to-be a famous playwright.

"It is," Mary agreed with a nod, her blond ringlets bouncing near her temples. "It likely would have been much easier to continue on, this close to opening night. But Nicolas made the best decision for the success of the show and all the actors involved. I'm very much looking forward to seeing the production."

Hearty agreement filled the drawing room.

"Apologies for our tardiness!" Fiona called out as she walked through the doorway.

"Oh, tosh!" I rushed to assure her. "You missed nothing. Eliza hasn't even eaten all of the ham sandwiches yet."

"I say!" Eliza turned and scowled.

I gave her a wink and tilted my head discreetly to our newcomer. Eliza dropped her faux porcine offense and turned to watch Kathleen enter the room, trailing uncertainly behind Fiona, Duchess of Compton.

Kathleen was our newest member and also the nanny to the duchess's young children. After a fortuitous meeting between Fiona and Kathleen, the younger woman was brought to live and work at the Compton residence. But she wasn't just a trusted and valued employee in Fiona's household. Kathleen had become a friend as well. It was unorthodox, but Fiona felt proprietary over the girl and her well-being. She encouraged her attendance at our meetings and longed to see her forge new relationships. This was, however, the very first time Kathleen had agreed to attend an embroidery salon hosted outside the Compton home. I was doing my best to draw attention away from this fact.

Perhaps if we all responded normally and without notice or our typical brand of exuberance, then Kathleen would settle and be comfortable.

"Oh, Kathleen! You're here! You never join us when we're away from Fiona's," Jane fairly bellowed.

I closed my eyes and Eliza both sighed and laughed quietly at my side.

Kathleen ducked her head and hastened toward the chair seated near the fire and farthest from the rest of us, but Fiona slid onto the targeted upholstery smoothly.

As a result, Kathleen's gaze darted frantically for a moment before Mary smiled and patted the place beside her on the small floral-patterned sofa. "Come sit by me, Kathleen. I'm eager to see the progress you've made on your lap blanket."

The young woman swallowed visibly, but finally straightened her shoulders and approached our circle, joining Mary and fishing her sewing out of her bag.

I cast a sly glance at Fiona to find her staring resolutely at her embroidery hoop with a tiny smile upon her delicate face. My friend, the duchess, was the epitome of grace and competency. Always the mother hen, attempting to push us toward what was best for us—usually with equal parts caution and concern.

Finding friends who simply wanted you to be the happiest version of yourself was a rare thing indeed. Acquiring a roomful of them was my very great fortune.

While Mary and Kathleen conversed quietly over their sewing, I attempted to draw the others into conversation so that the focus wasn't entirely on our uncomfortable newcomer.

"I met with Thomas this morning about our upcoming fundraising efforts for the Home. Ashleigh, he was curious if you still planned to resume your visits in the next month or so."

"Aye," my friend confirmed, looking up momentarily from her work. With blue eyes bright and earnest, she said, "I'm eager to return. I've been knitting some wee caps to bring upon my next visit."

I smiled. "Wonderful! They will love that, and your time and thoughtful attention."

Ashleigh was often brutal in her honesty, but she had a wonderful way with children. The ailing youth as well as the staff at the Home had been surprised to meet someone so witty and strikingly beautiful. Her humor and heart were only matched by her gorgeous features and her fierce protective instincts. I loved her dearly, and I knew that those children would benefit from her regular presence in their lives, as we all did.

"I wanted to let you all know," Mary began, her smile hopeful and barely contained. I got a sour feeling in the pit of my stomach as she continued. "David is returning from the Continent soon. Mother plans to host an engagement ball. Actually, she is already planning it. But she and David's mother are both so thrilled. And we're all happy to have David back home. Perhaps he'll even see fit to marry while in London. I know his family is quite eager to see us settled."

I didn't dare meet Ashleigh's or Fiona's eyes as I listened to Mary's happy news.

Working to make my tone enthusiastic, I offered, "That's brilliant, Mary."

She smiled sweetly, eyes shining brightly on her lovely face.

Lady Mary Harris was one of the kindest and most well-regarded ladies of my acquaintance. A brilliant dancer and conversationalist, Mary was invited to nearly every event. She came from a wonderful and supportive family. She cared deeply and was a devoted friend.

And Lord David Shepard didn't deserve her at all.

They had been promised to one another practically since birth through close familial ties. Mary honored that agreement and their lifelong friendship by hoping and praying for her future wedding. Her fiancé showed nothing but disrespect as he gallivanted between locales, conducting himself poorly, neglecting his betrothed, and flirting with anything that breathed. He'd been featured consistently in the gossip rags and was even openly mocked in a recurring column in *The London Post*. His mistreatment of Mary went unnoticed by no one —save Mary Harris herself. Her devotion to a man so unworthy made nearly every woman in this room contemplate bodily harm to his person.

And lo and behold, an opportunity might have presented itself. For if he embarrassed my dear friend at her own betrothal ball, I'd be happy to relieve him of his bollocks and, in turn, his hurtful philandering ways.

At the very least, Lord David would be expected to attend his own ball. He and Mary hadn't been in the same room in nearly a year.

Following suit, the other ladies chimed in with their well-wishes and eager anticipation of Mary's upcoming celebration. We would all be in attendance to support our friend. And to keep very close watch on Lord David Shepard, the Marquess Tweedale.

I could see Eliza aggressively stabbing through the linen on her embroidery hoop while Ashleigh shoved another biscuit in her mouth—likely to prevent her speaking and cursing Mary's fiancé with enthusiastic Gaelic barbs. Fiona watched Mary with a sad expression on her face. The room descended into somewhat awkward silence—which was very unusual for our gatherings. Mary fidgeted uneasily with the fabric in her lap.

Well, we couldn't have that.

I clapped my hands together lightly and pasted on a brilliant smile. "Well, ladies, you may have missed it during my birthday celebration, but did you hear about Viscount Bunsen's duel?"

They all turned to face me wearing shocked expressions, gasping in surprise.

"He was very brave and showed great determination."

Fiona frowned at my assertion. "But who did he duel, Cassandra? I cannot imagine Lord Bunsen challenging anyone."

I quirked a theatrical brow and waited for just the right moment. "He faced off against a rather sour nemesis."

Ashleigh had stopped chewing and was listening intently. In fact, all sewing had paused while I relayed my dramatic story. Kathleen chose that moment to carefully raise her teacup to her lips.

"Lord Bunsen fought valiantly and prevailed in the end, but it was a near thing. I thought for certain that the lemon rind would best him as he choked on a drink garnish while we conversed last Friday evening."

The ladies began laughing, with poor Kathleen snorting and nearly dropping her teacup as a result.

Eliza chuckled, "Oh! Nicolas and I saw him bolting away from you with tears in his eyes. But we couldn't find you afterward to inquire as to why. I thought you'd trod all over his toes during your dance."

I started to defend my superior dancing skills but she continued unbothered.

"But Nicolas disagreed and said you'd likely wounded his masculine pride with your unrivaled wit and intelligence."

I nodded sagely. "Well, I did indeed wound his masculine pride by witnessing his near death by citrus. But I prefer Nicolas's suggestion, so I've declared him the winner. Also, Eliza, excellent job on landing such a wise and wonderful husband."

She grinned. "He is delightful, is he not?"

We all chimed in our agreement. And as the ladies continued their discussion about Nicolas Morgan and his many virtues, including his upcoming play, I met Fiona's knowing brown eyes and gave her a little wink.

Order had been restored to our Tuesday afternoon gathering. Nearly every meeting required a ridiculous Cassandra story. It was understood.

And if I felt an uncomfortable ache beneath my ribs, it did not matter in the slightest.

I took a deep breath and asked Jane to pass the tarts.

Three

In mid-September, more than a fortnight later, our group gathered once more. This time without Kathleen in attendance, and at the home of James and Rose Harris, the Earl and Countess of Huffleton.

Mary and Lord David's betrothal ball was in full swing, if slightly underattended. From what I could deduce, Lord David had failed to invite any of his acquaintances and close confidants. The guest list was made up of nearly all Mary's and her mother's friends.

Guests had enjoyed a fashionable supper in the formal dining hall. Course after course had been served, and Mary had helpfully arranged to have me seated beside Lord Benjamin Harding, the Marquess Renfield. He was a mysterious gentleman who'd been away in Greece for years. Whispers around town said the man had returned after a summons and subsequent quarrel with his father. Apparently now he was on the hunt for a wife. Mary had thoughtfully inquired after her mother's seating arrangements and placed me directly in the path of the dark-haired and brooding marquess.

Dinner had progressed nicely, and I'd drawn Renfield into reluctant conversation. I could tell he'd been unsure what to make of me, but as we'd reached the fish course, he'd seemed fairly interested in the topics I'd discussed. Perhaps after some friendly banter I would have secured a dance from the gentleman by the time dessert was brought around.

However, it was not meant to be. Lord Renfield suffered an unfortunate reaction to the fish in delicate white sauce and needed to excuse himself once his lips and ears swelled to thrice their normal size. With watering eyes, the marquess had bid me a good evening with hardly a backward glance.

Which was fine. To be expected.

I'd forced a bright smile and turned my conversational skills to the young ladies on my other side—Miss Ashleigh Winstead included—for the remainder of the meal.

Now, I found myself in the ballroom surrounded by Mary, Ashleigh, Fiona, Eliza, and Jane. Eliza's husband, Nicolas, was somewhere with Jane's husband, Quinton. Probably drinking brandy and smoking cigars or taking part in card games. All the entertaining things that women were not allowed to participate in at these events.

Nevertheless, it afforded us the opportunity to support Mary in feminine solidarity.

Lord David was in attendance after all. He'd sat stiffly beside Mary at supper, doing his best impersonation of a statue as opposed to an attentive fiancé. Currently he was flitting around the ballroom, greeting guests and absorbing well-wishes for a wedding he clearly did not want.

Mary looked painfully happy. Happy in that she wore a smile. Painful in how forced it appeared.

I was going to murder Lord David.

We were keeping up a steady stream of conversation to detract from the fact that Mary's betrothed was ignoring her handily and had not even once asked her to dance. I could feel my back teeth grind together every time I caught Mary tracking her wayward fiancé around the room.

A footman approached our circle with a serving tray of bite-sized cakes. The delicate morsels were beautifully decorated and I looked forward to stuffing at least three in my mouth.

Grateful for the interruption, I pasted on a flirty smile for the footman and reached for a treat. I'd planned to make a quip about his timely arrival, perhaps attempt to charm him out of multiple cakes. But the grin died a quick death as I finally took in his face.

Before I quite knew what I was doing, I growled an uncharacteristic, "You!"

Jane's recitation of facts surrounding engagement traditions and customs from the sixteenth century was suddenly cut off. I could feel all the eyes of my friends turn to me in surprise. It was typical of me to be outrageous with servants and staff. I never went further than causing a quick blush on a footman's cheek or a sudden laugh drawn from a surprised maid.

But the unexpected urgency and rudeness in my tone—gone completely unchecked—had stricken my friends speechless.

"Good evening, ladies," the thieving faux footman said, unperturbed. "Can I offer you anything this evening?" He proffered his tray of sweets as all eyes swerved dramatically his way. The man looked markedly different compared to a fortnight ago in my father's study. Dressed all in black—like all the servants here this evening—he appeared impossibly tall standing at the edge of our circle.

His voice was low and scandalous. He sounded like…like he was offering much, much more than tiny cakes.

I swallowed convulsively, my heart vibrating beneath my skin. I hadn't told anyone about my encounter with this man—not my parents and not my friends. The reality of my flesh-and-blood secret stood right in front of me.

"Aye, thank ye," Ashleigh said, breaking the awkward silence that had descended. She reached toward the serving tray as did Eliza and Jane.

Dark blue eyes alight, the ridiculous footman smiled easily at my friends before sliding me a fairly victorious look.

I narrowed my gaze and opened my mouth to demand, once again, that he explain himself. However, before I had the chance, Fiona reached for the silver tray and gasped suddenly, pulling back and clutching her side. I focused my attention on my friend.

"What's the matter?" I demanded, taking an involuntary step in her direction.

"Oh, it is nothing," the duchess assured us all with a convincing smile. I scrutinized her features. "I took a little tumble outside with the children this week. I'm just a bit tender, I'm afraid." She laughed lightly, and I noticed the skin around her mouth tighten. "And it looks like I've missed my chance for sweets."

I whipped my head around to see the blasted footman striding away from us, tray still in hand.

Turning back to Fiona, I smiled. "Fret not, my dear. I shall retrieve some for you."

She tracked the movement of the dark-haired servant before turning narrow eyes on me. "That's not necessary, Cassandra."

"It's no trouble," I assured her, already backing away, poised to follow. To pursue. To seek. To prevent any escape.

I heard confused murmurs and Fiona saying my name, but it was too late. I was already weaving my way through the crowd, gaze focused and intent on the man doing his damnedest to get away from me.

Trailing behind, I exited the ballroom into the wide entrance hall. Casting about, I spotted the runaway footman and gave chase. The vestibule was deserted at this hour. Everyone was in the ballroom, dancing and making merry.

Caring less than I should, I gathered my skirts and took flight. My long legs carried me across the entrance hall and directly behind the mystery man. My slippers announced my quick approach, but it was too late. I snatched the serving tray from his hand and grasped his very firm upper arm before dragging him into a nearby alcove.

The man easily outweighed me. He could have resisted and pulled away, shoved me down and cast me aside. But he did none of those things. Merely regarded me incredulously and allowed himself to be directed into a deep recess in the corner of the wide corridor.

I relinquished the nearly empty serving tray to a nearby table and took a brief glance over my shoulder before pulling the footman into the shadowed alcove behind me. The space was perhaps large enough for three people comfortably. However, my skirts were abundant and the man occupying the space was tall, with the broadest shoulders I'd ever seen. The fit was decidedly cozy.

My hands were damp inside my lace gloves.

I stared up, and he stared down expectantly. Once again, I belatedly realized my rash behavior. It was as if I'd been possessed by a reckless ghost and then woken up in this unbelievable situation with a strange man who was mysterious and achingly beautiful and smelled of warmth and spice. I would not exacerbate my recklessness by inhaling his delicious scent. And I definitely would not be reacting prematurely and speaking first. I'd given too much away already in my wild pursuit.

Let him make an idiot of himself. It was clearly his turn.

"Well," he drawled, "you have me here now. What shall you do with me?" The words were low, the same seductive tone he'd used when offering a tray full of sweets to a group of women.

My swallow was overly loud. "I demand to know what you are doing here."

"Well, Your Highness, you may not be familiar with the concept, but I am working. It's referred to as *employment*." His smirk was unforgiving.

My answering glare was incendiary. "That," I replied pointedly, "is not what I meant."

He simply stared, amused and giving nothing away, those captivating blue eyes fathomless and focused.

"Are you planning on stealing from Huffleton? Mary is my friend. Please do not make me have to turn you over to the authorities." My question had been assertive, voice strong. But by the end of my statement I'd turned pleading. I could hear my determination waver in the whispered edge of my request. And what was worse, I knew he could hear it too.

Brows lowering, he studied my face silently for a moment before visibly shaking himself and stepping away. However, there was no more space to be had. He merely backed deeper into the recess, the abrupt movement jostling a still-life painting of apples and grapes.

With a frustrated sigh, the footman scowled, making the slight divot in his chin appear deeper. "There is no reason for you to turn me over to anyone. Haven't you tortured enough men this evening already? You're persistently bloodthirsty, I'll give you that."

I frowned. "And what is that supposed to mean?"

He looked expectant. "The marquess with the fish lips?"

"How did you—"

"Although you haven't maimed anyone on the dance floor as of yet. This *has* been a mostly successful event for you. Only one damaged gentleman so far."

"Now wait a mo—"

"I suppose the night is still young." His grin was cheeky. "I do not reckon I'd qualify for an encounter with the famous Lady Cassandra. I'm definitely not in the market for a wife. But for all the rest of these dandies, perhaps it is worth it to suffer whatever misfortune befalls them with you if they are guaranteed to meet their future wife soon thereafter."

My mind halted dramatically as whatever quip I'd been prepared to impart refused to fall from my lips despite my mouth dropping open in a surprised O.

He stopped talking, jaw snapping shut audibly at whatever expression he saw on my face.

"What does that mean?" I prompted, voice glacial.

"Pardon?" he replied primly, reaching up to grasp the back of his neck with his black-gloved hand. His elbow bumped the painting once more and he lowered his arm with a curse.

"Explain."

The footman, looking increasingly uncomfortable, risked a glance around the edge of the patterned draperies held back at the entrance to our alcove. "We should not be here. I think it best—"

Stepping into his space and closing the remaining distance between us, I tilted my head up to maintain eye contact. The heat from his body was embarrassingly distracting, but I pushed the awareness aside and said evenly, "And I think it best if you told me exactly what you meant about the dandies who are guaranteed to find their future wife after suffering an encounter with me. Is that how you phrased it?"

Flinching back at my nearness, the man's gaze turned scrutinizing. His eyes trailed over my features, cataloguing and assessing. It felt disconcerting to be inspected so intensely. The footman's expression went from suspicious to confused before landing on reluctant understanding. With a resigned sigh, he finally questioned, "You really do not know?"

"Obviously not, if I am asking you," I bit out, growing cold at what I suspected was about to come out of his mouth.

Sighing, he eventually admitted, "There is a bit of legend—lore or gossip, I suppose—surrounding you and the gentleman you bestow your attention upon."

He paused as if awaiting recognition or perhaps feminine hysterics, but I made my expression even and unaffected, prompting him to continue.

"It's fairly common knowledge among the unmarried men of the *ton*, that if they have a misfortune or accident or mishap as a result of, um, interacting with you, then the next woman they meet—or perhaps dance with, I'm unsure of the specifics—will be the woman they are meant to marry."

My mind reeled, considering the unfortunate instances, the failed courtships, the damn geese attacks. Confusion gave way to speculation, before finally settling on painful clarity.

I was a means to an end. A stepping-stone. Common knowledge and a cautionary tale. A curse. Don't dance with Lady Cassandra unless you're ready to get married. Oh, not *to* her! Just manage to survive the encounter and your intended shall be appointed to you by destiny forthwith.

I could feel anger and disappointment and frustration welling within, but I refused to be embarrassed in front of this menace—this man who thought so little of me. His disdain I could wade through. His pity, however? That I would grind beneath my heel.

With a steadying breath, I shrouded my emotions, buried them behind a charming, elegant mask.

Later. Later I would feel the pain of this realization—however truthful it might be. I'd analyze and consider the ramifications for my future. At some point tonight, alone in my bedchamber, I would allow my feelings to manifest before I swallowed down the resentment and the hurt and moved on.

This...this gossip from a footman—it changed nothing. My life would continue. I would have suitors. Perhaps they would even be laughing at me behind my back. It mattered not.

Ignorance wasn't always bliss. Sometimes it was injustice.

Something must have slipped through the cracks in my facade because the man I'd practically abducted looked confused and worried.

I sighed.

The intelligent thing to do would be to excuse myself, pray no one noted my absence, and hope I never saw this enterprising footman ever again. I'd behaved recklessly tonight—again—but part of me could not regret it. For at least now I had this bit of truth to ponder. A truth I hadn't even realized existed. The reason why I was so popular among unmarried gentlemen. The motivation behind the dances and the sunny afternoon rides on horseback. The constant attention and the very different goals I had compared to the men who sought me. Well, I supposed our aims were one and the same. We both wanted marriage. They simply never intended to marry *me*.

I valued my reputation. I guarded my purity. I wanted what all young ladies were supposed to want. And I'd dedicated the past four seasons to acquiring it.

Show you're interested, Cassandra, but do not overreach. Be demure, but engaging. Make sure you listen attentively. No, gentlemen are not required to extend you the same courtesy. Compliment your companion. Engage men in thoughtful conversation about hunting and horses and hounds. Make yourself presentable. Maintain your figure and never indulge.

I'd been the good girl my whole life.

What had it ever gotten me?

I opened my mouth to correct my irresponsible behavior this evening and retreat to the ballroom, but what came out was, "I'm calling in my boon."

The worry and sympathy washed away from his expression—thank God. "What boon?"

I sniffed. "The one you owe me for allowing you to escape my family home after attempting to steal from us."

He rolled his eyes. "Allow me to escape? Is that what we're calling it?"

I raised a determined finger and tapped his sternum. "Yes, it is. Because we both know I could have screamed at the top of my very ladylike lungs and had you arrested at any point during our brief exchange."

Eyes narrowed distrustfully, he challenged, "Fine. What do you want?"

"One. I want to know your name. And two—"

"It's one boon, Princess. Not two."

"And two," I said, speaking over him, "I want to kiss you."

There it was. I'd said it. I'd barely even thought it. And yet it was true. I wanted to kiss him. He was a thief! But he was pleasing to look at. And I could reluctantly admit—to myself only—that I enjoyed this little game between us, whatever it was. No one ever talked to me the way he did. The snipes and jabs and complete disregard for my station. I liked the odd tension in our exchanges. And I wanted to know what his full bottom lip tasted like.

There was a vulnerability in admitting what you wanted—out loud and to the very source. My request was out there in the air between us, expanding and heating the tiny space.

To my immense relief, the faux footman did not immediately balk. He was surprised, to be sure. I could see it on his face, his indigo eyes wide and mouth parted in bewilderment. But he didn't appear disgusted by the prospect of my request, merely skeptical.

Although, he did not look particularly eager. My pride was such that I could admit—again, to myself alone—that I obviously found the man more attractive than he found me. In all of our brief exchanges he'd either regarded me as a very strange animal, necessitating he be cautious with sudden movements, or he'd turned his nose up at me outright. It was very clear he did not know what to make of me. And it was equally obvious that he did not respect nor like members of high society.

"Why?" His deep voice brought me out of my internal musings and the growing discomfort I felt.

I frowned. "Why what?"

"Why do you want to kiss me?" He scrutinized me, gaze firmly fixed.

"It's a boon. I don't need a reason," I replied in a manner I hoped was more coquettishly cheeky and less petulant schoolchild.

I could see his mind working. Considering options and ramifications. I only hoped he wasn't rejecting me entirely. After the news of my status among gentlemen of the *ton*, I wasn't quite ready to be dealt another dismissal.

And truthfully, his control was something to witness. Perhaps this complicated man was truly not attracted to me in the slightest. Maybe his curiosity didn't drive him to allow kisses from frighteningly direct women. I should end this painful staring contest and retreat before…

Just then, his blue eyes strayed to my mouth. And lingered.

My lips parted of their own volition and his gaze jumped back up while an encouraging flush painted the tops of his cheekbones.

Heartened by his seemingly involuntary slip, my answering smile was slow and celebratory.

Clearing his throat, the footman narrowed his eyes once more. "There are a dozen men in that ballroom who would gladly kiss you."

"I've kissed all of them already," I deadpanned.

He choked out, "What? Truly?"

"No, not really." I fought the urge to laugh at his scandalized tone before amending, "A few." Once he'd recovered his delicate sensibilities, I went on. "I've never actually kissed anyone. They've always kissed me."

He was quiet a moment, considering, but then finally spoke. "I want to know why me specifically. I'm a servant. Barely anyone of note in your world."

I interjected before he could continue this point any further than he needed to. "I'm not demanding you kiss me because you are a servant. I'm not ordering you to do anything. That wouldn't be… I wouldn't do that. Yes, it's a boon I'm calling in, but I would not force you if you opposed. Or have you sacked because you defied me. Let's be honest, you don't exactly treat me like a lady. So, if the answer is no, simply enunciate clearly and we'll be done here."

An uncomfortable silence passed while he regarded me once more. "Is this some twisted fantasy you have? Do you imagine we'll promenade in the park together and I'll tell you my favorite color is green?" He quickly looked away from my eyes before continuing, making his inflection overwhelmingly highborn and mocking. "Does the lady assume we'll join forces in an adventure and fight French spies? I am not a one-eyed duke and you are the furthest thing from an orphaned governess. There is no future here for whatever silly little ideas are floating through your head."

I could feel an embarrassed flush heating my skin. I hadn't asked for any of those things, hadn't even considered them. But knowing he had—and discarded them outright—made the painful ache of being dismissed return. Realities were often made more uncomfortable by pointing out that they were, in fact, real.

Bitterness rose swift and ugly then. Who was this man to be so circumspect and distrustful? I was not asking for a marriage proposal. All I'd wanted was a bloody kiss. Was that such a trial?

"You know, the nameless thief doth protest too much, methinks," I replied.

His eyes narrowed but his lips twitched. "Do not quote Shakespeare to me, Princess."

"And why not? I think you're trying very hard to convince the both of us that a little old kiss would be such a tragedy." He opened his mouth, but I pressed on with my theory—it having coalesced in the last few moments. "I wager you enjoy seeking me out. All this goading. You've provoked me for the better part of a year all over Mayfair. Why else would you approach me so blatantly? I think you like this little game we play or you would not have antagonized me tonight." I'd risen on the very tips of my toes to deliver my parting line and was close enough to feel his warmth and see the dark outer edge of his irises.

"Maybe," he breathed, the word heating the short distance between us, "I just liked your dress."

And then his gaze traveled leisurely. He took in the decorative feathers adorning my red curls before journeying to the slightly scandalous neckline of my gown. He stared too long at the deep red I should most definitely not be wearing as an unmarried young lady.

But I liked that he was looking. It was improper and outrageous, but I was exhilarated by it nonetheless. His labored breath. His intense focus. His hands fisted at his sides. All of that *meant* something. His body gave him away, making secrets impossible and pretense a distant daydream.

Thus far, I'd been the one giving too much away. I wanted him to look, I realized. I wanted him to want me—not as a means to an end or a stepping-stone to some grand destiny, cast aside after I'd served my purpose.

Gaze still locked on my bodice, he murmured, "My name is Alexander," before his eyes flicked up to mine once more.

Taking his sudden offering as agreement and acceptance, I closed the bare inches that separated us and pressed my lips to his. I feared he might remain passive, allowing the kiss to merely happen *to* him. But he reacted immediately, mouth parting. He was tentative at first, seeking entrance and awaiting my response. But once my tongue met his own, he grew bolder and so did I.

Opening to my invasion, he gasped a desperate breath that had me leaning in, pressing closer. My heart thrummed forcefully in my chest, marking time with its frantic beat.

Tilting my head, I used my teeth to pull gently on his lower lip. He released a groan that had me smiling before diving back in.

I craved this honest reaction from him. It was clearly instinctual, and that was what made it so meaningful. He'd questioned my request our entire time in this secluded alcove. We'd argued and bickered. But now...now he was reacting. I wanted to draw him out from behind the wall he'd built around himself. Turn the key and open the careful cage of his self-control.

I kissed him slow and deep—how I wanted to be kissed. None of the hurried, closed-mouth touches out of sight of a chaperone or hidden in a garden. But something completely forbidden and utterly passionate. I couldn't say where my courage came from, for I was neither adept nor expert at these types of kisses. I simply wanted and acted as a result.

And from the way Alexander's mouth moved over mine, he didn't seem to mind.

Footsteps, loud and quick, had me pulling slightly back. Our mouths were still touching, quivering with our panted breaths. The sound of hurried feet continued on, but I knew the spell had been broken. My time was up and our one kiss—and my favor—over.

I was slightly confused to find my hands curled around the lapels of Alexander's footman jacket, and when I glanced to the side I realized I was quite alone in my desperate embrace.

I gently extracted myself and lowered my heels to rest once more on the ground.

"Apologies for manhandling you," I whispered, still eyeing his fists clenched at his sides. "You could have touched me, you know."

Alexander straightened as voices permeated our little cocoon. But before he stepped around me and out into the main vestibule, he said in a low voice, "You're not mine to hold."

Four

Alone in the alcove, I pressed a steadying hand on the wall and took a deep breath.

That had been…intense, unexpected, dangerous, addictive.

Before my thoughts could obsess over what had transpired between Alexander and myself, I heard Mary's voice from nearby. Frowning, I peeked out and saw my friend through an open door in a corridor leading out of the large entryway. She and Lord David were in a tense standoff.

"This betrothal is a farce. You cannot actually think I'll marry you just because our families decided it before either of us were even old enough to walk. Come now, Mary. This has gone on long enough." The voice was clipped and mocking, edged with cruelty undeserved.

Mary's back was to me as she faced the man she'd always thought she'd wed. I could see her folding in on herself. "It's been years, David. Why would you choose now of all times—at our engagement ball—to inform me that you never planned to marry me?"

"Because I like my life the way it is, and I'm not willing to sacrifice it for you or my mother or anyone else. And honestly, I don't know how this is surprising to you," he scoffed. "I rarely return to London, and when I do, I hardly make you a priority. It's time you accepted that this marriage is never going to happen. Go back to your little party, Mary." David turned to continue his exit down the hallway.

I stepped toward Mary, intent on consoling her, but she moved quickly, following her fiancé.

"David, wait. Please."

He whirled around, patience suddenly gone, his eyes flashing a warning. I paused at the expression he wore. "Now, listen here," he gritted out, grabbing my friend around the arm, hand squeezing the delicate skin just above her gloves. "You are embarrassing yourself…"

Whatever else he said was drowned out by the blood rushing in my ears as I hurried forward, eager to come between them and remove Mary from this situation. But before I'd made it more than a handful of steps, a large form brushed by me.

Alexander's sudden looming presence startled Lord David enough that he released my friend. The footman placed a hand lightly at her elbow and guided her to stand behind him, placing himself squarely between the two of them.

I rushed forward and gathered Mary in my arms. "It's all right, darling," I murmured.

"And what is this? Your savior?" David looked amused but only for a moment. "If you know what's good for you, boy, you'll go back to the servants' quarters where you belong. This discussion does not concern you."

"It did not look like a discussion to me. You should leave. Before someone gets hurt." Alexander's voice was bored and unaffected, but his body was tensed. Fists balled and shoulders taut.

I shuffled a shivering Mary back a few paces. I could not truly see David engaging in fisticuffs, but it was better to be safe in situations like this. Men were unpredictable creatures, especially when their pride was at stake.

David's chin lifted and he replied with venom, "I'll make sure you're out of a job."

"You do what you must… And so will I."

The threat was implicit. Lord David looked so disgustingly offended that a servant would challenge him thus. Mouth twisted in an ugly sneer, he spat, "Then so be it."

I flinched away from the spectacle, but before David could lunge or raise his fist—as was his obvious intent—someone reached around from behind his back and grabbed his forearm. Twisting violently, the slight form—*dear God, Fiona*—brought David's arm around and pinned it behind his back in one smooth motion.

Mary and I both gasped in tandem while Alexander jolted in surprise. Fiona, the Duchess of Compton, was a petite mother of two. Slender and unassuming, the woman barely came to David's chin. She had approached soundlessly from the rear in the shadowed hallway and completely subdued an angry marquess.

What is going on?

"Lord David," Fiona said with another firm yank on the man's arm, the angle of which could not be comfortable, "I think it's time you take your leave. I'm releasing you now so that you may be on your way."

The Marquess Tweedale turned sharply once freed, bringing his arm around to cradle against his chest. His anger died a quick and useless death upon viewing his tiny vanquisher. "Your Grace?" David was utterly confused and shocked.

I could honestly say this was the one occurrence in which we shared something in common.

"Indeed," Fiona confirmed. "Now, off with you."

Cheeks flushed with obvious embarrassment, Tweedale cast one more incredulous look at the duchess before scurrying down the corridor, away from the ball, the sounds of the musicians, and whatever had just happened before our very eyes.

Once he'd departed, Fiona placed a hand against her side, a spot high on her ribs, and grimaced. The moment passed in the blink of an eye but Alexander stepped forward. "Are you all right?"

Fiona straightened easily—so easily I might not have even remembered that she was in pain. She'd clutched the area earlier in the evening when she'd reached for Alexander's serving tray.

What in the world is Fiona involved in?

Finally, she looked to Alexander and smiled. "Yes, I'm quite well." A quick glance to Mary and myself before she turned back to the footman. "Thank you for assisting. I think we shall take Lady Mary and escort her to her private quarters."

The words were kind, but the dismissal was clear. Alexander executed a short bow before saying, "Of course, Your Grace." He turned and passed by me without a backward glance. Making for the exit, he returned to the vestibule and, I assumed, the ballroom beyond.

I gently led Mary over to Fiona. "You go on ahead. I'll be up shortly, and I'll bring reinforcements."

Despite Fiona's short stature, she expertly gathered Mary about the shoulders and nodded before directing the younger woman toward the family wing.

I allowed myself a brief moment to settle my nerves. Tugging my gloves higher on my arms, I looked down to make sure my appearance was orderly before returning to the ballroom. I supposed it was a good thing that Alexander had kept his hands to himself. I didn't know how I would have explained a disheveled coiffure or clothing askew. I'd exited the alcove on instinct and hadn't taken the time to put myself back together. Luckily, there had been no assembly required.

Moving cautiously through the crowded space, I spied my circle of friends across the ballroom and made my way there. Eliza, Jane, and Ashleigh did not question me when I told them we were needed in Mary's chambers. Nicolas assured me that he and Quinton and Compton could entertain themselves for the evening and they'd be waiting when our affairs were settled and Lady Mary was feeling better. I smiled gratefully before subtly scanning the space.

Alexander was nowhere in sight.

Before exiting the ballroom with my ladies, I stopped a nearby footman with my request. And then together we navigated toward Fiona and Mary on the second floor.

I briefly detailed what had happened and the scene I'd overheard—leaving out several tidbits including what I was doing in the vestibule beforehand, who I was with, and Fiona's actions—ensuring Mary would not need to rehash events upon our arrival. She was likely upset enough.

"I cannae believe he said those things," Ashleigh fumed. "On tonight of all nights. What a selfish arse."

"I know," I agreed. "I wish terribly that Mary did not have to suffer through this."

Tonight would not be for analyzing the situation nor looking for a solution. She could manage her emotions tomorrow. Here and now, surrounded by her friends, Lady Mary should commiserate. We'd provide a safe place for her to land. She could cry or rage, and we would do our utmost to provide solace.

Sometimes you could not explain away the bad behavior of others. You simply had to endure it. But Mary would not endure this alone.

The door to Mary's rooms was slightly ajar. In a jumble of skirts, we pushed our way inside. Fiona and Mary were seated near the fire in a spacious parlor. The lamps were burning and cast the room in a golden glow. The doorway to Mary's bedchamber was open, the fire lit within. The duchess's soft voice broke off as we entered and seated ourselves.

Moments later, before any words were spoken, a footman knocked gently and entered with a large, overflowing tray. I thanked the young man and assured him that we could manage the service ourselves.

The ladies all stared at the glasses and bottles of champagne I'd requested be sent up.

I eyed Mary as she stared woodenly forward. "I thought the night ahead called for something a little stronger than tea."

Her nod was small in response before she reached over, liberating a full glass from the low table. "You're right." She continued nodding. "Shouldn't let it go to waste." Before the crystal touched her lips, she paused. "We should have a toast, I think. It is customary, after all." Her gaze moved to each of us in turn before she spoke. "To my friends. Thank you all for being here tonight."

We all quickly grabbed and filled the remaining glasses and joined in, crystal chiming merrily. The sound was in direct opposition to the events of the evening and the prevailing mood of the room.

Well, we couldn't have that.

Swallowing the excellent vintage, I cleared my throat. "To Lady Mary…who looks utterly breathtaking in her ensemble this evening." My friend smiled weakly, absently smoothing the fabric of her pale blue gown. "I believe I saw Lord Ramsey trip over a floral arrangement when you walked by."

The ladies chuckled.

Another swallow of wine.

"I picked out those flower arrangements." Mary's quiet voice drew our attention. "I selected flowers that had meaning. Purity and prosperity. Happiness and health. Because I— I— I thought it meant something." She took another long swallow from her flute. "I thought it mattered."

Ashleigh's concerned gaze met mine, but I shook my head.

Mary continued, voice rising. "But he didn't care about the flowers. He didn't care about my gown. Nor the desserts. The guest list. Or my very existence!" Her breaths came fast as her jaw clenched. Anger radiated, but her eyes remained dry. She took another gulp, finishing the glass and reaching for an open bottle.

Instead of refilling her empty flute, she took another drink straight from the source. Jane's eyes widened but Ashleigh nodded approvingly.

"So, here is to Lord David Shepard, the Marquess of Tweedale," Mary said, raising her bottle in the air. "He always chewed with his mouth open. Thank God I will not be dining across from him for the rest of my life." She took a healthy swig from her bottle and then hiccupped adorably. Mary started laughing then. The laugh of the inebriated and perhaps the considerably overwhelmed.

We drank along with her, our hesitant laughter mingling in.

"Oh! And he smelled like onions!" Mary laughed again. "Inexplicably! I was always worried that when we married I'd smell of onions as well."

I smiled at my friend as she swallowed more wine. Taking up her mantle, I announced, "To Lord David! His head is abnormally large. Mary, I was honestly worried for your future childbearing." We all drank as Mary dissolved into fitful laughter.

I met Eliza's astonished gaze and raised my eyebrows meaningfully.

"Oh!" she exclaimed. "To Lord David. He always mispronounced 'supposedly' as 'supposably.'"

Ashleigh shuddered. "Aye, that's true! Horrifying."

More giggles rang out, Mary's the loudest as she nodded emphatically.

"I have one!" Jane declared. "To Lord David. He was terribly affectionate with his hounds. No one should allow that much dog tongue to enter their mouth."

Mary howled as Jane continued discussing the possible transference of illnesses between animals and humans while Eliza chimed in with her professional opinion.

Ashleigh contributed next and we continued toasting Lord David for the next half hour. Until a quite drunken Mary fell asleep heavily against Fiona's side.

As the giggling tapered off and Mary snored quietly from her slouched position, I raised my glass one final time before we tucked in our friend and disbanded to our respective homes. "To Lord David. May his regrets be as deep as the ocean. May they swallow him like the tide."

Five

The following Wednesday, I found myself at my weekly visit to the Home for Incurable Children. Fiona had canceled our regular Tuesday embroidery salon. She'd indicated in her letter that she wished to give Mary some time before we converged on her once more. But after the events of the engagement ball, I was not so sure.

I wondered if Fiona was still injured, and what could have possibly caused the soreness in her side. I did not believe for one moment that she sustained a fall while playing with her children. Not after having seen her graceful violence against Lord David. Something was afoot in the Compton household. But it was not my place to demand it of the duchess. I hoped she'd confide in me, but I would not force her. Yet.

Thomas joined me this morning and we planned to visit every child and adolescent in the east wing. I had knitted garments to deliver and prepared entertaining stories to tell. This was the most difficult yet most rewarding aspect of my life. Learning to smile in the face of such heartbreaking suffering was a great effort that often had me expressing my emotions on the carriage ride home when I could not allow them to show on my face within a patient's room.

"Beatrice, darling, you look radiant today." I smiled at the twelve-year-old child who suffered from a general weakness in her limbs. Some days she was unable to raise her head from the pillow. Walking was oftentimes too tiring and she spent most of her life abed.

Today seemed to be a good day, as she was propped up and braiding the hair of the doll I'd brought for Yuletide last year.

Her sweet face and excited greeting touched my heart. But when I felt my throat constrict with emotion, I forced a smile instead. "Doesn't she look positively aglow, Lord Blake?"

"Indeed, she does, Lady Cassandra. Why, if only I could dance without treading upon her dainty toes, I would be inclined to waltz right down the halls with her." This was the only time Thomas allowed himself to be fanciful and silly. He knew how important it was to keep up the spirits of the children here. It was why he attended to his brother Paul nearly every day.

Beatrice giggled and I felt the threat of emotion tugging insistently behind my eyes, but I didn't allow anything beyond a conspiratorial smile to appear. "It's true, Bea, dear. Lord Blake is an unfortunate dancer. Something about the music makes his feet confuse themselves. If even a fiddle is playing on the street corner, he'll occasionally stumble his way down the sidewalk."

The girl laughed again.

We stayed for another quarter of an hour while I offered to plait her dark hair to match her doll. Thomas read to her from a children's storybook he'd brought for our visit today. And just as we were leaving, her mother arrived to share the girl's luncheon.

Our rounds continued for another few hours. Several siblings and parents and extended family members were present to call upon the Home's ailing residents as well. We provided friendly smiles and comforts to many guests as well as patients. I brought a delivery of warm socks that Ashleigh and I had knitted, perfect for these chilly evenings in drafty hospital quarters. A hamper of muffins for the staff baked by our longtime cook, Mrs. Chapman, had rounded out the afternoon.

The sun was working its way across the sky on this mild day as I returned home from Northwest London with my chaperone. Mrs. Ridley acted as my escort when necessary. She was the widowed sister of our cook, and proved to be the best sort of companion. We shared a love of romance novels, and when Mrs. Ridley was not reading or discussing books, she was nearly always sleeping.

As she was doing now, snoring soundly in the carriage on our journey back to Dameron Hall. The conveyance slowed before the horses clopped to a stop altogether, and Mrs. Ridley jostled slightly before resettling unaffected.

Peeking out the window, I spied an overturned cart. The delay reminded me that I'd forgone a midday meal in favor of extending my stay at the Home. My stomach rumbled plaintively as my early breakfast was nothing more than a distant memory.

Eventually our coachman pulled off and took an alternate route down Baker Street. I continued gazing from within the carriage, taking in the unusual course. The avenue was fairly busy with foot traffic, tradesmen and working class alike. Brick and stone buildings lined the narrow street. I noted several shops: a solicitor's office, a grocer, a cigar and pipe emporium, two pubs, and finally the Baker Street Coffee House just ahead on the corner.

The charming corner storefront would do nicely, I decided spontaneously.

Rapping sharply on the roof of the carriage, I waited as our coachman pulled to the side of the lane. In the time it took Landers to climb down from the box and open the door, I'd pulled on my shawl and gathered my reticule while also ensuring that Mrs. Ridley was still sleeping like a babe.

"My lady," Landers sighed.

I smiled brightly and held out my hand. "Thank you, Landers."

Forced to assist me in descending the conveyance, the coachman looked pained as he pleaded, "Lady Cassandra, it would not be appropriate to stop here for a bit of shopping." With a quick glance at the elderly woman asleep on the green velvet bench, he amended, "Especially with Mrs. Ridley indisposed."

I stepped easily over the muddy wheel tracks and alighted on the cobblestone walk. "Well, lucky for you, my good man. I do not wish to shop today." The middle-aged coachman did not appear relieved. "I am feeling quite faint after spending the whole morning and part of the afternoon in Maida Vale with no luncheon nor tea. I thought I might stop for a bit of light repast at this rather appealing establishment."

I indicated the Baker Street Coffee House. A short staircase led from the main throughway up to a narrow, three-level brick building with a green awning. The sign hung from a corner post, hand-lettered blocks save for the *B* which finished in a scripted flourish and a long tail that swooped prettily and underlined all the letters.

Landers regarded the restaurant before aiming a concerned frown my way. "'Tis not appropriate for you to dine unaccompanied, my lady."

"I know. But I do promise to be very quick indeed. And look, there are several empty tables near the glass. It is but a slow afternoon and I'm sure they have an excellent and discreet staff available for a lady such as myself."

And by that, I, of course, meant a troublemaking rule breaker, but a genteel lady nonetheless.

Landers inhaled deeply in preparation for arguing, but I smiled, confident nearly all my teeth were showing, and forged ahead. "Do look after Mrs. Ridley for me! I'll be back quicker than two shakes of a lamb's tail."

And with that sorted, I bustled determinedly toward the stairs. I pushed open the wooden door and noted the delicate tinkling of a bell above. The space was warm and bright from the large windows on either side of the front door.

I had been correct in my assessment of the restaurant's occupancy. There was a well-dressed woman and a professional-looking gentleman at a small table within the interior. Another man dined alone in the back near the open doorway —likely the entrance to the kitchen and storage area. But the remaining tables, approximately twelve in total, including those visible from the street, were unoccupied.

Wandering away from the windows and to a central table, I took in the warm and earthy scents of the Baker Street Coffee House. A board on the wall displayed a menu including olives stuffed with anchovies, fried eels, entrées of mutton cutlets and tomato sauce, wild duck, fish and vegetable curries, and deviled sardines on toast. Despite the name of the establishment, there was more than coffee to be found.

Placing my reticule in my lap, I settled easily in the wooden chair. Everything about this establishment was comforting, from the framed calico prints on the wall to the elaborately patterned draperies. I felt welcomed and utterly at ease.

That was until Alexander, the nefarious footman, stepped through the rear doorway.

I stiffened in my chair, knowing he'd look up any moment and see me. Undoubtedly the tinkling of the bell over the main entrance had announced the arrival of a new customer. And judging from his appearance from the back of the restaurant, my assumption was that Alexander was an employee of the coffee house and was on his way to serve me. Dressed simply in a white shirt buttoned to the throat and a fitted black waistcoat, the man approached.

Finally, the inevitable happened. Alexander's head rose and his shocked eyes collided with mine. Truthfully, it was an impact. His feet stopped involuntarily upon spying me and he nearly stumbled.

Very interesting.

What a mystery this man was.

Alexander regained his composure and approached warily. With a discreet glance at the three other patrons, he swallowed visibly before narrowing his eyes in my direction. "You just keep turning up."

I smiled—over my shock—and was now dangerously curious. "I believe it is you I keep finding in unexpected places."

My reference could have been about any one of the events I'd attended where Alexander had acted as a footman. Ballrooms all across central London. But also in my father's study and in a corridor, protecting my friend.

I'd tried not to think about the kiss we'd shared. Too much introspection on something wild and reckless nearly always led to rationalizing bad behavior. I'd acted carelessly. My hasty decision to hide in an alcove and demand a kiss from a servant had been the height of irresponsibility. But if I allowed myself to consider the feel of Alexander's surprisingly soft lips and the slight scrape of his stubbled chin, I would start to justify what I'd done.

And then I'd try to figure out a way to do it again.

That slope was indeed slippery. And I lacked appropriate footwear.

"Is this your alternate place of business?" I inquired mildly.

Alexander's stare had not abated. It seemed my unexpected appearance had disturbed the natural order of things, and he'd yet to recover. "Yes, I am employed here."

His accent was different. Not the lowborn "my lady" he affected for ballroom service, and not the mocking high-society intonation I'd heard in my father's study. Was this his true voice?

Alexander swallowed visibly and the movement brought my attention to his throat. Without the cravat that I typically saw him wearing, I could now note a scar along his jaw. It was slightly ragged and uneven, beginning near his ear before extending down into the high collar of his shirt.

I fought to keep my expression even despite the disquieting sight. The former injury wasn't unsightly nor anything as simple as vanity. My uneasiness came from the knowledge that someone had likely attempted violence upon Alexander. From the look of the wound, years ago someone had very well tried to slit his throat. The mysteries surrounding this man were boundless.

Smiling brightly, I offered, "Well, this establishment is quite charming. I was traveling by and decided it would be an ideal place to have a late luncheon."

Frown in position and going absolutely nowhere, Alexander sniped, "I don't know that this is really the best place for…someone like you."

I frowned at the implication. I recalled that he seemed opposed to those sorts of reminders as well. I deduced his words were an attempt to place distance between us once more. Did he truly believe I'd followed him here? Or that I would announce to our meager audience that we'd shared an intimate moment less than a week ago?

I fought the urge to roll my eyes, and replied simply to be contrary. "Perhaps this will become my new favorite eatery in town. I could foresee weekly luncheons. Mayhap I'll have my friends join me for an outing."

Alexander grimaced. "Please do not return with your legion of admirers. The spice and flavors would undoubtedly overwhelm your delicate English suitors. I would hate to witness yet another grown man suffering by association."

Well.

I did not wish to admit that Earl Hansen had indeed fallen victim to a spice-laden delicacy at Lady Vega's masquerade two autumns ago while in my unfortunate presence. Our acquaintance had ended with his watering eyes and a "Farewell" forced through a painful-sounding wheeze. I supposed it had all worked out neatly because Lord Hansen seemed quite besotted with his new countess the last time I saw them.

I huffed a humorless laugh and dropped my gaze to the scarred tabletop.

The reminder of my unlucky nature caused a painful twinge. I did not wish to discuss my suitors with this footman-turned-restaurant-employee. Our last conversation on the topic had revealed the painful truth behind my continued failure on the marriage mart.

There was nothing I could do about how I was perceived by others. Alexander clearly thought me a fool. And the gentlemen of my acquaintance saw me as no more than a means to an end. These new truths, however painful, were still there. I could control none of that, so it was useless to worry over it.

Nevertheless, his words now struck true and sharp.

I feared I had not hidden my reaction in time, for Alexander cleared his throat, drawing my attention. With his brows relaxing, his frown loosened and he said, "I'm— I should not have said that." Those dark blue eyes appeared apologetic, likely as repentant as they were capable of…for someone like me.

I waved away his near apology with a shake of my head and a close-lipped smile.

Meanwhile, the man and woman who had been dining upon my arrival stood and exited the Baker Street Coffee House. Alexander and I watched their departure, the tiny bell above the door announcing their exit into the stilted silence.

With a quick glance back toward the only remaining patron, Alexander pulled out the chair opposite me and folded his large body onto it. Speaking so low I had to lean forward, he said, "I should not have said that about your suitors."

"But you're not sorry, are you?" I accused.

He continued without answering my question. "I am not sure why you are here. Our interactions have been such that I'm afraid I am incapable of polite servitude despite it being suddenly required."

"I'm not here to threaten you. I assure you, my arrival on Baker Street was entirely coincidental. Truly, I came in to enjoy a meal." The man still appeared skeptical, so I teased, "My intentions were honorable…mostly."

At the mention of honor and intent, Alexander's eyes strayed briefly to my lips. I licked them involuntarily at the attention before his eyes snapped up to mine once more.

Without giving him the chance to argue or order me away, I said, "May I please have the vegetable curry?" Perhaps if he saw the truth of my words, he would be less uncertain regarding my presence here. Although I was beginning to expect that distrustful was his standard behavior.

He eyed me for a moment longer before offering a brief nod and standing to retreat to the staff area through the rear doorway.

While awaiting my meal, I studied the colorful prints and decorations from my seat. The colors and patterns of the wall hangings and draperies spoke of foreign origins. I enjoyed the warmth and the comfort of the space. I wasn't simply teasing Alexander. I would truly like to return with my friends. Ashleigh would love it here, I had no doubt.

But perhaps my presence and that of other ladies such as myself would not be welcome. Whether from our kiss or my knowledge of Alexander's dubious employment as a roaming footman, he was clearly disturbed by my continued presence in his life.

The only remaining customer eventually folded up his paper and took his leave. Then I was alone.

Moments later, Alexander stepped through the archway with a dish in hand. With an unreadable expression and a brief pause, he placed my meal on the scarred wooden tabletop.

I made a decision—undoubtedly ill-advised—and said, "Would you care to join me? It seems we are alone for the moment, and I find myself in need of company."

Alexander swallowed hard before glancing toward the doorway at the back of the restaurant.

"Only if you would like to. I don't wish to cause you any trouble with your employer," I rushed to assure him.

He turned back and gave a short nod. "Business is slow today. I can spare a moment."

In a decidedly unladylike maneuver, I took my heeled boot and nudged the chair he'd occupied earlier out and away from the table, indicating he should sit. For whatever reason, my response eased the line of his shoulder and softened his hard jaw. I was beginning to suspect that any reminder of my genteel status was irritating for Alexander. He didn't seem to like highborn ladies very much. And so I would try to restrict my natural inclinations. The fewer reminders of my station, the better.

Alexander eventually lowered himself to join me.

The curry smelled wonderful, moderately spiced, the steam leaving the surface and warming the air. Alexander placed down cutlery I hadn't noticed and a linen napkin for me as well.

"This looks wonderful. Thank you. Do you cook as well?" I made my tone mild, forcing my innate curiosity to recede.

"No, I'm afraid my talents do not extend to the kitchen."

I raised an accusing brow at that. I wagered the man before me had many talents, and I doubted they could all be seen with the naked eye.

"Mr. Patel does the cooking and baking," Alexander finally answered. "He's the owner. Along with his daughter."

"I see." I spooned up some of the rich golden sauce and blew on the surface to dispel the heat. When I glanced back to Alexander, I noticed his gaze lingering on my lips.

After a quick bite—delicious and flavorful—I inquired, "How long have you worked here?"

Shaking himself slightly and focusing on the tabletop, he said, "Is this an interrogation, then?"

"Not at all. Just polite conversation." I smiled. "You can ask me questions if you want. I am an open book."

His expression turned thoughtful. "I don't believe that for a second. Honesty cannot be so easily won."

Well, that was a telling statement.

Unfazed, I replied, "Perhaps not. But it can be earned."

His gaze was scrutinizing. "And I have earned your trust, have I?"

Our conversation had taken a turn from all the others before it. Alexander was not questioning me for sport. There was no stimulating banter nor amused exasperation. He hadn't addressed me as *Your Highness* once. Something had changed. I didn't know if this was due to our setting. We were very clearly in *his* territory. I was the one intruding unexpectedly here. Or perhaps something had shifted since we'd shared a kiss in the alcove outside Mary's ballroom. I couldn't say the reason.

But while this new interaction seemed serious in a way that attempted thievery had not, I didn't mourn the loss. This felt like seeing a new side to Alexander. And I was learning more about him regardless of his hesitancy to answer my innocent questions.

On Baker Street he wasn't the charming footman nor the smart-mouthed ne'er-do-well. I had a feeling that the man before me—the one seated close enough at this tiny table that our knees brushed—might have just been the true Alexander.

Swallowing down the uncomfortable realization along with a bite of potato, I attempted to answer his question about honesty while also backing away slowly from the serious turn the afternoon had taken. "Well, all the men that I kiss automatically earn a modicum of truthfulness. It's standard on my part."

He choked a little at my ridiculous response.

I smiled before scooping up another spoonful.

Incredulous blue eyes met mine. "I honestly do not know what to make of you."

"Thank you," I replied.

He didn't acknowledge my cheek. "I am typically very good at understanding society and their motivations because most people are extremely predictable and rarely original. But you…you are something else."

I laughed genuinely. "You are not the first to call me odd." But he hadn't called me odd, not truly. Not in the way others had—with an air of incredulous amusement or the more frequent disapproval. As if I were doomed to a life of oddity with no future whatsoever and a house full of cats.

Alexander's assessment felt like a thorough guess at an intriguing puzzle. And maybe, just a tiny bit, like a compliment.

I didn't know if his attention was something I should want. Yet an unexpected warmth settled low in my belly when I considered his attempt to work out the very idea of me. And while it was not prudent or wise, I liked that he was trying. Did he lie awake at night considering my unpredictable behavior? Did I hold his attention the way he held mine?

"Hmm," came his thoughtful reply, neither correcting my assumption of oddness nor endorsing it. "You said you arrived here by coincidence. How so?"

"I was returning from Maida Vale and an overturned cart blocked our normal route. Out of necessity, we redirected our carriage down Baker Street, and the rest—as they say—is history." I spooned up another bite from my dish, the flavors bright and vibrant.

Alexander's expression was less severe now that I was eating and we were conversing. I expected it was difficult to appear threatening while wielding a spoon. "Why were you in Maida Vale?"

"I volunteer with the Home for Incurable Children, and so I regularly make my way through this part of London."

"Volunteer? What does that mean?"

He sounded so suspicious that I fought a laugh. But instead I described my work with the Home and the long-term residents there while he made inquiries throughout. I discussed the fundraising, the organizing, the visitations and donations. It wasn't until sometime later when I was recounting several events from the morning's visit that I noticed Alexander had turned quiet, his follow-up questions ceased. His expression could only truly be described as befuddled.

"What is it?" I laughed. "You are making a face."

He blinked and straightened in his chair. "It was easier before. When I thought you an empty-headed debutante."

The rare moment of honesty made my heart beat inexplicably faster.

I smiled, quiet and soft at his admission. "And here I thought you just liked my dress."

It was his turn to smile, just a reluctant tug at the corners of his lips. But it was enough to initiate the magic that transformed his face. The intensity of his features lessened and amusement softened nearly every one of his rough edges. He looked younger and freer and so handsome that my heart continued its rapid pace.

"I am, indeed, an admirer of that dress," he said as the grin melted away. "But I fear it's no longer the loveliest thing about you."

His praise warmed my cheeks. How strange to find this sort of conversation just as stimulating as our verbal barbs and heated exchanges. I supposed there was something to be said for truths being revealed. Once they were out, you couldn't shove them back. The possibilities twisted, swooping pleasantly in my stomach.

These were the facts as I saw them: Alexander was a mystery. A handsome, intriguing mystery, and I liked the pull of discovery almost as much as I liked a challenge. I was attracted to his face and his form as well as the odd freedom I found in his presence, as if I was the very truest version of myself and I didn't need to apologize for it. And I enjoyed his honesty in return, the utter reluctance and condescension that marked our early encounters. Alexander did not treat me like any other man had ever done. He was interesting, and I wanted to know him better.

Something peculiar was happening between us. And I'd be mad to think anything could come from it, but desires were often selfish in their nature. And I found I was not immune.

My future was one of those desires. It lived fully formed in my mind. Marriage. Children. Household. Dinner parties. Country holidays. Every single thing I'd ever wanted. Only the faces of my future were these hazy approximations. General children scampering about—some with red hair like mine and some without. A husband with indefinable edges. A ghost of indeterminate age and eye color.

But for once, my desire had taken the shape of something living and breathing. Perhaps he'd never be my future, slipping easily into those long-lived expectations. But he was whole and solid. Deep blue eyes under slashing dark brows. Tall and strong. And a tantalizing bit of skin between trousers and shirttails.

I gathered my courage that, frankly, never strayed very far, and asked evenly, "So, am I allowed to return to the Baker Street Coffee House, if I wish?"

Alexander's eyes were still on my face, drinking me in until surely there would be nothing left. "I suppose."

I smiled in victory before inquiring pointedly, "And might I see you working in Mayfair anytime soon?"

He gave me a flat look before raising one dark eyebrow in my direction, and I knew he understood my meaning.

Will you be stealing anything at a society event in the near future?

"I have no plans of which you speak."

My smile broadened at his words, happy that he'd replied and relieved that he would not be attempting any more crimes.

Alexander rolled his eyes before looking away, color dusting the high arches of his cheekbones. "I should get back to work," he mumbled before rising to collect my dishes.

"I should get back as well before my chaperone wakes up from her nap," I said brightly.

Alexander huffed a laugh before shaking his head. "I do not know why I am surprised."

"So, I shall see you again, Alexander?" I tested his name aloud for the first time and watched his gaze heat at my boldness.

That transformative smile claimed his features as he backed slowly toward the kitchen. "You know, Princess, I think you just might."

I didn't quite realize how much I'd missed his little moniker and this style of flirting. He was still distrusting, to be sure. But I couldn't explain the difference. It didn't feel as if he was using the name to keep me at a distance—to remind me of my station, our obvious incompatibility, and my lunacy in seeking any sort of acquaintance with him.

Now it simply seemed like a reminder of our meeting—something playful and light from a man who contained so much unknowable darkness.

I placed my payment on the tabletop before rising on unsteady legs to depart. Making note of the hours and days of operation, I hatched a harmless little plan.

And two days later on Baker Street, while I waited in my carriage to invite Alexander for an innocent stroll in nearby Regent's Park, I watched him get into a hack with a beautiful young woman instead.

Six

"Cassandra, we have some news." My mother's voice pulled my attention from the plate of coddled eggs and bacon I'd been enjoying.

"Are you planning to run away with the stablemaster? I shan't tell Papa if you're intent upon it."

My mother laughed at my absurd jest. "Cassandra! You silly girl."

My father, seated to my right at the head of our large dining table, simply turned to the next page of his newspaper and said in an unbothered voice that was familiar with my antics, "Well, if Mr. Fisher is interested in taking her off my hands…"

I smiled, amused that my dry-witted father had joined in my silliness. "Do make sure you leave my mare when you go. I have grown quite attached to this one from Brightleaf Farms. It would be a real disappointment to lose Delilah."

"Oh, you'd be sad to lose Delilah, would you? What about me?" Mama was all affronted amusement—an interesting combination—but I was thrilled she was playing along.

My family often did indulge me in my dramatics and ridiculousness. They'd never made excuses for my uncharacteristic and outrageous behavior—never showed embarrassment at my absurdity. I'd much rather spend my days being happy, and I thought they appreciated my efforts to bring lightness and joy into our lives. I was so very lucky to have a mother and father who spoiled me with their kindness.

"Mama, are you truly planning to run away with the stablemaster? I was simply jesting. Perhaps you should tell me your news before you become too invested in this plot. Do tell Mr. Fisher I have my eye on him."

My mother shook her head, a smile lingering about her lips. And my father's newsprint rustled once more. I took a bite of eggs while my parents proceeded to inform me of an unexpected trip to Hertfordshire to commence immediately. My mother's sister had written and implored my mother to stay for a fortnight at the very least. Papa would escort her and I was to stay in London with Mrs. Ridley in residence so she could accompany me as needed.

I was highly amenable to this development.

"Well, I hope you have a lovely trip to see Aunt Rose."

"Thank you, darling. I'm looking forward to it," my mother said as she stood from the table and straightened what I now recognized as her traveling dress in jade-green wool.

I turned to my father and gave him a serious look. The edges of his gray mustache twitched. The man suspected what was coming and it made keeping my somber expression in place that much more difficult. "And, Papa, take care to keep Mama away from the coachman. Her nefarious plans might extend beyond the stablemaster."

His patient amusement had me laughing outright before I rose and hugged my smiling mother goodbye.

"Lady Cassandra, might I have the honor of the next dance?"

Under normal circumstances the voice of Lord Hayden wouldn't have grated quite so much. But I'd found that my mood had shifted rather drastically during society events of late.

If the inquiring baron had asked to take a turn about the dance floor a month ago—before I'd learned the truth—I would have smiled fetchingly and said that a waltz with him was just the thing I'd been missing all evening. Chances were good that I would have thrown in some fluttering lashes and a playful jest as we made our way toward the musicians and other dancers.

But that was before.

Before Alexander the intrepid footman had shone a rather unpleasant light on the motivations of the gentlemen of the *ton*. Before I eyed every invitation or request suspiciously. Before I questioned each man who approached me. Before I felt a painful clenching in my stomach at these exchanges. Before every event since Mary's failed betrothal ball stoked the fires of my disappointment.

I did not wish to be a novelty in London.

"Lady Cassandra," Lord Hayden prompted quizzically.

I wasn't behaving normally—as I was expected to. And therefore, the baron before me was confused and perhaps slightly frightened. Men often were when women defied their expectations.

"Apologies, my lord. I find I am not quite myself this evening. I fear I must decline your generous invitation." My smile was small, apologetic.

Lord Hayden's brows lowered before he took an embarrassed step back. His feet had recognized my refusal before his mind made the connection. "Of course, my lady. Perhaps another time."

"Perhaps," I replied noncommittally.

Indeed, perhaps someday I would stop fixating on the truth that had been so neatly revealed. Perhaps I could enter a ballroom in the future and not see all the connections I'd facilitated with my legend and lore. Perhaps there was a man somewhere who craved my companionship and not the means my misfortune could apparently provide.

I felt like a laughingstock. What percentage of all my male acquaintances had only sought an association because they'd been told that surviving a disastrous encounter with me would facilitate a sound match with the woman they next encountered?

The thought made me feel bitter, and decidedly not like dancing. So I'd turned down Lord Hayden. And Earl Cassian. And the Viscount Warrick before that.

I was a stepping-stone to the future. Just not my own.

I hadn't discussed any of this with my friends. I felt too raw and sensitive about the revelation. I wasn't ready to laugh it off quite yet, if I ever would be. But I knew, without a shadow of a doubt, that if any of my ladies had heard even a whisper of this curse—legend, what have you—they would have told me straightaway.

Bitter, reckless thoughts often spurred others on. One week had passed since I'd nearly made a fool of myself over Alexander. Admittedly, I'd felt disappointment as I'd watched him meet a young woman on the steps in front of Baker Street Coffee House. I'd been nearly out of the carriage at the sight of him. But instead I'd paused with my hand on the door latch as a lady with brown hair and a pale lavender day dress approached. Alexander hadn't appeared friendly so much as familiar, which was somehow worse. It had been painfully clear: he knew this lady. Even more so, when she indicated the waiting hack, they'd climbed in together.

Truly, it was not my place to judge or question Alexander's whereabouts nor the company he kept. But a part of me—the tiny, hopeful part that had enjoyed our spiteful barbs as well as our simple conversation—had been disappointed. I'd allowed the emotion until the count of ten and then I'd shaken myself out of my frustrated stupor and realized I'd dodged a rather ludicrous bullet. I hadn't been thinking very clearly at all. I'd been curious, which was far more dangerous.

My intention—a stroll with a restaurant employee—was foolish at best and hopeful at worst. There was no future, no relationship, no *anything* remotely feasible for Alexander and myself. Even before the entrance of a fetching violet gown and the woman attached to it.

I had a plan. I was the daughter of an earl. My future was laid out before me —idiotic love curse or no. And it didn't involve ridiculous musings about a thieving footman. It was marriage to an acceptable match. I needed to focus my efforts and go back to dancing. Perhaps I could find my sparkling personality in the bottom of a champagne flute, and I looked about for a passing tray.

"Lady Cassandra," greeted Unlucky Dancing Hopeful Number Seven of the evening, drawing my attention.

My bitterness stirred at his tidy bow and friendly smile. Well, it appeared friendly enough. But how much of that was for me or for the thought of the woman who came after?

Stop thinking about the idiotic curse, Cassandra!

"Good evening, my lord," I stated woodenly. This was not going to happen tonight. Best to get it over with. "I find I'm in poor spirits and will refrain from subjecting you to my admittedly heinous company."

Lord Number Seven's smile wavered at the corners before abject uncertainty claimed his features.

I should have probably just said my feet hurt.

My unfortunate companion cast about, perhaps looking for a friendly face or an explanation for my rude behavior. When I made no move to respond or soothe his fragile male ego, he executed another neat bow, muttering under his breath, "I wonder if this counts."

Indignation flared hot, warming my cheeks. How dare he seek me out to fill a tidy role? To be this ridiculous harbinger of matrimony. It was lunacy—

not witchcraft or superstition. What these men claimed was utter bollocks, frankly.

But it obviously didn't stop them from believing.

Well, I could end this madness. Futures could change. My friends were walking, talking, embroidering proof of that. Ashleigh had been all but married in Scotland before moving to London and taking her future in her own capable hands. Jane's family was riddled with scandal but a chance meeting with a mysterious gentleman altered the course she was on. After profound loss, Eliza had resigned herself to a life free from love, but that changed with time and distance and sheer force of will. And Mary. Mary would be walking a new path as well, one she hadn't expected. And yet she would survive because she was strong. And she had the support of family and friends who wanted only the best for her.

Loss was a difficult but necessary part of life. I could part with my eager expectations. If not separate myself entirely, I could adjust them. Perhaps my future was not so orderly and linear as I had imagined. Courtship. Betrothal. Marriage. Family. I still wanted those things, but achieving them didn't feel so neatly assured any longer. Happily accepting invitations from any suitable gentleman offering was not agreeable any longer.

I'd felt sick all evening as I watched each man approach with ambiguous motivations. I craved truth. I wanted something real. Now that the wool had been removed from my eyes, I longed to live in the light. And why was the thought of Alexander's belligerent honesty so much more preferable when compared to dancing with every disingenuous lord in this ballroom?

All my life, I'd followed the path I'd been prescribed. And what was my reward?

Four full seasons. Eight courtships. Six proposals. Countless embarrassing encounters. All fodder for deception and someone else's happiness.

No longer. It was time I did something for myself.

I'd followed society's mandates. I was a diamond and still alone. What would happen if I was reckless and did something solely for pleasure?

Instinctively, my eyes searched the ballroom for a tall footman in liveried black. But he wasn't here. I knew it. I'd been searching him out at every event since our impromptu time together the previous week on Baker Street.

And still, the disappointment was sharp as a blade.

What would I say regardless? Would I be brave enough to try again? Could I be satisfied with an innocent stroll after all?

Looking down, I worried the empty dance card hanging from my wrist. *I should go.*

Leave, before I considered returning to Baker Street and extending an offer that could never be undone. My chaperone was likely in the ladies' retiring room. The majority of my friends were elsewhere this evening. I'd seen Fiona circulating, but she was the only one. I'd been intentionally brooding and alone beside this column for most of the night. It was time to put this melancholy to bed and figure out what to do with my life.

"You look quite serious, tucked away against this lonely wall. I never took you for a wallflower, Princess."

The quiet words had my head snapping in his direction.

Alexander faced forward, but his dark blue eyes slid my way and held.

Inexplicably, I felt a sudden stinging pressure that threatened damp lashes and feminine hysterics. But I willed it away despite everything. All I'd hoped for —all evening—was something definitive and true. An honest encounter to hold the tide against all the things I could not control.

And here he was, as if willed into being by the strength of my desire and the dangerous musings I could not hope to tame.

Therefore, it was with painful and regrettable honesty that I breathed, "You're here."

Alexander proffered a tray in explanation. But when I failed to retrieve a drink, he turned to face me more fully. "What's happened? Are you ill?"

I frowned. "No. Why ever would you think so?"

"Your nose has gone all red and you haven't danced once all evening."

Instinctively, three of my fingers rose to press against the offending appendage. But then Alexander's words registered and my eyes snapped back to his. "Were you watching me, then?" The implications caused my stomach to hollow agreeably.

He didn't look away—as any typical man would. Alexander was unashamed as he regarded me evenly and said simply, "Yes."

I bit my lower lip to prevent my victorious amusement from registering. Blue eyes tracked the movement. I pressed a little harder, the smooth flesh tingling beneath the abuse.

This was inappropriate on so many fronts. I should not delight in the fact that Alexander had been watching me tonight, registering my mood and my repeated refusal of suitors. His attention should not please me so. I definitely should not be biting my lip and remembering how it felt when I did the same to him. He likely had a sweetheart who wore lavender dresses, and there were approximately one thousand other details about his life that I was unaware of.

But hadn't I been wishing for this very scenario? A way to get to know him better? An opportunity to ask for more?

Alexander cleared his throat, the sound a physical embodiment of his attention dragging away from my lips. "Have some lemonade," he finally managed.

I slowly lifted the crystal from the tray, considering how to ask for what I wanted.

While I'd never lacked for bravery, this was something else entirely. I wasn't flirting or jesting or encouraging someone's suit. This was not batting pretty lashes or telling an outrageous tale. It wasn't even brazening through to confront a thief.

I was offering something true for the first time in my life, something solely mine. Alexander had the power to take this tentative desire—beating on fierce gossamer wings—and crush it in his gloved hands. He wasn't bound by decorum nor society's expectations. And what I planned to ask would not be proper by any stretch of the imagination.

I held the glass but didn't move to drink. "Might I see you again?" The words were out and hovering in the air between us. Those delicate wings fighting to stay aloft.

Alexander scrutinized my words, as if he too could see them fluttering wildly. He didn't laugh outright, for which I would be eternally grateful. "Why?" he demanded, for it could hardly be called a question.

"I want more." I couldn't admit all the things *more* meant to me. Not here. Not now. It would simply have to be enough. Perhaps another time—without prying eyes and eager ears—I could explain that I wanted more from this life, more from my expectations, more for myself, and the most foolish *more* of all… more of him.

It was improper. And it was unwise. Obscenely reckless. It could very well cost me everything. But it was the truth. There were moments in your life that required wild honesty, so you wouldn't break apart from all the gentle lies.

Alexander regarded me, eyes touching on every part of my face before bringing my gaze back into focus. He didn't nod or voice his agreement. But a moment later he swallowed, the movement pronounced, throat working beneath his white cravat. As if his acquiescence was an indulgence that needed to be swallowed down.

I didn't want to wait for his rejection.

Refusing to feel embarrassed or any other useless emotion, I spun away. But before I could lift my slipper toward the ballroom exit, I felt a hand close around mine and an urgent "Wait, Cassandra."

I could hardly register the desperate plea because standing directly in front of me was Fiona Bowen, the Duchess of Compton. I would have barreled right into my friend in blind humiliation without Alexander's staying touch.

"Cassandra! There you are!" Fiona's words conveyed surprise at having located me, but her tone said she'd known exactly where I was…and who I'd been with.

The hand clutching mine evaporated like smoke, and I knew without turning that he would be gone.

My heart was pounding with the threat of discovery layered upon the frustration of missed opportunities. Just barely resisting the urge to growl, I made my tone even and greeted my friend. "Hello, Fiona."

Fiona's gaze flicked over my shoulder so quickly I might have imagined it, before she wound her arm through mine and pulled me into a stroll. "It's been an eventful night. I've been meaning to make my way over to you all evening."

"You've been busy. It's to be expected." Fiona was beloved among our peers. I was not put out by her delay in seeking me out. Not at all.

Her worried brown eyes met mine momentarily. "And you've been rather hidden. Is everything all right?"

It seemed Alexander wasn't the only one who'd observed my odd behavior. I was beginning to think the duchess saw more than most.

Smiling to reassure my friend, I replied easily, "I'm afraid I don't feel like entertaining this evening."

Fiona's brows rose in surprise. Admittedly, it was unusual for me to remain out of the spotlight and away from conversation. Boisterous laughter generally punctuated my time in the ballroom in between bouts of energetic dancing.

"Is there anything I can do? Anything you need?"

The stinging behind my eyes returned suddenly at the quiet reassurance from one of my staunchest supporters. I sniffed indelicately before waving away her concern. "Truly, I will be fine. Just not feeling like myself."

The duchess remained unconvinced. She steered us along the edge of the dance floor before tucking us into a corner next to a potted fern. "Does it have anything to do with that footman?"

Dammit.

Reading my expression, Fiona hurried on. "I just want to make sure he didn't do or say anything to put you into this state." I was already shaking my head but she continued. "I know he was the same footman in the corridor at Mary's betrothal ball. What I don't know is why you were there with him, then or now. You don't have to tell me, Cassandra. But I am concerned. I would just ask that you consider whatever it is you are doing. Be careful, my dear."

"I will, Fiona. I'll take care," I said earnestly, pressing close and squeezing her arm in a reassuring grip at my side.

"Good." She nodded, seemingly satisfied, but inquired anyway, "Do you want to tell me what you were doing with him?"

The first genuine smile of the night tugged the corners of my lips into a grin. "I'm not sure. Do you want to tell me how you were able to appear out of thin air and manhandle Lord David into submission?"

"Touché," she offered good-naturedly before plucking the lemonade I still held and finishing it in one go.

It seemed I wasn't the only one with secrets and questionable decision-making.

How refreshing.

~

LATER THAT NIGHT, after conversations with Fiona and a few others who approached, I returned home with my chaperone, Mrs. Ridley. Mama and Papa were still away in Hertfordshire and would be for the next month. Mama had written recently, having decided to extend her visit with my aunt. So Mrs. Ridley would be my companion for any outings. She was to remain in the guest quarters at Dameron Hall and share meals and accompany me to any events as was required.

Jansen, our butler, greeted us upon our arrival despite the hour, helping Mrs. Ridley with her cloak and cane while I ignored decorum and slipped out of my shoes before anyone could scold me. My sigh of footwear-free satisfaction was interrupted by my butler's surprising announcement.

"Lady Cassandra, a letter arrived for you."

"For me? At this time of night?"

"Yes, my lady. A footman dropped it off not a quarter of an hour ago."

The word *footman* set my heart to racing.

In a distracted fog, I took the letter from the butler's outstretched hands before mumbling good night to Mrs. Ridley.

Moving swiftly from the foyer, I strode up the staircase and to my rooms, paper clutched tightly in my hand. There was no identification in the wax seal, no crest, and no writing on the outside either. But I had a suspicion. An inkling, really.

I closed the door to my chambers and leaned against it. My bedroom was warm, fire stoked and candles lit for my arrival. With a deep breath, I broke the seal and unfolded the letter.

I scanned the correspondence four times before I allowed myself to smile into the empty room, certain the words would disappear as easily as the one who penned them. The missive was brief, no formal signature, no calling card attached. Just a time and location, an initial, and a single word scribbled hurriedly on a half sheet of paper folded, sealed, and delivered to my doorstep under the cover of night.

The London Zoo. Eleven o'clock, Monday morning. More.
-A

It was that one word—OUT of place and meaningless to anyone who hadn't heard my plea in that ballroom—that had my stomach swooping in anticipation.

Following Fiona's interruption, I hadn't spied Alexander again. He'd vanished just as I'd feared, like smoke in the cool night air. But perhaps he hadn't quite relinquished his hold. Because I was standing in my bedchamber holding a letter by his hand. And in three days' time I would do something wild, something reckless and decidedly improper. Something just for me.

Something *more*.

Seven

Monday morning emerged gray and chilly. Clouds hovered, blocking any sort of meaningful sunlight, but appeared mostly benign.

I excused my lady's maid to assist below stairs for the day, and dressed in a simple muslin day dress with a matching pelisse of pale green. Forgoing a bonnet, lest I rouse suspicion in my intent to depart, I tugged on short white kid gloves and made for the rear garden entrance.

I'd sent word to Landers early this morning to have the carriage prepared for an outing, but I failed to inform Mrs. Ridley.

Oh dear. My mistake.

On swift, booted feet, I approached the mews and found Landers nearly ready to depart.

"Lady Cassandra?" he said, confusion lacing his tone. "I would have brought the carriage around for you and Mrs. Ridley. You needn't have come all the way out here."

I smiled brightly. "Good morning, Landers! It was no bother. In fact, Mrs. Ridley is still abed and I did not wish to disturb her. So it will just be me today." My coachman frowned. "We're off to the zoo. Whenever you're ready, if you don't mind." I smiled again, even more brightly if possible.

Landers regarded me. He was well aware that I required a chaperone or companion, but he was also indulgent and kind. And it was a rare servant who would question their mistress. With the earl and countess away, he really had no one to appeal to unless he planned on dragging me back into the house and locating Mrs. Ridley. I hadn't been lying—she was still abed. The old woman seldom rose before luncheon. I'd effectively cornered Landers and he knew it.

With a deep sigh and obvious resignation, he moved toward the side of the carriage and opened the door before holding out his hand.

"Good man," I said, patting his shoulder before ascending into the conveyance.

"Just, please be careful, my lady."

I sat primly on the velvet bench before replying earnestly, "I shall be the picture of discretion."

With another sigh that had me stifling laughter, Landers closed the door and then we were off.

Nerves were a living, breathing thing. While I was admittedly anxious, it was mostly in eager anticipation rather than fear. I had no idea what to presume from this upcoming encounter with Alexander, but I fairly vibrated with the expectation of it.

Twenty-two years seemed an awfully long time to go without a clandestine meeting.

Forcing my hands to stop twisting in my gloves, I peeked out the window as the carriage trundled on. Hoping the rain held off, I forced calm and inhaled slowly. It felt like an effort more than a breath.

The ride passed sluggishly and then quickly all at once. And before I knew it I had reassured my coachman, paid my admission at the north entrance, and was standing in front of the lion enclosure attempting to slow my frantic heartbeat.

I refused to entertain nervous dawdling, looking in every direction, awaiting someone so obviously. Alexander would arrive when he arrived. Instinctively, I knew he would find me.

A short while later I felt a presence at my side. I did not turn, but it was a near thing. I'd never had a fondness for delayed gratification.

"I *would* find you here," the newcomer mused.

A month ago I would have never heard it. But now I could detect the faint edge of amusement, though I would wager he wore no discernible smile.

Still facing forward, I responded slowly, "Of course you would. You instructed me to meet you here. Or are we pretending that did not happen? Just like we are pretending we did not kiss."

I felt his attention shift from the big cats, gaze lingering on the side of my face. Only then did I turn to meet his flat expression.

"I meant *here*," he explained, hand waving forward to indicate this particular enclosure.

I glanced back to the three lionesses before meeting his unwavering stare. "Are you insinuating that I am a predator? A threat to those around me?" The implication—first made in jest—had me flushing suddenly. I didn't want to think about those unfortunate and embarrassing encounters with other men.

Alexander smiled, small and secret, before replying. "That is not what I meant at all. But now that I consider it, you are quite dangerous indeed. And yet not in the way you think."

I frowned, but instead of asking for clarification I attempted levity. Flippancy often made a handy shield. "Well, are you worried about our outing, then? Thus far you've escaped disaster. Most men of my acquaintance by now have succumbed to my famous bad luck. Are you worried you'll fall in with the man-eaters?" I laughed lightly to show just how *fine* I was with my lot. Categorically unbothered. Amused, even.

But Alexander didn't join in my amusement. In fact, his tiny, mysterious smile fell away as I spoke. Now he was merely watching me. It continued long enough to have me turning back to the lions. I did not wish to be examined for the truthfulness of my words nor the spite hiding beneath the surface.

"I fear I have not escaped anything, Cassandra." His words were low by my ear. "Being with you, like this, out in the open where anyone could see us, feels utterly dangerous."

Eager to read his expression, I turned back to see his dark blue eyes focused and intense. "But surely—in your line of work—you face true threat and uncertainty."

"Just the troubles commonly faced by servants," he deadpanned.

He knew what I meant…his life as a thief. But apparently we weren't discussing that either. "Right," I agreed before changing the subject. "Well, shall we set off? There is the giraffe exhibit open for viewing as well as the reptile house and public aquarium. I'm afraid Jumbo the elephant is no longer on display, having recently been sold. Pity that, I was hoping for a ride."

"Those rides are for children."

I smiled. "I'm fairly certain I could have charmed my way into an elephant ride."

His smile was all reluctant admission. "You are probably right."

"I generally am."

He bit his lip to keep his grin from growing. "Shall we?" he finally asked, indicating the path toward the north pond and aviaries beyond. He didn't offer his arm, so in answer I fell into step beside him.

I noticed he was dressed similarly to the time I saw him on Baker Street. Dark trousers, white shirt buttoned to his throat, and a dark waistcoat. The scar along his jaw was visible once more. Additionally, he wore a dark jacket. A top hat sat low on his head, and it made me wonder if this was a disguise. Was he hiding this…this…whatever this was with me? Was this the true Alexander I was seeing or was this a role he was playing? The most innocent version of himself—a restaurant worker from nearby Marylebone—presented for my benefit. Was there a darker, more dangerous version being parceled out and hidden away?

The thought of only being offered parts of this mysterious man did not sit well with me. I was greedy for every version of him.

But it was not my place. And this was not the time to demand it. I had a feeling Alexander didn't take kindly to being ordered about despite how he spent his days and his nights. Instinctively I knew that demanding the truth would have him retreating from me, and I didn't want that.

"So," I began easily, "you have no work today…for Mr. Patel?"

Alexander shook his head. "I am only employed at Baker Street four days per week. Mr. Patel and his daughter, Miss Shirra, manage just fine without me most of the time."

It was on the edge of my tongue to ask about his work as a footman. If he needed to steal in order to supplement his income. But I knew I should not address either topic. It was the quickest path to him pulling away from me, initiating it with my own hand.

Our stroll through the zoological grounds and gardens continued, leisurely and meandering.

"Have you been here before?" I inquired, reaching for topics that were safe and innocuous.

Alexander eyed me. "Yes, I've been to the zoo. I didn't visit as a child." A pause. "Not all children in London are so privileged that they may ride elephants." Some bitterness entered his tone, but he swallowed visibly and then resumed. "But I come here—and Regent's Park—often." Another quick sidelong glance. "It's nearby to my rooms. I let one of the apartments above the restaurant."

That little speech might have been the lengthiest and most informative I'd witnessed yet. His words told me much: where he spent his time, how he'd lived.

And if I hadn't already suspected, his utter disdain for the wealthy aristocracy was easily confirmed.

"I'm afraid that horses are the only wild beasts I've ever been fortunate enough to ride." I made my tone purposely suggestive—mostly to see how Alexander would react. His step faltered before he recovered, but he didn't look my way. Smothering any amusement, I continued. "Do you ride?"

"No, I've never been on a horse." His response was matter of fact, no shame in acknowledging his lack of a gentleman's hobby.

But he wasn't a gentleman, was he?

Eager to continue conversing, I remained upbeat. "I ride quite a bit. That's how I met the Duchess of Compton. Our shared love of the activity. When the weather is fine, we typically exercise our horses together regularly. You remember the duchess? You met her at the Huffleton ball."

Alexander looked at me, slightly taken aback. "I didn't *meet* her, Cassandra. We were not introduced. We did not exchange pleasantries. I served her champagne and we briefly shared a corridor."

"Well, you spoke," I argued, despite knowing he was accurate in his statement, and sounding petulant to my own ears. I didn't know why it was important to note this perceived familiarity. Probably because he seemed so determined to emphasize the lack thereof.

He was an enigma, this man. So very eager to place walls between us. He wanted to remind me of our differences—our positions in society—with nearly every breath. And yet he continued to use my given name, as if it was customary, as if I'd given him leave to do so.

Remembering suddenly, I stopped walking. Alexander noted my hesitation and turned toward me, expectation lifting his dark brows.

Lowering my voice, I said earnestly, "I never thanked you for that night. For coming to Mary's aid and placing yourself between us and Lord David. It was brave and— And— I just wanted you to know that I was grateful—am grateful."

Alexander's brows lowered as I spoke until they finally rested in a confused frown. "Of course," he said slowly, acknowledging my thanks while making no move to discuss the events of that night. Not the confrontation with the marquess nor apparently the kiss we'd shared, tucked away in that alcove.

I nodded once and then resumed walking. Alexander fell into step alongside me, bringing with him the scent of warm herbs and spice. He wore the aromatic trace of Baker Street on his skin, but there was something else, perhaps citrus as well. Something sharp beneath the surface, much like the man himself.

"Can I ask you a question?"

His quiet words broke through the fog of girlish fantasies and my ridiculous attempt to discern his male scent. *Thank God.* "Well, you just have. But I'll allow another."

He gave me a flat look.

I smiled cheekily.

After a sigh that I generously interpreted as nearing amusement, Alexander finally said, "Before we were interrupted...the other night. Why weren't you dancing? You never said."

I didn't wish to discuss this. Not really. And not with him.

How could I admit that my pride was bruised and he was applying pressure to the wound? That I didn't trust any invitation I received? That I wanted to be wanted for me?

But that I would accept a dance with him for a multitude of reckless reasons, the least of which was knowing he wasn't using me to gain someone else.

Despite being out of my control, the secret of my popularity was humiliating. Alexander and apparently every other man in London knew the truth, but I had been the agreeable, accommodating woman who had been completely in the dark.

Alexander was waiting for an answer to his question. And I supposed if I was expecting honesty and familiarity from him, I must offer it in return. "I find I can no longer stomach the idea of socializing as I once did. Now that I know the truth of my companions and why I was sought after in the first place."

It was his turn to stop walking, just as we approached the pelican enclosure. Turning to face him, I jolted when his hand found mine, urging me off the main thoroughfare to a bench a short distance away. The stone was cold as we sat close to one another but not touching.

Dark blue eyes searched my face. "Because of what I told you? You turned away those men?"

I nodded, looking down at my gloved fingers, anxious and twisting in my lap. "I don't like feeling used, apparently. And I do not trust their intent." Laughing softly, I admitted, "What is that saying? The grass is always greener? Well, I'm not even the lackluster grass. I'm the bridge to the other side."

The man beside me turned slightly, the knee of his trousers just brushing the edge of my green skirts. I stared at the contact for a moment before meeting his serious gaze.

"I wouldn't have— I'm sorry for the way I told you, thoughtlessly and without care. I never dreamed— I thought you knew."

"You thought I welcomed any sort of attention? Whatever I could get? No matter how disingenuous or insincere. That is what you think of me?" I could feel my blush heating despite the chill in the air.

"I don't know," he admitted on a frustrated exhale. "I keep expecting you to be one way and…I am continually surprised."

Curious, I hedged, "And who do you expect me to be?"

"Spoiled. Two-faced. Dramatic. A gossipy chit who is nothing if not boring." His recitation came easily enough, as if the words had been rehearsed in his mind a thousand times with regard to me.

I knew what he wanted. He needed me to be the spoiled princess. He wanted to hate me like all the rest. I was supposed to fit in his tidy little box for a genteel society lady.

Well, I was sorry to disappoint him. I'd never fit in any mold.

"Tell me, Alexander, are you bored?" The challenge lay not only in the question but in the knowledge that I already knew the answer. It was why he'd kissed me. Why he'd planned a secret meeting today.

Despite our stations and his obvious disdain for the *ton*, he couldn't help himself. He wanted me. Or at least he was curious enough to peek in the window at the pretty little impractical trinket that he could not afford.

With a clenched jaw and gritted teeth, Alexander finally admitted, "Unfortunately, I am not."

There was satisfaction to be had in the admission, but I held back the gloating smile that threatened. "Well, I will admit to being a touch dramatic. Perhaps you are not entirely wrong in your assessment."

A small smile claimed his features, large enough to perform the magic that transformed his face from intimidatingly handsome to incandescent. "Oh, aye. I've seen your flair for the dramatic. I was definitely right about that."

I thought back to my father's study. Throwing back those curtains and surprising Alexander. I wondered if he was remembering the same. "Can I ask you a question?"

Alexander's gaze turned wary. "That depends."

"On what?"

"There are some things I cannot discuss with you, Cassandra."

There it was again. My name on his lips. Low and deliberate—like a heavy press against my sternum.

Perhaps I was wrong in assuming he used my given name for anything but a challenge. Because the way he was looking at me, gauging my reaction and waiting, he was daring me to correct him, to demand an honorific. Alexander was reaching for a reminder.

Well, I wouldn't be the one to give it to him.

"Why is that, Alexander?" I said pointedly.

His nostrils flared. "Because there are things that are not safe for you to know."

I narrowed my eyes, considering. "If I ask something…dangerous, you have leave to decline. Does that meet with your approval?"

He watched me for a long moment before offering a decisive nod of agreement.

"How did you get that scar?"

His fingers, clad in black gloves, rose to the jagged line along his jaw for a moment as if his touch recalled the memory. "I got caught by footpads when I was a boy. They tried to cut my throat. Nearly succeeded."

I fought a gasp for I knew he would not appreciate my show of emotion. "Why would thieves attack a child?" I managed in an even tone.

"The reason most people steal, I would imagine. I had something they wanted."

I filed that away for further consideration. "Did someone save you?"

Alexander's eyes were dark and fathomless before he shook his head slightly. "Not that one, Princess."

Hmm. So there was the first boundary, someone he didn't want me to know about. Which reminded me incidentally of the young woman in the lavender gown. "Do you have a sweetheart? An intended? A paramour? A mistress?"

Alexander's eyes widened. "No, Cassandra," he rasped. "I am here with you, am I not?"

"You are surprisingly missish." I scrutinized him while keeping my amusement at bay. Perhaps that woman had been a family member. "Most men have no trouble entertaining multiple offers." But I was secretly pleased that he considered this meeting between us…*something.*

The tops of his cheekbones were warming and I didn't think it was due to the late September weather.

"Did I embarrass you with my questions?" I asked, delighted.

"I did not know that ladies such as yourself could be so forthright about delicate matters," he groused.

I laughed. "Shall I tell you a secret?" I didn't wait for confirmation. "I am hardly delicate."

"It's difficult to reconcile," he said after a moment, eyes alighting on every part of my face. "You look the way you do—inexplicably beautiful, so perfect I'm afraid you'll shatter under my gaze alone. And yet you open your mouth and destroy the illusion of a delicate flower by asking out loud, in public, if I have a mistress. Good God, Cassandra."

A giggle threatened before I laughed outright. I quite enjoyed his exasperation. Getting a reaction out of this man gave me a dangerous sense of satisfaction. But the way he'd described me—*inexplicably beautiful*—had a pleased, swooping sensation hollowing my stomach. It was reluctant, his admission. And that made it all the more meaningful. Every measure I'd gained with Alexander had been hard-won. Ground, and forward progress, earned on an incredibly difficult battlefield.

Perhaps I'd had it far too easy all my life.

He watched me while I was consumed with amusement, an indulgent smile on his full lips and something warm in his extraordinary gaze. Finally a huff of laughter escaped him, and I grinned so wide that I felt my cheeks straining to contain my joy.

After a moment, Alexander stood and extended his arm cautiously in my direction. "I'd best return you."

I fought the urge to ask if he'd like to keep me instead. It felt like another conversation that would reveal too much of me and cause another blush to climb his cheeks.

Instead I stood, slipping my hands around the crook of his elbow, leaning closer than was proper and enjoying the warmth of his side perhaps a little more than I should. We walked back the way we'd come, passing children and families as the zoo grew busy at midday.

When the entrance gates were in view along with my carriage waiting on the street, Alexander asked quietly, "Is this…what you were after? The *more* you were wishing for?"

I met his gaze, my own undoubtedly sparkling with mischief and delight. "It's certainly a start."

Eight

A few days later, Thomas and I were once again ensconced in the informal drawing room at Dameron Hall. Our monthly planning meeting for October had wrapped up a quarter of an hour ago. We'd discussed the necessary arrangements and upcoming events for the Home for Incurable Children, and now we were sipping tea and enjoying Mrs. Chapman's light repast.

I felt suddenly like I should confide in Thomas about the confusing relationship I was developing with Alexander, surname still unknown. While I'd met with my friends yesterday for our Tuesday embroidery salon, I couldn't bring myself to broach the subject. I wasn't ready to discuss with them what was happening. Reality had a way of encroaching without remorse, and I didn't wish to imbalance the scales between reckless illusion and willful ignorance. Besides, the possibility of Alexander felt secret and covetous. Revealing the circumstances of our acquaintance to my friends would paint the situation in a painfully realistic light—one with consequences and judgment. I was not ready for whatever was happening between us to end.

However, Thomas was a trusted friend and brought an interesting perspective to nearly every topic of conversation. Perhaps his outlook could provide support for my continued behavior. Lord knew that common sense and rational ladylike conduct had not. And deep down, I knew that my friends would disapprove. Fiona in particular would have much to say regarding my safety. And as I'd already considered, I wasn't ready for my association with Alexander to be over.

Logically, I knew there was no future for us. No marriage and family—none of the things I'd been working toward since my society debut.

"So, are you betrothed yet?" Thomas's standard luncheon inquiry jolted me out of the daydream I'd been considering.

I hesitated, deciding if I should mention Alexander. The momentary pause had Thomas's dark brows going high on his forehead.

"No. No, of course not," I hurried out.

"Then what was the delay in your response? Is there something happening on that front?" He relinquished his teacup and saucer to the low table between us, giving me his undivided attention. Thomas seemed invested in any sort of movement on the topic of my future. Perhaps he regretted offering a marriage arrangement before we were both old and gray.

I dawdled, aligning my own teacup just so. "Not in the way you think. There is someone though," I finally said, the admission forcing my eyes lower.

"Perhaps your new suitor just needs time before arrangements are made for formal courtship."

I smiled sadly. "That is not the case. There is no promise of a future for us."

Thomas looked affronted. "Good God, Cassandra. Is he married?"

"What? No!" I said, aghast. I glanced over my shoulder to make sure Mrs. Ridley hadn't overheard our conversation from her seated position across the drawing room. Thankfully, her nose was buried in her novel.

He sighed, relieved, before leaning back in his chair. "Then why the devil can you and this gentleman not solidify a future together?"

I swallowed. "I would not consider him a gentleman in the traditional sense."

"What other sense is there?"

"Well," I hedged, "he's not titled, and even if he wanted to marry me—which he does not—I cannot imagine my father would allow such a union."

The viscount scrutinized me. "I see."

"We're not a good match," I felt inclined to add. "I cannot envision…this working out." I forced a laugh. "You're not rid of me for a future marriage pact regardless."

Thomas gave me a flat, unamused look. "But you care for him?" he guessed.

I swiveled the handle of my teacup another quarter turn. "I suppose I do. He's not like anyone I have ever met. And I feel like he's honest with me in a way that no man has ever been." Another thought occurred. "Thomas, have you ever heard gossip about me regarding a curse or legend that any man who suffers my acquaintance will then meet the woman destined to be his wife?"

My friend frowned and sat forward again. "No, of course not. What utter rubbish."

"I know," I agreed. "It was brought to my attention, but the more I consider my past suitors, the harder it is to deny the validity of the claim. There's the recent betrothal of Patrick Morley. And the Marquess Windthorpe. Lord Grant is now wed following the champagne disaster during our brief association last spring."

Thomas looked thoughtful. "I did hear that Barrington proposed to Miss Whitmoore recently following that whole lemon peel…incident."

"What?" I exclaimed. "But…"

I knew—rationally and logically—that all of these instances with all of these newly wed or engaged men were simply coincidence. But the vulnerable parts of me didn't know it. My pride certainly didn't either.

There was no weight to this silly, small-minded gossip spread by ridiculous men who had their self-importance inadvertently wounded by an unfortunate, embarrassing encounter with me. Perhaps they'd simply redoubled their efforts at companionship after our meeting. Or they'd sought a safe woman—exactly my opposite—to seek a future with. There were any number of reasons.

Sensing my spiraling thoughts, Thomas cleared his throat pointedly. "Cassandra, you know this tall tale regarding you is complete nonsense. I am rather out of fashionable social circles, as you well know. Had I heard an inkling of this gossip, I would have told you, and I would have argued against it."

"Thank you, Thomas. You are a good friend."

He nodded, his typically unaffected expression softening briefly—for my benefit, no doubt. After a moment, he asked, "Is that why you're interested in this unsuitable match? Because you know he's not using you for marriage to someone else?"

My friend was astute. I should have realized he would make the connection. "I suppose it started that way. But I can no longer claim that as my sole reasoning."

He nodded, as if in understanding, before reaching for his tea once more. "Well, I feel it only right to caution you if you proceed with this improper man."

I dipped my chin, expecting as much.

But Thomas went on. "However, there is something to be said for trusting your instincts. Perhaps the future isn't quite as decided as you think it is, Cassandra."

Hope unfurled in the wake of his words. This felt suspiciously like support for fanciful musings, a surprise coming from my practical friend. But it was what my heart wanted to hear, in the moment. I wasn't ready to give up the pull of Alexander, nor the mystery of him. Something in him called to me. And the possibilities were not yet ready to loosen their hold.

Knowing Thomas would not appreciate any sort of sentimental display, I quickly changed the subject. "Are you attending St. Clair's upcoming masquerade?"

"Doubtful. Andrew extended an invitation, but I can't imagine I'll go."

Of course not. Thomas wouldn't see the entertainment in something as frivolous as a masked ball. But I was rather warming to the idea. In my current state, having some measure of anonymity—no matter how contrived—would make a society event bearable.

And then there was the possibility that Alexander would be in attendance. Andrew Castel, the Earl of St. Clair, spared no expense for his annual masquerade. It rivaled Lady Vega's yearly event. The guest list was large and additional staff would be required. I was hopeful that Alexander would be there.

Two days ago, we'd said our farewells across the street from my carriage, just outside the northern zoo gates. He'd merely said that he would see me soon and watched as I climbed into the conveyance and trundled away. I hadn't wanted to push for details of when or where that would be. He was attempting to provide the *more* I'd requested. What that looked like, I did not know.

And determining when *more* became *enough*—well, that was the question, indeed.

~

THE ANSWER CAME SOON ENOUGH. I received a missive from Alexander that evening. Once again delivered to my butler, the note provided simple instructions: meet at the rear kitchen entrance of Dameron Hall, Saturday morning at eight o'clock.

Despite my naughty imaginings, the appointed hour was far too early and unfashionable to get up to any trouble. The timing would also afford me ample opportunity to avoid Mrs. Ridley. And if the other servants noted my absence, well, it would be too late by then.

At the appointed time, dressed in a warm and serviceable wool day dress with matching pelisse and hat, I made my way to the kitchens. I waited until

Mrs. Chapman entered the larder before scurrying to the door and tugging it closed quietly behind me.

A mischievous smile broke across my face as I considered my successful escape. My excited breath burst forth, fogging the chilly morning air with my exuberant exhale. Upon first glance, the dim garden was devoid of enterprising footmen, so I startled when Alexander pushed off the wall nearby and entered my space. He'd obviously witnessed my triumphant departure from the kitchens, but I could not feel embarrassed by it. He was smiling and making his way closer to me, looking youthful and roguish. And despite the early hour, the gardens suddenly felt very illicit.

"Good morning, Cassandra." His voice was deep and a bit rough, as if he'd yet to speak this morning and his first greeting was for me. The intimacy of that possibility had sensation twisting low in my belly. Alexander was once again daring me to challenge the use of my given name.

"Good morning, Alexander," I replied in kind. "What is your surname?"

I could tell my abrupt question surprised him. He hesitated for a moment. "It is…Hill."

Mr. Alexander Hill.

"How old are you?"

Another long pause, as if revealing details about himself required some working up to. "Twenty."

He was two years my junior. There was no denying his appearance, face unlined and fairly radiant. His features sometimes held the stubbornness of youth, with stern brows and a pouting lower lip emphasized by the crease in his chin. Yet in many ways he seemed far older than his twenty years—smart, capable, perhaps a touch jaded and world-weary.

"How old are *you*?" he asked cautiously.

"Two and twenty," I answered easily. "Practically on the shelf."

He scoffed in amusement, a deep sound, and warmth flared in my chest. I enjoyed shocking him and even more so making him laugh. I had a feeling that Alexander had not experienced nearly enough laughter in his life thus far.

His eyes seemed to linger along with his smile before he shook his head dazedly and said, "Come. Our conveyance awaits."

Alexander led me along the garden path before he snaked between two hedges and emerged on a neighboring cobblestone drive. I moved swiftly to follow along the perimeter of the property, feeling awash with excitement. Alexander remained alert, head on a swivel as he took in the minimal sights and sounds of the street. On the next block, a hackney waited. Alexander handed me into the enclosed carriage, and, after signaling our readiness to depart, quickly followed me inside.

We sat facing one another as the carriage trundled along the lane.

Our eyes met and held. "Where is it we are going so early on this fine morning?" It was indeed fine. The autumn morning still held a chill but the sun was gaining strength and would soon give way to an exceedingly agreeable day.

He snorted. "It's only early to people like you."

"People like me," I confirmed.

"Yes," he agreed. "Lords and ladies who enjoy their entertainment until the wee hours of the morning and then stay abed until half the day is nearly gone, only to repeat their efforts again and again."

I refused to show any offense despite the intended slight. Alexander was eager to remind me of our differences and to keep me firmly in the box he'd set aside for me: a useless young lady with no responsibilities who selfishly sought enjoyment and recreation above all else. Nothing like the hardworking laborers who rose with the sun and proved their worth through their backbreaking work.

While I lived a privileged life with wealth and frivolity, I did have responsibilities. However, reacting defensively to Alexander would do nothing but support his claim. I would not point out my philanthropy efforts, nor would I remind him of my volunteer work and charitable contributions. I refused to allow his unreliable mood to affect our outing.

With brightness—neither false nor forced—I said, "Well, I am awake with the morning now." My companion's brows furrowed, but I continued on unbothered. "Where is it we are going? Wait, wait, don't tell me. I should like to guess." Tapping my chin thoughtfully, I mused, "Is it a music hall?"

I looked to Alexander for confirmation or denial, but he was still staring at me.

"Well?"

"No," he finally answered after blinking several times. "It's too early to attend a music hall."

"I should like to go to one someday. I've never been."

"It's not really the place for a lady," he argued, but there was no heat in the rebuke.

My nose wrinkled. "Does that mean we *are* going somewhere fit for a lady?"

Alexander turned thoughtful before shaking his head slowly. "No. Not really."

My brilliant smile had him rolling his eyes, but I could see the grin threatening. His pink lips were curling at the corners, and something low and indecent in me twisted again at the sight.

"Fine, no music hall. Are we going to a tea garden?"

"No."

"A circus? To the Royal Exhibition Hall? Wait, it's a street performance with sword swallowers and salamander men?"

He grinned, shaking his head all the while. "No. No. And definitely not. You'd convince them to let you participate."

I pouted in mock annoyance. "The theater?"

"No matinee for you, I'm afraid."

I peeked out the window but could really only discern our direction moving south toward the river. "Are you running away with me, then? Shall we board a ship and become pirates?"

"What did I tell you about one-eyed dukes and orphaned governesses?"

The reminder of that night—our kiss and the threat of fanciful notions—didn't ache as it once had, for I was here with Alexander, after all. Our acquaintance had not ended there with his warnings and mocking. We were presently alone together in a carriage. *More* was on the agenda for the day, and I could not regret it.

Acknowledging his question, I nodded. "No adventures for us. I remember."

His gaze lingered once more on my face, touching softly everywhere. "Perhaps some small adventures."

"Come now. Don't be a dullard. Surely we can manage a moderate adventure."

He hadn't quite managed to stop smiling. "Perhaps," he echoed, and I took it as tacit agreement whether he intended it or not.

Feeling emboldened from his attention and amusement, I asked suddenly, "Might I kiss you again?"

My words caused Alexander to go still and cautious once more. I nearly cursed myself for my impatience and impertinence, but then he swallowed thickly and moved to sit beside me on the worn bench.

His face turned, and his words were quiet and intimate when he spoke. "Would kissing me constitute an adventure?"

"Well, based on experience, kissing you and adventuring have much in common," I replied, suddenly breathless with anticipation.

"Is that so?" he murmured as his lips drew closer to my own.

I nodded, brushing my nose along his. "Both make my heart race. My breathing turn shallow." As if to demonstrate, I took a large inhale, my chest grazing his jacket. Then I reached for his gloved hand and placed it on my belly. "And here. I get vicious butterflies in both scenarios."

Alexander's fingers flexed, clutching the fabric of my dress, and then before I could even react I was moving—positioned astride him, skirts bunched all around us. Firm thighs tensed beneath my bottom as I wound my arms behind his neck and brought our mouths together.

The kiss was not tentative or delicate or any other mild form of affection. Alexander's hands gripped my waist as our lips fused, tongues seeking and searching, rewarded by unrivaled heat. I tightened my hold and brought our bodies flush together, all of my softness pressed firmly to his long, strong lines. I was impatient and encouraging, making little sounds that might have embarrassed me if I hadn't been so consumed by the moment—so consumed by him.

I threaded my fingers through the short, dark strands at the base of his neck, eagerness making my grip rough. Alexander made a sound, half growl and all approval, before he bit my lower lip. Then he was shifting down, kissing the edge of my jaw as I gasped out a short-lived protest.

This was madness. I wasn't even sure this man liked me and yet we were attacking each other in an indecent display. Nothing about this was proper or expected. But it was real. I wasn't worrying over intentions now. Alexander was making himself and his desires known quite plainly. He had long since gone beyond kissing me as some sort of experiment or granted request. There was no questioning the way he held me. I could read every line of truth between us in his ragged breaths and clutching hands.

In the next moment, the carriage wheel found a sudden ditch. I bounced hard on Alexander's lap and the contact pulled a broken "Oh God" from my lips as he groaned into the skin of my throat. The carriage trundled on, even and unbroken while we froze in our ministrations. I could still feel him, hard and insistent between my legs, but I was too afraid to move. The urge to bear down was just there…hovering on the edge of complete madness.

But Alexander pulled back. His fingers still clutched my sides desperately. The touch was covetous, and when he finally relinquished his hold, it was as reluctant as a child refusing to release his favored plaything.

Alexander's flushed cheeks showed that I was not alone in my desire. This pull between us—this overwhelming attraction—was evident in his pupils, blown wide and dark. He leaned forward and placed a surprisingly gentle kiss on my mouth. Our parted lips caught and held for a beat before he leaned back once more.

"We're nearly there." The rawness of his voice had me forcing a swallow. He sounded awed and reverent in equal measure. Finding myself the inspiration was addictive.

I felt grateful just then that he wasn't a gentleman. I did not wish to hear platitudes or apologies. If Alexander had shown a sign of remorse or a modicum of regret for our highly inappropriate exchange, I would have never forgiven him. Women didn't want to feel sorry for the things that brought them pleasure. They did not wish to feel shamed for them either.

I smiled as I smoothed the collar of his jacket I'd mangled with all my furious clutching. Alexander reached forward and straightened my hat, wearing a satisfied grin of his own.

The hackney pulled to a stop, and he helped me off his lap before opening the carriage door and descending. I exited the conveyance in a daze as I met the sights and sounds of the Covent Garden Market.

Chaos was the best way to describe it. The main thoroughfare was lined with sellers. Booths and tables filled with all manner of produce were on display. Autumn vegetables—beets, carrots, parsnips, cabbages, squash, and pumpkins—colored the central piazza as well as the surrounding streets filled to capacity. The yellows and golds of flowers caught my eye in every direction. The purple and blue of delphinium. The soft green and pink of delicate hydrangea petals. There were freesia and lilies and more shades of beautiful blooms than I could possibly name.

The sights and sounds of the costermongers hawking their wares played the accompaniment to my utter delight. The avenue was absolutely teeming with people. Basketwomen balanced impossible loads and young girls called to shoppers in their high-pitched voices.

I was charmed by the disorderly, overwhelming wonders, a variety of dazzling colors displayed as far as the eye could see.

A barra boy pushing a cart nearby forced me to crowd close to Alexander. I slipped my arm through his and let him lead me through the throng.

He glanced over to see my undoubtedly elated face, before leaning down to be heard. "I knew you would love it here."

My smile sobered slightly. The idea of being known by someone who was little more than a stranger to me felt intimate, nearly more so than what we'd just done in that carriage. Was I so easy to read? Or was this acquaintance with Alexander becoming more dangerous, more fraught, just...*more?*

"I do love it," I said, my admission made bolder as I met his warm gaze.

We meandered among the crowd, listening and watching. Alexander was alert, the way he so often was, scanning the passersby while I simply took in our surroundings, absorbing the energy that overflowed here.

"Do you come here often?" I asked, eager for the details of Alexander's life.

"Not as much anymore," he replied before glancing away. "I made my home in Covent Garden for many years."

"But it's still home?" I guessed.

He shook his head. "No. It was only ever a place to lay my head. I moved to Marylebone when I was sixteen and had saved enough for a small flat. Mr. Patel was kind to allow me as a tenant. I started helping him with heavy lifting or any work in his home that required an extra set of hands or a strong, young back. He eventually offered me a position at the restaurant. I help with deliveries or errands that occasionally bring me to the market here, but rarely anymore. It seemed like a fine adventure for you today, however."

I smiled gratefully. This was a marvelous outing for me—just this side of scandalous. It so happened I frequently walked the border between what was ladylike and what was not. Here, though, I was fairly anonymous—just a lady in a nice frock collecting mud on my hem the same as everyone else. And Alexander had offered so much of himself just now, more than he'd ever admitted before.

"Then you must be close to the Patels," I wagered. "They are your family." I didn't imagine there was a mother or a father in Alexander's life. But I could be wrong.

A brief hesitation on his part. "They are as close to a family as I have, yes."

We continued strolling past wares of fried eels and silkworms, fresh fish and live chickens. "I'm fortunate to have my family. They indulge my high spirit."

Alexander laughed. "You make it sound as if they tolerate a particularly willful horse."

"I suppose that is as fine a comparison as any. I'm often dramatic with strangers, frequently stamp on gentlemen's toes, and can be swayed into an improved mood with a bit of sugar."

His smile was luminous, and I felt, once again, that warm surge of satisfaction.

Just then a little girl approached. "Please, kind lady, buy my flowers. Do buy a bunch, please do!"

"Of course, darling." I reached for some pin money in my reticule, but Alexander had already pulled out a coin for the young girl—far more than the pittance the flowers warranted. She handed over her offering before maneuvering past, voice once again rising to tempt new buyers.

I took the pitiful sprig of greenery and said quite solemnly, "Thank you, Alexander."

Voice tight, he replied, "It was nothing. You are used to far finer things, I am sure."

I wanted to sigh aloud at his assertion. The reminders of my station were growing tiresome. Of course I'd received elaborate bouquets from gentleman callers, but I'd never received a gift like the one Alexander had given me. This adventure to the market was planned with me in mind. During calling hours I was interchangeable with any young lady receiving flowers. But this—this moment here—was mine alone. I would treasure this outing and the wilting blooms I held as a result.

"I am accustomed to all manner of things," I said slowly. "When my friend Ashleigh—Miss Winstead—and I were first acquainted after her arrival in London, she was interested in learning to knit. So we spent a great deal of time getting to know one another over our knitting needles. We typically embroider during our weekly meetings, but she and I continue our knitting efforts for donated items in our own time." I waved my hand to indicate that was beside the point. "Anyhow, when she was learning to knit, she made a scarf for me. It is uneven and lumpy with more than a few dropped stitches. But that scarf is my very favorite. I wear it all winter long and she smiles and shakes her head every time she sees me all wrapped up in the warmth she created for me."

Alexander was watching me, face serious, gaze intent. But he said nothing. So I went on.

"The value we place on objects cannot always be measured, and certainly not by comparison." I held the flowers tightly to my chest, protecting them from those passing by. Circling my hand once more around Alexander's arm, I squeezed gently. We continued on the path through the busy space.

It wasn't until we reached the fringes of the market that I felt Alexander tense. We'd spent the last half hour walking easily with one another, viewing the Floral Hall, pointing out various items for sale or remarking on the traveling marionette show set up on one corner. So his sudden rigidity was noticeable all along my side.

I followed his gaze to a man standing on the edge of the street. He was beneath a striped cigar shop awning and looked entirely out of place. His dark hair threaded with gray was oiled generously away from his face, the majority of which was hidden beneath a dark top hat. The man was middle-aged and dressed in a fine patterned waistcoat, a tailored jacket, and dark trousers. Most of the crowd was attired simply, as they were laborers or shopkeepers—firmly lower- or middle-class Londoners. But the mysterious man who had drawn Alexander's attention held a gentleman's air along with an elegant walking stick. Yet nothing indicated he needed it for mobility or ease of movement. He looked hard and exacting and perfectly capable of walking all on his own.

And he was heading right for us.

The crowd had thinned so his path was largely unencumbered. Alexander halted our movement and seemed to be scanning for an escape. He glanced to me momentarily but I could not read his expression. His handsome face was all hard lines and firm resolve.

"Well, Alexander. What an unexpected surprise." The man's tone held an edge of warning, but his voice was surprisingly formal—one better suited to upper-crust London than the muddy streets of Covent Garden.

Alexander did not respond or acknowledge the newcomer in any way.

But the man carried on, unaffected. "Aren't you going to introduce me to your lovely companion?"

Still, nothing from the man at my side, nearly vibrating with tension.

A lifetime of good manners had me swimming in discomfort. After a long moment, I smiled gamely and stuck out my hand in greeting. "Good day, sir. I am Cassandra Fields."

The man grinned, all teeth, and took my hand gently. "*Lady* Cassandra Fields, I'd wager." I confirmed with a tight nod. "I am Elias Blaidd. It is a pleasure to make your acquaintance."

I did not return his platitude. Nothing about this was pleasant. And I was honestly a little put out that this interloper had intruded upon my outing with Alexander.

"Where have you been hiding her, m'boy?"

With the strain obvious in every part of his body—from his clenched fists to his taut jaw—I was stricken with surprise when Alexander replied in an entirely bored and unaffected tone. "I have been hiding her nowhere."

The man laughed, all cutting amusement. "Is that right? My guess would have been Mayfair." It did not sound complimentary.

I swallowed nervously against the implication that I wore my upbringing so blatantly.

"The lady can go where she likes," Alexander drawled.

Mr. Blaidd's expression turned pitying. "That's not actually true though, is it? A fine lady—an unmarried daughter of an aristocrat, no doubt—requires a chaperone for any public outings. Surely you know that from all your hard work at society events as well as the restaurant. And it is extremely unlikely that she would be permitted an excursion with someone such as yourself, Alexander. I'm guessing this little trip to the market is some manner of secret rebellion."

Alexander glanced toward me as if remembering who I was, expression pained with self-recrimination. Mr. Blaidd had pulled a curtain back, revealing a truth Alexander had momentarily allowed himself to forget. My chest felt tight with discomfort and the bittersweet knowledge that for a time today Alexander had forgotten to see me as a lady. He'd just seen me as…me.

"Or did you plan to steal her too?"

Mr. Blaidd's words had me looking sharply his way. This man knew all about Alexander. He knew of his work not only as a footman in Mayfair and a servant on Baker Street, but also of his double life as a thief.

The stranger met my stare, cool and calculating. He was waiting for a reaction, but I would be damned before I gave him one. I kept my features impassive and, for the first time in Alexander's presence, assumed the role I'd been born into.

I straightened my spine and said with as much condescension as I could muster, "I'm afraid we should be on our way. As amusing as it has been to meet one of Alexander's acquaintances…" I let my voice trail off as my eyes traveled over Mr. Blaidd's form in an unimpressed perusal. "We really must press on."

"Good day, Lady Cassandra." The man smiled in utter delight and tipped his hat before glancing to Alexander. "We'll talk soon."

I tightened my hold on Alexander's arm and pulled him forward. Without missing a beat, he fell into step and we walked easily around the man who'd ruined our morning.

I could feel a storm brewing in Alexander. There would be no recovering from this interruption. Alexander's worlds had collided, and I'd witnessed something I was never intended to see. The separation between our lives was first and forefront now. Alexander's blinders were off and whatever he'd allowed himself to believe about me was left trampled somewhere in the market behind us.

I knew better than to speak. He would not offer an explanation and I didn't have the courage to pull one out of him.

He steered me determinedly down an empty connecting lane that was hardly wider than the two of us walking side by side. I matched his long-legged stride in my heeled boots, but after a moment I slowed. Alexander pulled easily out of my grip as I stopped altogether.

"Are you all right?" I asked firmly. Showing any sort of pity or concern would likely end this conversation before it had even begun.

He stopped ahead of me, facing away. Hands resting on his hips, his head dipped down to stare at the packed dirt beneath his feet. "This was a mistake."

Grief rose like a wave, hollowing my stomach before stealing my breath and prickling just behind my eyes. Before I could object or do something horrific like cry, Alexander moved swiftly and aggressively, slamming his fist into the stone wall beside him. The sound was dull and harsh at the same time. I startled, lips falling open at the display of violence as I clutched my hands to my chest, crushing the wilted foliage I still held.

Alexander's arm pulled back and repeated the gesture twice more in rapid succession before he braced both hands on the wall and hung his head. I started to reach for him, but his profile was angry and defiant. And I could see the newly scraped and ragged glove of his injured hand.

I was ashamed to admit that I was frightened in that moment—in a way I hadn't been in my father's study, alone with a potential thief and criminal. But here—in this broken alleyway, mere yards away from a crowd of people—I was afraid of the raw strength and unpredictable man before me. Perhaps foolishly, I still believed he wouldn't hurt me in his anger, but I now knew the damage he was capable of inflicting on himself. And the knowledge did not sit well.

"It's time to go," he said, voice empty as he pushed off the wall.

He covered the remaining distance and exited the alley. What else was there to do but follow?

We emerged back onto a crowded side street off the central piazza but I kept pace and trailed a stiff-shouldered Alexander. He moved away from the sellers toward Catherine Street where carts were loaded and carriages moved past.

Finding an unoccupied hack, he engaged the coachman and pressed money into his hand before opening the carriage door and waiting while I approached. He hadn't looked back at me once. I almost admired his blind faith that I'd follow. Almost. If I hadn't been so angered that I'd done so.

I walked up to the steps of the carriage but didn't climb in. Alexander looked over my head, refusing to meet my eyes or even hold out a hand to help me in.

I waited, and it did not take long.

"Get in," he growled, eyes flicking once in my direction.

It was now or never. "So, this is it? You won't explain what just happened."

"This little adventure is over," he said through gritted teeth, ignoring my question.

I nearly smiled at his attempt to minimize what had occurred between us here today. "You're just going to smuggle me back home? Send me on my way?"

Finally he gave me his attention. His face was incredulous. "What? Did you think I'd escort you home? Walk you up to the front door? Greet your neighbors warmly and remark about the fine weather?" His laugh was disbelieving…and a touch mean. "Well, Princess, I'm afraid the only entrance I'm accepted at is the one around back."

And with that he pressed a warm hand—not the one I could see bleeding through the tears in his glove—to the center of my back and urged me forward. Despite the acidity in his tone and the force of his words, his touch was gentle against my spine. The contrast was confounding and frustrating.

I understood that he was pushing me away—physically and emotionally. After a joyful morning spent together, he'd nearly forgotten who I was and where I came from. But the run-in with Mr. Blaidd had narrowed his focus.

I sighed and pulled away from his reach before handing my damn self into the carriage and closing the door behind me. I knocked an irritated fist three times on the roof of the conveyance and mercifully the coachman pulled away from the curb.

This felt very much like the unsatisfying end of a particularly good novel. Did it ruin the entire experience? No. But it certainly left a bitter taste in my mouth.

We'd hardly been moving, and I hadn't even had the time to consider my feelings on the events of the morning, before the carriage paused and the door opened.

I had but a moment to be hopeful, to think that perhaps Alexander had changed his mind and was boarding to apologize for his behavior and have a rational discussion with me.

But a woman entered the carriage just as it resumed motion. A woman I recognized. A woman I'd seen enter a carriage nearly a fortnight ago on the arm of Alexander Hill.

Nine

"Lady Cassandra Fields," the stranger said plainly. It didn't sound like a greeting so much as an appraisal.

"At your service," I remarked dryly.

The young woman I'd seen with Alexander on the cobblestones of Baker Street regarded me curiously. There was no malice that I could discern, simply genuine interest. She watched me the way I'd watched the flamingos at the zoo.

I supposed I was, indeed, a strange bird.

With rich brown hair plaited loosely, the woman was dressed much more simply than the last time I'd seen her. Her plain gray skirts and sturdy black boots offered ease of movement. She wore a tidy jacket over a cream shirt. Both had very little in frivolous adornment.

Weeks ago, this attractive young woman could have passed for a debutante enjoying her first season. Today, however, she looked closer to my age and ready for a busy day as a shopkeeper or governess. The difference was striking and notable. But the only commonality I could discern in her repeated presence was a close proximity to Alexander.

I assumed she'd tell me what she wanted me to know when she was ready. I wouldn't beg for an introduction or demand answers. That would reveal a little more than I was comfortable with. This woman already had the upper hand.

Moments passed and the sounds of the market faded behind the horse and carriage. Finally, the woman laced her fingers together on her lap and offered, "I am Ember Bellamy."

"How do you do?"

She eyed me, allowing a bit of amusement to creep across her expression. "I am trying to determine what you were doing in the market this morning."

"Oh, that's easy," I said. "I was shopping." Reflexively, I squeezed the mangled greenery still in my hand.

She tracked the movement. "I can see that." When I did not elaborate, Miss Bellamy continued. "I feel as if I should warn you, Lady Cassandra. Alexander is not who you think he is."

I noticed she used my name and honorific as a challenge. To remind me of my place, the fundamental differences between us, and the implied wall separating our lives. And yet the sound of my name on her lips reminded me not of the dissimilarities between this woman and myself, but instead of that impenetrable wall and Alexander on the other side.

"Is that so? And who is he?"

She smiled, sly and knowing. "He is a great many things to a great many people. Your association, if discovered, would be just as detrimental for him as it would be for you."

"We hardly have an association," I argued. A small pang resonated within when I considered the truth of my words and how little I actually knew about Alexander.

"Enough of one. Which is an anomaly in and of itself."

Miss Bellamy's speech and diction indicated that she was well educated. Her accent and clipped tone told a different story. A strange dichotomy, this woman. While her words posed a warning, there was no threat present. I was beginning to think Ember Bellamy thought she was doing me a favor. "And why is that?" I asked, attempting to focus on her statement. There would be time later to dissect her intentions.

"Because Alexander does not allow associations, acquaintances, or connections of any kind. And certainly not with a diamond of Mayfair."

My eyes narrowed. Was she saying that Alexander was entirely alone in this world? He had the Patels, of course. And some sort of relationship with the well-dressed Elias Blaidd. "Well, he obviously has an association with you, judging by your unexpected presence in this carriage."

"I don't know that my place in Alexander's life truly counts."

"And why is that?" I repeated…to be insufferable.

"It was never his choice. Our relationship is one of circumstance." Before I could interject and question this, Miss Bellamy pressed on. "But *you* have a choice, Lady Cassandra. You can protect yourself and your reputation. And protect Alexander as well."

"By making the choice for him? As others have done?"

Miss Bellamy nodded, lips curving, as if to acknowledge the point I'd made. "It would be a kindness in the end. Before any irreparable damage is done." She leaned forward and banged on the roof of the carriage, four quick raps.

"You know I don't have any idea what you're truly talking about."

Her grin was devilish, one dark brow lifting—a challenging slash on her cunning face. "I'm counting on that for all our sakes."

And with that, she opened the latch and swung herself down from the carriage, landing easily before the horses had drawn to a full stop.

I heard her instruct the coachman to be on his way and to return me to Dameron Hall. I didn't wish to consider how she knew my name or where I lived. I was at a steep disadvantage where information was concerned.

After the confusing and frightful events of the morning, I wondered if today was the last day I'd ever see Alexander Hill again.

"HAVE YOU HEARD?" Eliza asked. "Lady Helm reported her priceless jewelry collection missing."

I placed my biscuit on the edge of my saucer and finished swallowing. "When was this?"

Eliza shook her head, blond brow furrowed. "Unfortunately, there is no way to tell. The family heirlooms were in her safe. She had no cause to open it in recent months. However, with the betrothal of her son, Lord Clayton, she wished to pass along a gift to the future Lady Clayton. But when she opened her safe, all of the jewelry was missing."

"That is most unfortunate," Mary said, frowning.

My remaining friends in attendance for today's embroidery salon—all but a busy Nicolas—made similar sounds of sympathy and regret.

Something niggled in the back of my mind, but I cleared my throat and reached for a biscuit.

Thievery was not unheard of. Many aristocrats had obvious wealth and means. That often made them—and their well-appointed homes—a target for enterprising individuals.

Unbidden, I thought of Alexander and the scene I'd intruded upon in my father's study. He'd never confirmed my accusations, but there simply was no other excuse. I'd pardoned the instance because nothing had actually been taken, and I was admittedly still intrigued and attracted to the duplicitous footman. It was not rational, but human impulses often were not.

My mind snagged suddenly on the last event held by Lady Helm. A soiree the previous spring which I'd attended. It had been particularly memorable in that Lord Grant had been the unwilling recipient of a disastrous Cassandra encounter. A tray of champagne—carried coincidentally by Alexander himself—had ended up almost entirely on Lord Grant. We'd both left the event early and soggy. Grant had suffered great embarrassment in my company, thus terminating our courtship. But he was now happily married to Esther Hamilton—the young lady he'd courted immediately following the unfortunate champagne incident.

I could distantly hear Fiona asking questions about the theft of Lady Helm's valuables, but my mind was slowly connecting dots like the stars of a particularly dim constellation in the sky.

Umberland House—Lord and Lady Vega's London residence—had been burglarized nearly a year ago. That time the theft was noted immediately following their annual ball. The undisclosed items were thought to have been removed from Umberland House during the event as so many guests and servants were abound. We'd discussed the theft at another such Tuesday afternoon meeting. My mind spun, the lights shining brighter, becoming more distinct, looming overhead.

"Were Lady Vega's valuables ever recovered?" I blurted, interrupting whoever had been speaking.

All six ladies in attendance turned startled expressions my way, but it was Fiona with her scrutinizing brown gaze who spoke. "I do not believe her stolen items were ever returned. At least, it has not been noted among any of my acquaintances."

I considered every ballroom in which I'd seen Alexander the footman. Could he… "Jane, was anything taken during your ball this spring?"

My friend frowned in thought at my demand but answered matter-of-factly, "Not to my knowledge. But then again, I haven't anything of real value. Quinton did not mention our home being compromised in any way."

Alexander had been serving drinks at Jane's first event as Lady Sullivan. I'd seen him there this spring at Randolph House. Perhaps this was all a coincidence. I wasn't even entirely sure if he'd been hired as additional staff for Lady Vega's ball. There was simply not enough evidence to draw a damning conclusion.

And yet my heart was pounding forcefully behind my ribs at the possibility.

There was also his presence at Mary's betrothal ball. But I wouldn't be asking after her family's valuables. We had yet to bring up the event since Lord David's horrible display.

"What are you saying, Cassandra?" Fiona asked, tone concerned.

I swallowed and resisted the urge to place my hand over my pounding heart. It felt overly loud in the duchess's drawing room. My uneasiness was aided by the fact that Fiona was a dangerous combination of astute and suspicious. "Just considering the possibility of Jane and Sullivan being afflicted by whatever thievery is afoot." I waved away the theory and laughed lightly. "And playing detective at the same time. Ignore me, ladies."

"As if we could ever ignore ye, Cassandra," Ashleigh teased.

I could have kissed her square on the mouth for the distraction. All the ladies laughed...except Fiona. She was still watching me, gaze assessing.

I forced my hand to remain still in my lap and gave my friend a bright smile.

Alexander could not be connected to these thefts. Simply because I did not wish him to be. The alternative was painful and frightening. Accusing him of repeated crimes against members of the *ton* made me feel vaguely ill. Just because the circumstances of our meeting were steeped in suspicion did not give me leave to consider Alexander for these wrongdoings. He simply could not be the perpetrator behind these events. His disdain for the peerage was obvious. He was deeply distrustful, yes. But he'd also asserted himself and assisted Mary when it could have very well cost him his position, when he'd gained nothing by standing up to Lord David. How could I reconcile the bravery and determination I'd witnessed that night?

How could I also overlook his intentions in my father's study?

I did not have answers to these questions at present.

You don't want to know, my heart whispered, *because you already care about him more than is wise.*

You are being foolish, my brain responded with sensible accusation—the traitor.

Likewise, I did not know what was happening in Alexander's life. The encounters with both Miss Bellamy and Mr. Blaidd were so odd and cryptic. Mr.

Blaidd spoke like an exacting father, and Miss Bellamy like that of a jilted lover. Who were these people to Alexander? The man himself was not very forthcoming with information nor details about his life.

He is a great many things to a great many people. Your association, if discovered, would be just as detrimental for him as it would be for you. Alexander does not allow associations, acquaintances, or connections of any kind. And certainly not with a diamond of Mayfair.

But what did any of that mean? And how did his work on Baker Street coincide with his knowledge of Covent Garden?

He was becoming more enigmatic rather than less. I didn't know what to make of him, but the mystery of it all was drawing me in, more and more.

And who knew if we'd ever see one another again? The way we'd parted had been troubling. Definitely less than ideal.

I needed to put this matter behind me. No matter Alexander's allure and the pull of attraction I felt for him, it was time to proceed with my future as planned. Forget the enterprising footman.

I shook myself and attempted to dispel the lingering doubts and conspiracy theories. "Mary, may I ask how you are?"

It had been several weeks since the events at Mary's betrothal ball. The ladies and I had not pushed. We wanted to give Mary time to recover and to confide in us when she was ready.

My friend gave a small, sad smile. "I am…managing," she finally settled on. She leaned forward and placed her teacup gently on the low table before straightening her posture. "David has broken the engagement. The betrothal agreement between our families has been dissolved. But David has agreed to remain quiet about our separation. He'll return to his travels, as he is wont to do. And I will hope that I make it through the remainder of the season before the news reaches the four corners of London. I will endeavor to find a husband next year."

Sympathetic murmurs went up from those assembled.

"It's all right," Mary insisted on a sigh. "We were never a good match. Not really. No matter how much I wanted to be. You can't wish something into being. Positive thinking only gets you so far. I could not, in the end, deliver Lord David to the altar through willfulness alone." She paused to worry a loose blond curl resting elegantly at her collarbone. "Truthfully, when I thought of our future—as man and wife—I worried I'd be terribly lonely and…terribly humiliated by his indiscretions. Perhaps now I will have a choice. A chance to consider what and who I truly want. For once in my life. Maybe there is more to life than the minimum we're willing to accept for ourselves."

There it was again. *More*.

I wanted that for Mary. She was deserving of more in any and every way. My friend had subsisted for so long on the barest hint of attention from her fiancé. If anyone was owed more, it was Mary.

Her future wouldn't look the way she'd envisioned for so very long. But expectations were silly that way. They only existed in our minds, yet we held tight to them with both fists.

Perhaps Mary could adjust her long-held beliefs.

"A toast to Mary," I said suddenly, raising the fine porcelain china in my hands. I saw soft smiles around the room and I knew the other ladies were remembering the drunken toasts we'd made to Lord David the night he'd ruined everything. "May the fates deliver unto her a husband worthy of her unending love and devotion. So that they may be happy in life together, as equals and partners."

"To Mary," said the chorus of women as Mary's cheeks turned pink and pleased.

We leaned forward and carefully tapped our teacups, fueled by determination for our friend and the quiet hope that happiness would find us all.

Ten

"Cassandra! Do come in. Stop hovering by the doorway."

I jolted a little at Paul's words. I *had* been hovering outside Paul's room as he and his brother, Thomas, visited.

Paul was fifteen, and he was nearing his final year here at the Home for Incurable Children. Thomas and I hadn't discussed it, but I assumed Paul would come to live with him following his sixteenth birthday next summer. I knew Paul would already be in residence if Thomas could find in-home care at the level provided here at the hospital.

I still lingered by the wooden door which stood barely ajar. Truthfully, I didn't know how Paul had noticed me hovering in the hallway.

I'd spent my morning checking in on the patients of this floor—reading stories, drawing pictures, and playing games as the children were able. I'd brought some supplies for a few of the older girls and we spent nearly an hour knitting together in one of the common rooms for gathering. One of the girls' mothers had joined as well. I'd promised to bring more yarn in a variety of colors the following week. It had been a good morning, and I felt buoyed by the experience.

Thus my appearance outside Paul's door.

"It's fine, Cassandra," Thomas called from within. "He's having a good day."

My weekly visitation to the Home usually aligned with Thomas's regular visits to his brother. But we didn't always necessarily cross paths. A good day for

Paul usually meant very few convulsions associated with his epilepsy. I didn't want to intrude, especially on a good day.

Moments later, the door pulled open all the way and Paul grabbed my hand, tugging me fully into the room.

Thomas was reading a newspaper in an armchair beside his brother's bed. He pointed with the newsprint and indicated I should sit in the adjacent seat.

Paul climbed back atop the coverlet—sewn by me as a gift—and told Thomas to continue reading.

I'd made friends with Paul over the years of my volunteering, as I generally held the maturity and humor of a fifteen-year-old. We amused ourselves by joining forces and teasing Thomas, and he allowed it because it made his very sick brother happy. Thomas was a good sort.

Finally, Thomas's monotone recitation of the latest bill being put forth to the House of Lords was at an end. Paul straightened and asked after me.

"I'm quite well. And I'm even better now that I see what a fine day you're having," I replied with a large grin.

"Any new gossip to share? Exciting events you attended?" His eager questions made my heart squeeze.

"Well..." I paused, and then reached a decision. "I visited Covent Garden Market just last week."

I could feel Thomas turn to look at me even as Paul's eyes brightened. The young man's expression became animated. It was as if there was an allotment of emotions in the Burke family. Paul received them all and there was nothing left over for Thomas.

"Tell me everything," Paul begged.

So, I did. I told him all about the colors and sounds and smells. The fresh vegetables and fruits. I described the people I saw. As much as I tried to convey the general busyness and congestion of the streets, I didn't think I could ever do it justice. One had to experience the overwhelming chaos that was the market before they truly understood it.

Paul remained fully engaged, asking questions and seeking clarification as I spoke. We carried on for over a half hour, and yet the boy remained still—no horrible convulsions racking his thin, wiry body as they so often did throughout the day. This truly was a good visit for Thomas.

A maid interrupted with a luncheon tray for Paul.

"I should be on my way. It was so very good to see you, Paul," I said, standing.

"Tom, you should escort Cassandra out. I'm going to take my meal with Harold down the hall. I promised him I would on my next good day."

I smiled at the boy's sly intent and Thomas's corresponding eyeroll. Paul thought Thomas and I should have married long ago. I'd tried—many times—to explain that I too saw a brother when I looked at Thomas. And there was no possible way I'd ever mention Thomas's offer and our theoretical marriage pact. I didn't know if Thomas had ever shared his proclivities with his brother. It was not my place to judge or divulge. I would support him however he liked.

We said our goodbyes with Thomas promising to return in the afternoon to spend the remainder of his day with Paul.

Once we were in the hallway, Thomas turned to me as we walked. "Who did you go to Covent Garden with, Cassandra?"

I knew he wouldn't let that go.

"With Alexander, the unsuitable match."

His facial expression did not change and neither did speech come right away. We'd turned a corner toward the staircase before Thomas spoke. "And he thought that was an appropriate outing?"

"I imagine he didn't consider the suitability of the market until we were already there." Not until Mr. Blaidd pointed it out. "He seemed to think it would be something I would enjoy."

Thomas didn't immediately answer, as if his thoughts needed room to breathe. "I'm quite sure you did enjoy it."

"You are correct."

He pulled us to a stop at the end of the corridor. "What's going on, Cassandra? You clearly sought me out today." I opened my mouth to explain, but he cut me off with a quick shake of his head. "It's fine. I am not upset. Paul loves when you visit. You are far more entertaining than I."

"Indeed. In the way clowns are entertaining." My friend gave me a flat look that had me chuckling to myself, but I sobered when Thomas reached out and gently squeezed my arm.

"Tell me."

I hesitated. I didn't know what to say, how much to reveal. I would need to explain the basics of the mad plan I'd come up with in the five days since Alexander had unceremoniously put me into a hackney carriage. "Will you join me for luncheon at a nearby restaurant in Marylebone? I need your help," was what I settled on.

"Yes, of course," Thomas replied immediately, and my throat tightened a bit with his easy agreement and unwavering friendship. He was willing to do so much for me. I didn't know that I deserved him.

Once we were in the carriage, I explained that Alexander was an employee of the Baker Street Coffee House. I left out the part about him also being a footman in Mayfair at a variety of large events over the years, and his potential—unsubstantiated—involvement in thefts at those same high-society events. I elaborated on my visit to the market and admitted what had happened with Mr. Blaidd.

"So, he's faced reality. And likely realized—and finally acknowledged—that you are far above his station and there is no hope for an association," Thomas surmised.

"Yes," I agreed. "But I am not ready for that to be the end of the story. I want to see him and speak to him. And perhaps if he sees you—someone who is a suitable match—he'll find some competitive intuition in the face of adversity and stop being someone who gives up at the first sign of challenge."

Thomas regarded me from his place across the carriage, lips pursed. "But where is this going, Cassandra? What could you possibly be hoping for…for the future? You already acknowledged that you cannot marry this man. He is not on your path. He is firmly in the opposite direction."

"Well, perhaps my path deviates. Perhaps my path takes a few unexpected turns."

"Yes, through a bramble that will leave you bruised and heartbroken. Cassandra, this is a bad idea."

"I know," I admitted in frustration. "I know it is. But I— I cannot simply let this be the end. I have to talk to him. I have to at least try. Can you understand that? I need to know that he will be all right. That our time in each other's lives has meant something. That I'm not alone in that."

We'd already stopped on the side of the street.

Thomas heaved a sigh worthy of the stage and said, "Fine."

"Really?" I knew my voice conveyed my hopefulness.

"Yes," Thomas confirmed. "We shall go into the restaurant and I will behave as if I'm enamored of you. I am a brilliant actor. We'll draw Alexander's attention as you have *planned*." He said the final word as if it was unsanitary.

I squinted. "What do you mean you are a brilliant actor?"

Thomas descended the carriage and held out a hand to me. "Just what I said. I will make him believe that we are a true love match, destined for matrimony. I will rile all his competitive instincts with my devotion to you."

I grew slightly alarmed at how convinced Thomas was that he could successfully pull off this ruse. My worry grew as he placed my hand on his arm and crossed the street with the stiffness of an Egyptian mummified corpse.

"Thomas," I hissed, pulling him aside before he could "act" his way up the stairs to the restaurant front doors. "How will you be a convincing thespian?"

He frowned. "I will act besotted and never look away. I will laugh at your jokes. Show him how delightful you are and how amusing and entertaining I find you."

"Show me," I demanded. "Pretend I just said something and you are consumed with hilarity and utterly charmed."

Thomas blinked and then suddenly he was laughing—braying like a donkey, actually. His face had not changed at all. If it wasn't for his mouth, wide and gaping like a cavernous maw, I would have thought he was watching paint dry. But the sound was horrific. I actually raised my gloved hand to cover his lips before realizing the intimacy of the action on a public sidewalk and pulling back.

"Stop," I begged.

He did. Immediately. The inhuman laughter cut off like a garden hose, and the ensuing silence felt overwhelmingly like relief.

"What was that?" I said aghast, looking around to see if any passersby had noticed. "Is that your stage laugh? Is that how you think people express amusement, Thomas? Dear God."

Affronted, he placed a hand to his chest. "I have heard several men laugh at your antics in such a manner. It is entirely plausible that—"

"It is not. I assure you."

"Should it be more of a chortle, then?" He demonstrated by placing a hand on his stomach and leaning back, huffing his manufactured amusement in rhythmic grunts of *heh-heh-heh*.

My eyes widened. "No. That doesn't sound natural at all!"

"Was that register too low?" What followed could only be described as the giggle of a deranged schoolchild that had me simultaneously horrified and incredulous. So, naturally, that was when I started laughing—like a normal person—as well. And that was also when Alexander turned the corner onto Baker Street behind Thomas's back.

He walked with his hands in his coat pockets, and froze as recognition struck. His attention paused to focus on the sounds of our lunacy on the sidewalk.

My laughter died and I started choking. Thomas, however, did not see fit to cease until Alexander resumed motion and walked directly up to us, demanding in a low voice, "What are you doing here?"

I cleared my throat and ruined our entire plan with startled honesty. "I wanted to see you."

Alexander examined me for a moment—as if cataloguing the veracity of my claim. But then he looked over to Thomas and frowned in aggravation. "And what is *he* doing here?"

Thomas opened his mouth but no sound emerged. He looked to me helplessly.

Alexander rolled his eyes before sighing. "Come on." His warm hand eased around my arm, just above the elbow. I was moving with him before he'd applied any pressure.

Thomas found his voice after I'd taken two steps in Alexander's direction. "I say! Where are you taking her?"

"It's all right, Thomas," I assured him, pausing briefly in my progress. "Take the carriage and return to Paul. Enjoy his good day."

Thomas came closer and lowered his voice. "Cassandra, I cannot leave you unaccompanied."

Alexander looked irritated but he remained still, awaiting my decision.

"I will be fine, I assure you. Please trust me."

Thomas eyed me before nodding. "I am leaving the carriage. You will need it. Come back to the Home following your…conversation here. So that I know you are safe."

"She *is* safe," Alexander growled. "I would never hurt her."

I'd never seen Thomas look so stern. "She'd never let you know it, even if you did."

Alexander's frown deepened as he considered my friend's cryptic warning.

"And *she* is standing right here. Goodbye, Thomas. I'll return to the Home shortly. Thank you for your assistance today. Mission accomplished."

With that, I turned toward the street corner. Alexander tugged my arm once again to direct our steps.

"Careful," I said, removing my shawl from beneath his grasp. "I don't want it to get damaged. I sewed it myself." Not to mention the delicately embroidered edge.

Alexander's hand moved down to clutch my forearm instead. "You did?" His frustrated expression gave way to curiosity as he took in my shawl.

"Nearly every young lady can sew, Alexander."

His frown returned. "Not where I'm from."

He resumed our path, leading me around the corner to a small alleyway behind the restaurant, barely wide enough for a carriage. Up a short flight of stairs, a door stood open with wooden crates stacked neatly on the landing. We entered a storage area with boxes, cans, and more crates—these filled with autumn vegetables and other produce.

Alexander's steps never faltered as he made for the stairs, but his hand slid lower, interlocked our fingers, and pulled me easily along behind him. He did not pause on the second-floor landing but continued up to an apartment on the third floor. Unlocking the door, we went inside.

It was tidy but spartan. The main room held one chair next to a large window. No curtains and no table. Books overflowed from bookcases lining one wall and were even piled in three high stacks beside the chair. I could see an open doorway and a bedchamber beyond. Plain bedding and a bare canopy marked the simplicity of Alexander's private space.

The urge to linger over every corner and investigate every book spine was admittedly strong, but when I glimpsed Alexander's tight fists and pink cheeks, I endeavored to control my curiosity. "Were you not working today?"

"It is one of my days off from the restaurant," he confirmed.

If not for truly exceptional timing, Thomas and I would have dined together and missed Alexander entirely. The plan would have been simply moot rather than the explosive failure it had become.

Alexander's frustrated voice distracted me from my perusal of his rooms. "What are you doing here, Cassandra? Why were you at the restaurant trying to make me jealous? Why are you playing these games?"

"I will have you know that Thomas is my very dear friend. We've worked together for years. And we were at the Home all morning and thought to indulge in a bit of luncheon."

Alexander stared flatly and waited.

I swallowed. "And fine, yes. I wanted to see you. I hated how our trip to the market ended. I was worried for you." I glanced quickly toward his hand covered in black leather. "And perhaps I wasn't ready to be cast aside."

He sighed. "I wasn't casting you aside. Putting you in that carriage was for your own good. I never should have brought you to the Garden. It was thoughtless and dangerous."

"But why?"

Abruptly, Alexander took off his hat and placed it on the bookshelf. "Blaidd was right. You are a lady. Sneaking you in and out of your home will only rouse trouble. Your reputation is at stake."

I appreciated neither the reminder nor the resignation I heard in his tone. "Who is this Elias Blaidd person? Why did he have leave to speak to you that way? Who is he to you?"

Alexander's features closed off. "Believe me when I say it is better that you do not know."

"I am trustworthy, Alexander. I would not betray your confidence."

"I know that," he admitted, voice anguished. "I know." I witnessed the whispered repetition more than I heard it. Alexander's gaze was pained and remorseful, as if he wanted desperately to confide in me but he simply could not allow it, the words lodged stubbornly in his throat.

I knew what I'd told Thomas, that coming here today was some sort of final attempt with Alexander. But I could not move forward. That path was closed to me, impassable and unfathomable.

I stepped closer, bringing us within touching distance if he lowered his guard or if I was particularly encouraged. "I am not ready for this to be the end for you and me."

"There is no you and me, Princess." The word held no bite, just fondness. "We are too different in every conceivable way, and even more that I probably have not considered."

I met his stare and shuffled forward a pace. "What about what I want?"

"And what is that?" he asked.

You.

My voice betrayed me, refusing to say the full truth aloud, so I admitted the other part of it instead. "I want to be happy. I'm tired of being a stepping-stone for others. Wanted for some silly reason, and never wanted for me. But you, Alexander. You look at me like you *want*. Like you *need*. I should get a choice. And I want to choose you. I want to spend time with you and get to know you. And kiss you again." I omitted the full truth of my wants and desires: the feel of his skin under my wandering hands, the sounds he would make in the dark, and the absolute destruction of my carefully crafted future.

I couldn't read his expression. If he was considering the very improper offer we both knew I was making, he didn't show it.

"Do you know what you're asking for?" he finally said.

I closed the remaining distance and placed my hands upon his strong shoulders. "I believe I do."

"What about the season?" he demanded, bitterness bleeding through. "You're supposed to be looking for a husband."

I swallowed against the unfairness of our circumstances and the undiluted honesty in his tone—disappointed in a world where I was required to navigate a future of my choosing when it wasn't really my choice at all.

I didn't answer. There was nothing I could say, no argument I could make. I *should* have been looking for a husband. Instead I was in a third-floor apartment in Marylebone, staring at him.

He leaned forward, brushing his chilly nose along mine. "I would be nothing but a waste of your time and an unnecessary risk."

I squeezed his shoulders, a warning, an admonishment. "You could never be a waste, Alexander."

He sighed, the warmth ghosting over me. "If you are determined to be reckless, we should put a time limit on…on…this. After the new year, you should cut me loose."

I raised slightly on the tips of my toes, my words forming along the stubbled skin of his jaw. "I shall take that under advisement."

"Cassandra," he scolded.

I smiled, pressing a soft kiss beneath his chin.

"We can never be seen together."

"I can be creative," I argued. I was inching my way to his ear, one sweet kiss at a time. "And I know you can too."

His breathing was picking up pace under my ministrations. "It's too dangerous."

I pulled back, giving him space to answer, desperately needing this trust between us. "Why don't you explain a bit of that to me? Not all of it, if you're not able," I said quickly before he could object. Thinking of the inherent warning from both Mr. Blaidd and Miss Bellamy, I continued. "I cannot be cautious without knowing what to look out for, Alexander."

He was utterly still in my arms, but when he finally spoke, his voice was hoarse. "Covent Garden is too dangerous. That is where…my past is most insistent. And I don't want any part of that to touch you. No more trips there. Can we agree on that?"

"Yes, of course."

Alexander swallowed audibly. "Blaidd…he found me and he raised me. Since I was a young child. And he will never loosen his hold. He thinks he owns me. But I've spent the better part of four years trying to separate myself from him—put distance between us. If he thinks you are someone to me, he'll use you. Hurt you in order to hurt me."

"Why would he want to hurt you? If he raised you, doesn't he care for you?" I was confused by their relationship and sought to understand.

He shook his head before returning his gaze to mine. "I don't think he's capable of—of caring. He values money and little else. He does not think of me like a son, if that's what you're meaning. I'm more like a…" His voice trailed off, searching. "A possession. Valuable but worth destroying if it comes down to it."

A wave of sadness had me shifting my hold, moving my arms down and around Alexander's waist to clutch him more firmly. I was fortunate to have two kind and loving parents. It was difficult for me to imagine someone raising a child yet being unable to love them in return. Making my voice as even as possible, I asked, "How old were you?"

"When he found me?" Alexander confirmed. At my short nod, he continued. "I don't really know. Maybe four or five years of age. I have very few memories of my life prior to Blaidd being in it."

"Your mother? Or father?"

"I don't remember them. Not really. Just shadowy images of a woman with dark hair." Alexander's eyes were distant, looking beyond me and reaching for a life that was no longer there.

"I'm sorry," I said, and winced at the sympathy that had inadvertently bled into my tone.

His attention snapped to me, eyes going hard. "Don't. Don't pity me."

"I don't pity you," I said firmly. "I just want to know you, Alexander. You're so solitary. You needn't be."

"What good does it to tell you of my past?" His voice was resolute. "You want to hear that I was an orphan? That Blaidd found me barefoot, wandering the streets of the Garden with nothing but some papers pinned inside my clothes. That I was poor and hungry for most of my life? Starving and cold. And too much of all those things to even notice that I was lonely. Friendship and companionship are just frivolous possessions for people who can afford to miss them. People like you."

"People like you as well," I challenged. "You deserve to be cared for. You deserve friendship and love. What you've been through doesn't make you any less worthy. Can't you see that?"

He grimaced and stepped back. I'd gone too far.

We were both quiet, watching one another carefully.

Contrite, I said, "I apologize. I overstepped."

His eyes softened, and he breathed a sigh. "No, you didn't. I was offering information and then drew an imaginary line in the sand. You stepped beyond it without even realizing it was there. But if I give an inch, Cassandra, you're likely to take a mile."

"Is that a testament to my prowess?"

He laughed. "Something like that." His stare never wavered, but he finally said, "Come here." And held out a hand.

I stepped forward as he sat in the lone chair in the room and pulled me onto his lap. The ancient armchair groaned in protest, but Alexander did not seem concerned.

"Will you consent to seeing me in secret?" I sought to confirm.

He sighed. "You are nothing if not persistent."

"Thank you."

He smiled wide. "That wasn't a compliment."

"Really? Because I think you like that about me."

Alexander's smile softened, teeth disappearing behind his full lips. "I like a great many things about you."

Now it was my turn to laugh. "That cannot be true. If I recall correctly—and I do—you spent a fair amount of time attempting to evade me."

His warm palm settled on the outside of my thigh. "Avoiding you seemed to be the safest path forward. You are too perceptive and intelligent." I grinned under his reluctant praise. "And you are a troublemaker." His hand gently squeezed my leg through the fabric of my skirts.

"I think you aren't afraid of a little bit of trouble."

Alexander leaned forward and placed a lingering kiss on the column of my throat.

"Nor adventure." Another press to where my pulse was thrumming. I took a shaky inhale. "Neither do you fear my persistence. Nor my perceptive intelligence." The final word emerged as a squeak as Alexander's lips found the lobe of my ear.

After a moment, he pulled back. "Oh, Cassandra. How very wrong you are. For I am, without question, terrified of you."

Speaking became difficult as our lips became otherwise engaged. The hand warming my outer thigh began an upward journey, tracing the contour of my waist before settling over my breast.

I gasped into Alexander's kiss as his other hand stroked up my spine and into my hair. Our kisses and touches were lazy, lacking the ferocity and urgency of our previous interludes. It was as if this arrangement, now mostly decided, gave us the time and energy to enjoy our exploration. To slow our pace and give in to the demands of our desire.

Cupping his cheek, I relished in the intimacy of the action and the rough stubble beneath my palm. Instinctively, I knew Alexander did not allow closeness of this kind. It required trust and understanding.

The hand clutching my breast squeezed and plumped my sensitive flesh over the fabric of my bodice. I could feel his palm ghost over my pebbled nipple, dragging sensation and leaving fire in his wake.

I broke our kiss, breathing hard against his neck. Alexander's arousal was unmistakable from where I sat draped across his lap. The knowledge sent a spike of desire and feminine satisfaction through my body before settling low and deep, someplace hidden and waiting.

Eventually our labored breathing evened as we worked to gather ourselves, knowing instinctively that level heads should prevail in this moment. Knowing there would be more.

This wasn't the end. Only the beginning.

Eleven

"Cassandra, dear, I am going in search of refreshments. Enjoy yourself. I shall see you later."

"Yes, Mrs. Ridley. Please make yourself comfortable. I shall be quite all right." I attempted to withhold the excitement from my voice as I reassured my chaperone that I would be perfectly well on my own at the St. Clair annual masquerade.

As the elderly woman shuffled out of the crowded ballroom with the aid of her walking stick, I discreetly scanned the area.

Two days ago, when Alexander and I had finally parted, he'd removed me from his lap and escorted me from his rooms to my waiting carriage. He'd asked if I planned on attending the masquerade ball this Saturday and hinted that he would find me there. The street had been crowded and I wasn't able to ask all the questions I'd wanted, but I felt reasonably certain that he'd be making an appearance this evening as a footman.

And now, as I took in the elaborate space, my skin fairly vibrated with the possibility.

The room was alight with glowing candles and an eager crowd, all attired in stylish half masks—some plain, some beaded and bejeweled, and others feathered and as elaborate as my own. The servants were milling among the guests bearing trays of light hors d'oeuvres and sparkling glasses of champagne. They too were wearing masks—black domino in style.

I couldn't see Alexander from my position, so I moved about, scanning the area. I knew that none of my close circle of friends were attending this evening. Fiona's husband was in town unexpectedly and she was spending the evening with her family as a result. Mary was still avoiding public events following the dissolution of her betrothal to Lord David. Thomas had informed me that he wouldn't be present tonight. Ashleigh and Eliza were attending one of the final dress rehearsals for Nicolas's upcoming play at the Joc Collins Theater. And Jane and Quinton were off being married and happy in each other's company.

My pink gown swished agreeably around my legs as I continued onward. Elaborate sights and sounds greeted me in nearly every direction as St. Clair spared no expense for his grand event each year. Ladies and gentlemen danced in their finery around a raised dais for the musical accompaniment. I peered beyond a group of men congregating with their drinks near the open doorway to the gardens. I pardoned my way through and down the steps toward the hedge maze.

Revelers were fewer here, and I had no doubt that if I wasn't careful, I would stumble upon couples indulging in the cover of secrecy and relative darkness. The St. Clair masquerade was typically known for bad behavior. However, the perceived anonymity of being masked among one's peers seemed to provide the courage necessary to act improperly. As a young, unmarried lady, I was only permitted to attend with a chaperone, and my mother only allowed this because she was such good friends with St. Clair's mother, Lady Smithwicke.

It was not my fault that Mrs. Ridley sought the comforts indoors rather than remain steadfastly by her charge for the evening. But I would damn well use the extent of my meager freedoms to the very fullest.

Tugging my shawl tighter to ward off the chilly night air, I ambled farther into the greenery. The yew hedges must have been nearly six feet tall, and twisted and turned along the path. Torches were placed haphazardly, but in some areas I became completely engulfed by darkness before emerging into the warm glow beyond.

It was in one such shadowy corner that I collided most inelegantly with someone large and solid. A startled squeal rose in my throat as my chest made contact with…perhaps a shoulder. However, before the urgent sound could emerge, a warm, gloved hand covered my mouth, and lips by my ear whispered quickly.

"It's me. Stay quiet for me. There is a couple around the next corner."

My heart pounded hard, but I heard Alexander's deep voice in my ear and smelled the smoky spice and rich sandalwood scents of the Coffee House on his skin.

And then, just as quickly, he removed his hand, pressing a soft kiss to my cheek. His lips lingered and I felt my heart trip over itself for an entirely different reason.

It was nearly too dark to make out his form, but I felt strong fingers lace through my own and I followed eagerly in his wake. Finally, we entered the torchlight up ahead, and at the intersection Alexander turned left. He walked with purpose, as if he'd investigated this maze and already concluded the safest course. Eventually the path widened to showcase a row of young saplings and an inset in the hedge with a marble statue atop a pedestal depicting a barefoot young maiden.

I drew closer for a better look and placed a steadying hand on the pedestal. My grace faltered at the last moment as I tripped upon the grass. My hand pushed with more force than I intended and the marble statue wobbled precariously. I gasped and my eyes widened, but then Alexander was there, wrapping strong arms around the base and settling the sculpture back into place.

Our wide eyes met and I placed a calming hand to my chest. "Oh God! That would have been a tragedy. Thank you for righting it."

Suddenly we were both laughing at the absurdity of the moment.

"You know," I managed, "if we were courting, that would have been your Cassandra disaster and you would have broken our association to avoid a broken foot."

I laughed at my own jest, but Alexander's smile lost a bit of width. "I don't know about that. I don't scare easy."

It was then that I noticed Alexander's attire. He was not dressed as a footman. In black trousers and jacket, Alexander played the part of a high-society gentleman. His dark waistcoat was elaborate and perfect for tonight's event, interwoven gold threads catching the dim light. A black cravat and matching shirt lent completely to the look of a mysterious and unattainable aristocrat. He'd slipped into this masquerade tonight as a guest and not a servant. I knew well enough not to draw attention to this, so I focused on the near miss with the statue instead.

Alexander tugged me toward a shadowed stone bench. The next torch was some distance away, providing us the illusion of privacy in the relative darkness.

"What is that grin for?" he asked, both amused and cautious.

"Oh, nothing," I replied, my smile widening. I didn't know how Alexander would react to hearing how pleased I was that he'd found me tonight—that he'd been motivated enough to attend as a gentleman spy. And even more, that I'd known he would come for me. The knowledge and the expectation felt intimate in a way that—contrary to his recent claim—would likely scare him off. So I withheld the truth from my words if not my expression.

He snorted. "I'm not sure coy suits you, Your Highness."

I laughed lightly as I settled more comfortably on the bench. I moved to lower my shawl from around my neck, allowing it to fall from my shoulders and settle on either side in the crook of my elbows. "Am I being coy?" I said, tone impish.

There was no response for several long moments. I finally looked up from where I was straightening my wrap. Alexander's eyes were fastened on my bosom, and speech had apparently abandoned him.

I'd known that Alexander found me attractive, or at least appealing enough to return my kisses. I'd felt—several times now—the reaction of his manhood, hard and eager against me. But that was simply his body responding to a stimulus. I couldn't rely on that alone to indicate interest. So while I'd inferred his attraction to my physical form, he'd never told me he found me lovely or enticing or any other such romantic sentiment.

Sometimes it was nice to hear the words. And coming from Alexander, I knew they would mean something. It wouldn't be the expected compliments received in a ballroom or mindless chatter about the quality of my appearance. I wanted to know that he found me beautiful. The same way I thought him all things masculine and tempting.

But in the absence of those words, the look on his face right this moment would do nicely.

Admittedly, the bustline of my dress was scandalous, the beaded edge cut low and tight across my chest. The locket I wore nestled indecently between my breasts. I had never worn this gown to any other event. However, the St. Clair masquerade, with its mischievous air and reckless sense of anonymity, seemed the perfect choice. With the addition of my elaborately decorated shawl to cover all the inappropriate bits, I felt confident in my selected attire for the evening.

Our earlier conversation apparently forgotten, Alexander choked out, "Where is the rest of your dress?"

I fought the urge to laugh as his eyes rose to my face before being drawn back to my chest. They flitted around the garden in an impressive attempt at distraction before landing once more on the wide expanse of pale skin between my collarbones and the globes rising above the pink fabric of my gown. I did laugh then and his eyes snapped to mine.

"Did you wear that for me?" Alexander's gaze was dark and challenging behind his mask. But beneath that was the honesty I craved. He wanted. He desired. And he was desperate with it. For me.

I'd put that look on his face. A sense of feminine satisfaction rose like a wave, warming me. An answering heat flushed my cheeks and settled low in my belly.

The realization wiped the amusement from my face, and for one long and intense moment we simply regarded one another.

"I did wear it for you," I finally admitted, face still hot, the blood surging beneath my skin.

Embarrassed honesty had me suddenly self-conscious, wondering if I'd over-reached or missed the mark entirely.

When Alexander still said nothing, I blurted into the silence, "Do you think me pretty?"

My words awoke something within and he shook his head slowly. Reaching for my hand, he pulled it onto his thigh and cradled it carefully. "No, Cassandra. Never." His words were soft and gentle, spoken to our joined hands. Slowly he worked off the fabric of our gloves before stroking the skin he'd uncovered. His fingers were rough from a life lived outside of gentleman's clubs.

I frowned at his words and the implication, but Alexander continued speaking, caressing my hand all the while.

"You are loveliness personified. The brightest light in every room." The pad of his finger traced the line of my knuckles, dipping and rising slowly along an uncharted path. "Your beauty is but a part of your allure. I am charmed by so much beyond your face and your body—your honesty, your caring and giving heart. But your face and your body, Cassandra...could never be merely pretty. You are incandescent."

I swallowed with some difficulty. His tender manner and the solemnity in his words made me feel suddenly emotional.

Compliments came and went easily enough. The commonplace praise I so often received for my dress or my hair rarely touched on anything deeper. But Alexander's admiration dipped well below the surface. It felt real in a way that made my chest constrict.

When I had failed to respond and could only watch as the man reverently held my hand, he finally looked up.

I opened my mouth, but before I could speak the leaves on the hedgerow in front of us shook with movement on the other side. And then a feminine giggle erupted. Alexander rose swiftly. My hand—still enclosed in his own—allowed him to lead me from our bench and farther into the maze to avoid being seen by the encroaching newcomers.

Alexander walked silently. By comparison, I felt like a conspicuous oaf—my underskirts rustling loudly in the night air.

We turned a dark corner and abruptly came face-to-embrace with a couple wrapped around one another. I stared wide-eyed at the pair before Alexander urged me back a pace until we were safely hidden the way we'd come. Our eyes met behind our masks and the urge to laugh became nearly overwhelming. Smiling, he shook his head to discourage me, so I covered my mouth with my hand and he led us quickly around another turn and down an alternate path.

We were moving briskly now, away from the kissing couple and the giggling woman who'd interrupted us on the bench. Alexander was peeking around corners and I was looking over my shoulder. We scurried and then finally ran from path to path before suddenly bursting out of the hedge maze and into a line of trees surrounding St. Clair's property. The autumn leaves had already abandoned their tall branches so the night sky was hardly obscured. The moon shone brightly—nearly full—on a surprisingly cloudless night. The air was cool on my heated skin as our breathing slowed, loud in the quiet space.

Alexander pulled me along the perimeter of the shrubbery and I could not hide the smile from my face. "That was at least a moderate adventure."

He paused and drew me into his arms. "I'm inclined to agree with you."

I snuggled close, encircling his waist and resting my head on his broad chest. "That's a first," I teased.

I felt his laugh more than I heard it, and the intimacy of the action had me squeezing him closer. My mask pressed uncomfortably against my temples, and I ached to remove it. I'd never needed a disguise to feel brave. But something told me that Alexander appreciated the illusion—one that placed us on equal footing, here on this chilly night.

"Are you cold?" Alexander asked as I nuzzled closer. I shook my head, but he ignored me. "Here," he said, pulling back to take my shawl gently and tuck it over my shoulders. He looked mournful as he angled the fabric across my chest, covering the wide swath of visible skin. But he wrapped his arms back around me and held me close once more.

"Are you here tonight to steal something?" I asked suddenly, calling on that bravery. I was terrified of ruining the moment, the lightness between us this evening. But I needed to know why he'd attended dressed as a guest rather than a footman. And honestly, we'd ignored this long enough. *I'd* ignored Alexander's nefarious acts in favor of ignorance. I hadn't wanted to face the reality of his life posing as a servant. In the fantasy I'd created, Alexander was a handsome employee of the Baker Street Coffee House. He thought I was incandescent, and kissed me like a starving man. There hadn't been room to consider his alternate lifestyle. I'd filled all my thoughts to bursting with the man I wanted rather than the one standing before me this night.

Alexander stiffened in my arms but did not pull away.

"I—I just want to understand. You try to pretend that part of your life doesn't exist, but, Alexander, we met under less than reputable circumstances. I remember seeing you at events in which valuables were taken." I felt him swallow. "Lady Vega. Lady Helm. Lord Sullivan. I'm not trying to reprimand you or accuse you, but I want to know."

"Cassandra, I cannot tell you," he insisted on a sigh. "It would put you in danger, and I refuse to do so. I told you that my past would make you vulnerable."

"Is someone forcing you?" I persisted, ignoring him.

"We all have expectations. Even you," he admitted, voice flat.

"My expectations will not land me in prison," I argued.

He laughed without humor. "Your expectations would see you shackled in an entirely different way."

I flushed hotly at the insinuation of my future and the sort of marriage I could hope to expect. I kept my arms around him but pulled back to see his face.

Alexander's expression was defiant, prepared for battle. So I reached on tiptoe and kissed his nose—the tip just peeking out from beneath his black half mask. "I hope someday you will be able to tell me the truth, and trust me enough to hear it."

I had to believe that he would confide in me in his own time. Pressuring him would only lead to conflict and strife. Our time together was limited. I did not want to push him away with my insistent curiosity and badgering, but neither did that mean I would give up. Perhaps I was foolish enough to want to help him—to save him. That, however, was not something I was ready to admit.

He blinked before saying gently, "The only reason I am here tonight…is for you."

I didn't know who moved first but suddenly we were kissing, masks colliding inelegantly.

I gripped his shoulders as if he would disappear, and he clutched me back just as tightly. My mouth moved over his, eager tongue licking along the seam of his lips. He groaned into our kiss, the sound tortured and raw.

Alexander's hands found my backside and he squeezed me to him just as an explosion of sparks burst in the air. We broke apart and watched through the tree branches as fireworks turned the sky golden in a shower of light.

I turned in the comfort of his arms and together we watched the night transform to hopeful and bright, as if by magic.

Time passed, and at the intersection of very late and exceedingly early, Alexander led me back into the hedge maze. My lips swollen from our renewed affections following the fireworks display, we maneuvered through the nearly empty paths among the shrubbery. Alexander had placed his jacket on my shoulders some time ago, saying he needed to return me before someone noted my absence. Smiling to myself, I thought of his eager lips and wandering hands. I wore the mark of his stubbled jaw on the delicate skin of my breasts just as securely as the fine wool of his coat.

"The garden opens up just ahead," he said quietly by my side before pulling to a stop. He retrieved his gloves and my own from his pocket before removing his jacket from my shoulders and shrugging it on.

He quickly covered his hands in the fine dark fabric before carefully tugging my own long gloves into place. Grasping either side of my wrap, he covered the skin he'd so eagerly worshiped earlier in the evening.

His eyes lingered a moment before he swallowed audibly and met my gaze. "You have no idea what seeing your skin, so pink and perfect from my ministrations, does to me. Something primal. Something savage. To smell your lavender scent on my jacket for the remainder of the night will be the purest form of torture."

I grinned. "I have some idea," I said before reaching up, uncaring about my pale glove, and rubbing the rouge I'd left on his bottom lip. He followed the movement, nipping along my thumb and smiling devilishly in response.

With a quick motion he grabbed my hand and placed a kiss to my palm before stepping away. "Go ahead. I'll stay back a moment."

I nodded, uneasy with the separation and the deception required to simply exist in the same space. But I raised my chin and stepped forward toward the patio and stairs beyond.

I smoothly entered the congested ballroom. The crowd hadn't thinned in the slightest despite the late hour. Musicians played and couples still danced. My chaperone was likely in one of the retiring rooms, nursing a sherry or already asleep where she waited.

The urge to turn back and watch Alexander enter through the balcony doors was overwhelming, but I knew I shouldn't. It wouldn't be prudent or wise. So naturally I maneuvered to the opposite side of a potted palm and peered discreetly through the leaves, watching just as Alexander emerged. His gait was unhurried and unbothered. He appeared utterly confident and at ease dressed in his disguise. But I supposed people often saw only what they expected to see.

Alexander scanned the assembly before his eyes locked on something or someone on the edge of the dance floor. His expression never altered, but his steps faltered momentarily before he resumed his measured stroll toward an interior corridor and out of the ballroom. He hadn't noted my position at all.

Cautiously, I maneuvered to the other side of the plant and searched the area that had caught Alexander's attention. A woman in a shimmering violet gown lingered along the fringes of the crush. Her medium-brown hair was pinned effortlessly in place and her mask obscured the top half of her face. But I'd recognize the woman anywhere. I tended to remember individuals who entered carriages uninvited and issued veiled warnings.

I watched Ember Bellamy for a moment longer, noting that Alexander hadn't reentered the ballroom. Whether he disappeared as a result of his adventure with me in the hedge maze or the presence of the mysterious Miss Bellamy, I couldn't say.

The enigmatic woman turned suddenly and met my eye—as if she'd known I had been standing there observing her all along. I couldn't read her expression behind the beaded mask, but her lips quirked before she turned and meandered away, getting lost easily in the crowd.

I found her manner unsettling, as if she were a wild animal—both unpredictable and venomous. Her connection with Alexander was still unknown. The questions were mounting, forming a tidy brickwork, layered atop one another and solidified with curiosity. All the unknowns were building a frustrating barrier between myself and Alexander where physical ones already existed.

But the time was coming when I would no longer accept half-truths and secrecy.

I hoped Alexander was ready for it.

~

MRS. RIDLEY and I left St. Clair's a short while later.

We arrived back at Dameron Hall just after two o'clock in the morning. I'd shrugged off my slippers in the foyer, wished Mrs. Ridley and Jansen a good night, and carried myself to bed.

The fire was banked but my bedchamber was warm. I wandered in the relative darkness over to my dressing table and deposited my elaborate mask. Folding my shawl, I placed it on the cushioned seat before hearing a quiet tap on my balcony doors.

Something instinctual within told me who I would find. My heart accelerated with expectation rather than fear.

Moving cautiously, I went to the closed window overlooking the garden and down into the mews. I peered sidelong at the dark form standing just outside my exterior doors, on the second floor of my home.

Anticipation bloomed eager and hopeful, and I threw open the latch. Alexander stood sentry on the small balcony, his hair slightly tousled, expression guarded. His eyes dipped once again to my bodice, but returned admirably after just a moment.

"I was not ready to say good night," he admitted finally, acknowledging his presence here in my home.

"Somehow I don't imagine the lock would have posed a challenge for you."

"I thought it better to ask permission rather than forgiveness."

"That doesn't sound like you at all," I quipped.

He smiled, a weak and wounded thing. "Perhaps I am trying to be more respectable."

I reached forward and tugged the lapels of his jacket. "I wish you wouldn't."

As we moved within, I felt him smile against my lips before he reached low around my thighs and hoisted me up. His boot lifted and he pushed the balcony door gently shut. Then we were shuffling, in the dark, toward my bed. Alexander didn't bother turning down the coverlet. My back landed softly and he followed, lips still caressing mine.

His weight was a delicious press in the darkness. I felt both bound and safely ensconced. My legs were wide but the bunch of my skirts inhibited full contact between us. I felt his tongue ease forward and lick into my mouth, the heat and movements slow and seductive. One large hand still clutched my outer thigh while the other supported his upper body where he hovered above me.

I broke away from his mouth and squirmed in his arms, reaching for a candle and a match on my bedside table.

"Leave it," he begged, voice rough and strained. "If I clearly see your face, your body, I'll come to my senses and climb down your trellis, calling myself every kind of fool for forgetting my place."

"Your place," I said, "is right here. With me." And leaning forward, I took his lip between my teeth and bit down.

Alexander grunted as his lower body surged forward. I could feel him, just barely, at my center. But it wasn't enough.

Reaching down, I grabbed frantically at my skirts. Alexander realized my intent—kissing me all the while—and eased his weight off me slightly, providing room for me to maneuver and unpinning the fabric between us. My impatient fingers slipped along my dress before finding purchase and bunching the layers of silk above my waist.

Alexander kissed along my jaw as he lowered himself once more, our centers aligning in a rush of heat and desire. I moaned softly at the contact, so hard and eager.

This was madness. I was lost to the feel of him, the want and savage desire I so often saw in his gaze. Despite the darkness, I knew he'd see the same urgency reflected back in my own.

His erection pressed rhythmically with every roll of his hips. My desire was building, rising in me—instinctual and vital. Alexander placed open-mouthed kisses along my throat, his tongue licking expertly at my heated flesh.

My movements became searching. I matched his rhythm with the urgent press of my hips, soft sounds of encouragement falling mindlessly from my kiss-swollen lips. I knew what was coming. I was cresting higher and higher. Soon, the sensations I'd only ever sought alone in this darkened bedchamber would make themselves known with Alexander here, atop me.

He made no move to further our intimacies. He was fully dressed and my drawers remained in place. If he'd asked—if he'd wanted to remove all of our clothes and join our bodies—I would have said yes. Loudly. Resoundingly. My agreement in this moment wasn't in question. But he did not ask and he did not presume. And perhaps part of me worried that he would never cross that barrier, in an effort to keep me at bay.

But then I was spiraling in pleasure, and I could not think beyond the tightening of my limbs followed by the sudden release spreading from my core throughout my body.

"Fuck," Alexander breathed against the skin of my neck as his movements became wild and erratic. I could feel my intimate muscles clenching and releasing as the pleasure took hold. He thrust against me once, twice more before groaning quietly—the sound vibrating against my throat.

Alexander shifted slightly to the side so as not to crush me, but his head lay heavy against my chest. He smoothed the fabric of my skirt down my legs and then wound his arms tight around my waist. Our breathing slowed gradually, and with the return of regular inhales came awareness. There was a man in my bedchamber. We had engaged in highly inappropriate acts. And I couldn't bring myself to regret it.

My instinct was to feel embarrassed and I did somewhat. What happened now? Would we discuss our recklessness? Could I admit that this moment was etched in my life with intimacy and wonder? That I'd never felt so alive?

My feelings were settling like a wool blanket over us, oppressive and suffocating.

Just when I was prepared to address all the complications living and breathing in this bedchamber, Alexander asked suddenly, "Will you tell me something true?"

My inclination was to retort that of course I would. I was not the one who kept secrets. Instead, I cleared the roughness from my throat and said, "What would you like to know?"

"Just more," he replied simply. "What was your childhood like? What are your favorite things? Anything."

"Well, I spent a great deal of my childhood in Leicester at our family home called Lakehurst. I rode horses from a young age, went hunting with my father. Mostly ran wild in the country and behaved as the heir my father had hoped for but was never blessed with. I loved the land and I loved animals. I swam in the pond. But we also divided our time between Lakehurst and London. I loved the energy and bustle of life in town. Overall, I was fortunate to have a very happy childhood." I was conscious, as I spoke, of Alexander's own history—little though I knew of it. He'd never had the comforts and privileges I'd had and it caused a painful lump to form in my throat.

Just then, he made an amused sound instead of drawing attention to our differences. "I can picture you, wild and free. Causing trouble, climbing trees, getting all your dresses dirty."

"That is true. I used to drive my mother mad," I said, but there was amusement in my voice, remembering her stern expression that always gave way to her indulgent smile. "But then she'd pull a handkerchief out and wipe all the smudges off my face before sending me on my way and telling me not to bring any more animals home."

"I think I'd like to visit the country someday." His voice had gone sleepy and soft.

I liked him like this—open and curious, real in a way where he was typically untouchable. He'd never been so vulnerable, usually preferring to keep distance between us. But here in my bed he clung to me like a lifeline, taking and giving comfort, clutching me as if he'd never let me go.

My nose stung suddenly. "The sky is so wide and open. The air is fresh, and it's nice to…simply exist."

Alexander shifted a bit, nuzzling closer before his drowsy voice murmured, "I should like that."

My chin wobbled and one rogue tear fell from the corner of my eye. I wanted to take Alexander to the country. In my mind, I could see us at Lakehurst. Reading on a blanket by the pond, his head in my lap while we discussed the story and argued through our points. The thought of that sort of freedom had more tears threatening. The idea that Alexander could long for something so simple made my heart ache. A life I'd taken for granted was one he could only envision in his dreams.

"Keep talking," he urged. "What are your favorite sweets?"

I smiled against the top of his head. Threading my fingers through his dark hair, I spoke on and on. I told him my favorite dishes and some of my favorite memories. His breathing deepened but he insisted I continue anytime I paused. I told him stories about my friends. How Jane and Quinton met and fell in love. I told him about Ashleigh and her life in Scotland before she came to London. By the time I finished the tale of Eliza and Nicolas and their reclaimed love, Alexander was holding me in his sleep so tightly, his breaths deep and even.

I lay awake for a very long time, staring into the darkness. A few more tears fell unbidden as I stroked Alexander's hair and tried to figure out a way to reconcile the future and the very complicated path I now found myself on.

Twelve

I knew when I'd awoken that he'd be gone.

So much of that evening with Alexander had felt like a dream: running and laughing through a hedge maze at a masquerade, watching fireworks bursting overhead while safe in Alexander's warm embrace, and then the surprise of him in my bedchamber and what we'd done after.

However, instead of languishing in his arms or sharing an early morning kiss, I'd woken to cold sheets, a short note, and the salty remnants of the tears I'd shed the night before. Tears of helplessness and frustration.

I'd clutched the note he'd left. Written on paper from my own desk, Alexander had provided instructions for another secret outing the following week. Not Covent Garden Market this time. But the National Gallery.

He'd signed the missive *Yours, Alexander*. And I'd stared at his slanted script and those two parting words for a very long time, thinking how desperately I wished they were true.

I did not know what was going to happen with Alexander, but I could not for the life of me see a happy outcome. My vision of the future seemed inevitable—me, with a broken heart. And yet I could not say that would derail me. If Alexander was serious about the time limit he wished to place on our relationship, I had just over two and a half months. Ten weeks of secret meetings.

I didn't know how I felt about that. I preferred to live my life in the light—big and bold and entirely myself. But I knew Alexander was not in a position to be so daring. Additionally, I knew his concerns for my safety were founded in truth. I had the proof of the encounter with Blaidd reinforced by Miss Bellamy's continued presence. Speaking of, I needed to mention that to Alexander. Perhaps he would explain who she was to him. Seeing her at the masquerade, so easily shifting between worlds, was jarring.

While I wanted to demand answers to all my questions, I knew Alexander was not ready for that. I truly believed he feared my reaction as much as any danger that might come to me as a result of knowing the truth of his past and present.

Several days had passed. I hadn't responded to Alexander's note just yet. I needed to consider the way forward. And today was Tuesday, so I would see my friends. The thought of confessing my relationship with Alexander flitted in and out of my head, before hovering uncomfortably. *Perhaps…*

I surrounded myself with intelligent, caring, intuitive women, and now Nicolas. Perhaps they would offer a solution or at the very least a helpful opinion. Mayhap one of them could envision a future for Alexander and myself—one that didn't end in mutually assured destruction and resounding heartbreak for me.

Later that afternoon, I found myself at Randolph House—Jane and Quinton's residence in Mayfair. My friends were chatting amiably and enthusiastically. The embroidery hoops were mostly tucked away while everyone nibbled and crunched their way through tea cakes and delicious little sandwiches.

I sipped my tea and fought the nervous worry that threatened.

"You are awfully quiet over there, Cassandra." Nicolas's concerned tone pulled my thoughts out of the dread spiral they'd been engaged in. He was the only person not eating, choosing instead to work on the handkerchief he had in progress.

Perhaps I should make a handkerchief for Alexander. It would seem a frivolous gift to him, to be sure. But everyone needed a linen square for their pocket, and I could embroider something clever for him—something that would make him smile. While it was not appropriate to give a gift to a non-blood relation, I figured we were well beyond what was acceptable anyhow. In for a penny and all that.

Nicolas's words drew the attention of everyone else and suddenly the ladies quieted and looked my way.

Jane was the first to speak. "Cassandra, are you not comfortable? I can see if there are other refreshments in the kitchen more to your liking."

"No, Jane. It's nothing like that," I rushed to assure her. "This is a lovely spread and your home is magnificent. I am quite comfortable here."

Eliza leaned forward and deposited her teacup and saucer on the low table between us. "Are you feeling unwell?" She'd shifted expertly to physician and caregiver.

I smiled in gratitude for her concern. "I am the picture of health, I promise."

Before I could defend my behavior further, Ashleigh straightened and brushed a few biscuit crumbs from her coral patterned day dress. "There is something though. What is it, Cassandra? Ye look so serious. And we haven't heard about one of yer determined suitors in nearly a month."

Heads were nodding around the room. "That's true," Mary cut in thoughtfully, as if realization had just dawned. "I believe a teary Lord Bunsen and the enterprising lemon rind was the last such gentleman you reported."

More nodding resumed. My stomach felt a bit unsure as a result.

"Remember the Earl of Hansen?" Eliza called.

"Was that the one whose horse stepped on his foot?" Kathleen asked.

"No," Jane corrected, "that was the Viscount of Clayton. It was the Earl of Hansen who accepted the spicy canape from Cassandra, and he turned into a drippy watering pot as a result."

"Oh, right."

"That was it."

"And didn't Lord Chester snort whiskey through his nose after Cassandra made him laugh at his mother's house party in the summer?" Eliza asked thoughtfully.

"Aye, I was there for that one," Ashleigh confirmed. "Honestly, Cassandra, what is it with ye and crying males?"

"Well, as the unluckiest woman in London, it is apparently my effort at torture that facilitates their next successful match." I snapped out the words with intent. Hearing all of these examples laid bare on a day when I was feeling exceedingly emotional already was more than I could take.

Everyone was quiet following my pronouncement and I looked away.

So, so gently, Fiona moved onto the settee beside me and took my hand in hers. "What are you talking about, Cassandra?"

I realized then that I hadn't confessed this earlier revelation to my friends because I had been ashamed—not because I thought the claims or the lore were true, but because I didn't want *this*—these pitying looks and soft touches. Cassandra Fields did not need to be handled so carefully. And I did not intend to be the reason everyone looked uncomfortable and morose. That was not my role in our circle.

Fiona's hand squeezed once more.

I sighed and then I began speaking. "It is seemingly common knowledge among gentlemen of the *ton*. If they spend time with me—a dance, a conversation, a stroll—and some disaster strikes, as they are wont to do in my presence, then those same men are destined to meet their wife. It is foretold," I intoned dramatically, "that the next woman they interact with following an unpleasant encounter with me will be their future bride."

The room was quiet for so long that I risked a glance up. Then they exploded into motion. Jane hopped from her seat and quit the room with no explanation whatsoever.

Ashleigh said forcefully, "What utter horseshite."

"That's preposterous," Mary agreed, face incredulous.

Eliza scoffed, "That is madness, Cassandra. You must know this."

"Indeed," Fiona said, firmness creeping into her voice that had everyone else quieting. "That is a silly prophecy invented by prideful men struck by insecurity. Men feel the need to explain away their deficiencies at the hands of a woman. A ridiculous warning tale has been assigned to you for no other reason."

"Did ye know about this, Nicolas?" Ashleigh asked.

His head was already shaking. "No, truly. I had no idea. But then again, I'm a bit of a novelty due to my profession. Eliza and I rarely attend high-society events unless they're hosted by one of you ladies. The only gentlemen I spend any time with are Q and Compton, and my family, of course. I don't imagine I would have been informed about Cassandra's status, especially as a married man myself."

"I did not presume you would, Nicolas. Anyway, these men are not all bad sorts," I argued. "I don't know the origin of the claim. Perhaps all the others fell victim to the jest or played along. I do not know. But I discovered the truth at Mary's ball last month."

The group was quiet once more.

"Is that why you've been so reserved, Cassandra?" Fiona asked. "Refusing to dance at events and withdrawn from your peers?"

I looked down to our still-clasped hands, and shame rose swiftly to the surface for the way I'd let that silly legend affect me. How I'd made myself smaller and changed as a result of what I'd learned. When I should have been dancing with whomever I pleased, I'd questioned my instincts and played the part of the shy wallflower instead.

But before I could answer, Jane entered the room, drawing our attention and pulling a frowning Quinton Jameson, the Earl of Sullivan, in tow.

"I asked Q if he'd heard that bit of gossip about you, Cassandra," Jane explained.

All eyes swung to her husband who looked mildly alarmed before meeting my gaze. "I'd heard some rumblings after that incident in Hyde Park."

"Which one?" both Eliza and Jane asked in unison.

Eliza looked sheepish. "Never mind. Continue, Sullivan."

"It was so deeply preposterous. I ignored it as trivial gossip. It didn't even seem worth mentioning. Those men are idiots."

I nodded. Well, at least now Alexander's claims had been confirmed.

Eager for escape, Quinton slipped quickly out of the room with a kiss to Jane's cheek. We watched him go before Fiona turned questioning eyes on me. "You said you discovered the truth at Mary's ball. How did that come about?"

I pulled my hand out of Fiona's warm grasp and took a fortifying sip of tea. This was the moment. I could tell my friends about Alexander. Admit the truth of our relationship and gain their advice. Thomas was typically my sounding board. He was so staid and practical that I didn't always feel the need to assume the role of entertainer with him—my charms hardly affected him anyway. But the point remained, I didn't typically require assistance from my embroidery circle.

"You can tell us, Cassandra," Eliza encouraged. "You needn't always feign a distraction or make us laugh at your expense. We can be here for you—offer you guidance and acceptance. This situation seems to have affected you greatly. Let us help."

Swallowing awkwardly, I looked around the room at the concern I saw on the faces of my friends. Ashleigh nodded, expression fierce. Kathleen gave me a small encouraging smile.

"Well…you see," I began nervously, fingers twisting uselessly in my lap, "a footman at Mary's event accidentally told me about the legend or superstition or whatever you want to call it. About me and my suitors and their true intentions. He thought I already knew."

"What footman?" Fiona asked.

"The one from the hallway," I replied, looking directly at her. And then to everyone else, "His name is Alexander and I'm afraid I might be…falling in love with him."

The silence was palpable in the wake of my admission. I could have sliced it and served it alongside my tea.

Admitting the truth of my developing feelings to a roomful of people felt fraught and dangerous. Alone, in my wildest musings, I'd hardly allowed myself to consider what falling in love with Alexander might look like. But now the truth was no longer hidden in the most desperate corners of my heart. It was out —consuming all the air in this drawing room.

"Why don't we start at the beginning?" Fiona's voice, so gentle and beseeching, floated into the stillness of the room. "And, Jane, dear, why don't you bring the sherry?"

I looked to the duchess and offered a watery smile.

So I told them an abbreviated version of my time with Alexander. I discussed our introduction in my father's study, as well as the times I remembered engaging with him during events in the last year. The eyerolling, the laughter under his breath and general antagonism we'd engaged in. I admitted to feeling overwhelmed by the realization regarding my failed matches and the subsequent kiss I'd requested from Alexander as a result. Kathleen gasped when I relayed the chance meeting with Alexander on Baker Street. Continuing, I told them about our outings to the zoo and the market, touching briefly on the confusing warnings and lack of information about Alexander's life.

"Do you think he is dangerous?" Eliza asked, frown firmly in place.

Nicolas made an incredulous sound. "He is obviously a thief. It is quite likely he is dangerous. Whether he is a threat to Cassandra has yet to be seen."

"He wouldn't hurt me," I assured them.

The emotions reflected around the room ranged from concerned to disbelieving.

"Ye cannae be serious, Cassandra. Yer going to ruin yerself, running around and carrying on with this man ye can never hope to be with. Is yer future really worth all the secrets he is keeping? Is this some sort of rebellion? Is Alexander the forbidden fruit tempting ye?" Ashleigh's words grew increasingly frustrated, her brogue thick by the end. She obviously did not approve of my arrangement with Alexander.

"It's not any of those things," I said. "In the beginning, I think I knew I could trust Alexander's feelings toward me. He had no ulterior motive. Hell, he hardly liked me. There was no deception on his part regarding his intentions. I felt like I could no longer trust any gentleman to seek me out for anything beyond meeting their next match. I felt foolish and demoralized, humiliated and manipulated.

But, with Alexander, I knew I could trust the way he made me feel. And then I started to know him. And now I want…more."

Ashleigh was already shaking her head, but Fiona spoke before Ash's objections could materialize. "I think we are all merely concerned for your well-being, Cassandra. Obviously your secret encounters with Alexander could lead to a negative impact on your reputation and your future. I do think you should make him clarify the danger inherent in simply associating with him. You have a right to know." Heads nodded in agreement all around the drawing room before the duchess continued. "But my additional concern is that, as you spend more time with Alexander, your fondness will grow. Will you be able to walk away after the new year as you've both indicated?"

"I don't know," I admitted. "I need a solution. Some way forward that does not destroy everything." Resignation settled hard on my chest, unyielding and possessive.

There was not always a happily ever after in store.

Some paths led us on adventures that were more than we'd ever bargained for.

Thirteen

When I was a girl, I would wait for my father to have time for me, usually when we had planned to go riding together. He would be busy with a solicitor or a land manager or a steward, and I would be impatient—often loud and bothersome in the hallway outside his study at Lakehurst. There were times when my nanny or governess could not keep me confined in the nursery or schoolroom. I would escape and seek out my father in my excitement.

I felt that way now, bursting with anticipation and unable to moderate my expectations. My skin vibrated and I could not keep my hands still at my side as I waited for Alexander at the National Gallery. Despite my useless worry and the unknown future, I was eagerly awaiting his company, especially after our intimacies the week prior in my darkened bedchamber. He had been so open and vulnerable, trusting and affectionate. Would he remain thus? Or would our next encounter be awkward and stilted?

I'd written to Alexander and accepted his invitation after speaking with my friends during our Tuesday embroidery salon. We'd reached no conclusions for my situation with Alexander beyond emphasizing the need to understand any underlying danger he posed. There had been no magical answer from Fiona that would ensure a happy future. No logical reassurances from Jane. Ashleigh had been flatly opposed to any further contact with Alexander, and I felt so disappointed that my closest friend could not understand the desires of my heart.

Nevertheless, I was here on another early morning adventure, excitedly awaiting his arrival to the point that my mind refused to quiet itself and anticipation flooded my veins.

"And what is your opinion on this piece?" a low voice said just behind my shoulder.

I didn't turn, but it was an effort, to be sure. Biting my lip to contain my smile, I focused on the painting before me. It was a landscape painted by Joseph Mallord William Turner. The display named it *The Fighting Temeraire*. The retired warship was being pulled toward a dramatic sunset, all hazy warm reds and oranges. I was not well versed in Turner's accomplishments with the Royal Academy, but it appeared a large, attractive painting to me. "I think it's quite lovely."

Alexander stepped up beside me, and without looking my way, he asked, "What do you like best about it?"

I thought for a moment, desperate to simply take his arm or turn to look at him. Instead I replied, "I enjoy the colors of the sunset best. They are striking yet subtle." *There.* That sounded reasonable if not intelligent.

"And how does it make you feel?" His words were quiet and seductive.

The intimacy of the question had me fighting the urge to read his expression. However, I remained facing forward. Finally, after some thoughtful introspection, I said, "It makes me feel somewhat melancholy." I forced myself to really look—to battle away the nervous energy Alexander's presence wrought—and I spoke my opinion confidently despite no such mastery of the subject matter. "I suppose the sight of such a vessel, once grand and capable, being towed so inelegantly feels final and sorrowful. Heading toward a final sunset over the water. Whatever dramatic and daring battles it once fought are now over, and instead it is destined for an uninspiring end."

I pivoted then and found Alexander finally looking at me. "Hmm. Does that tarnish the journey and all the good along the way, to have reached an end such as this?"

He looked thoughtful and dear, watching me with soft eyes and a tender expression. I noticed his appearance for the first time. Alexander looked quite put together in a tailored jacket and patterned waistcoat. The wide gray stripes were threaded with silver and his cravat stood out, snowy white against his skin and dark hair. He wore a top hat pulled low over his eyes but I could still make out the dark blue color and the intensity with which he wielded his stare.

I didn't wish to think on his attire and the reason behind his fashionable choices today. So I considered the question he'd asked carefully, and couldn't help but draw a tidy line between Alexander's words and our impossible situation. Would I regret everything between us when the inevitable end came to pass?

"No. No, it does not," I answered finally, voice soft and subdued.

The nervous energy had quieted, dissipating in my thoughtful reflection. I still ached to reach for him. But now that he was here, sharing the same space, I would instead appreciate the time we had together.

"This is the *Temeraire* being towed by a steam-powered tugboat down the Thames. You were right about the finality of the story. The warship was being retired and scrapped. It is unlikely that Turner actually witnessed the passage, but that did not stop him from creating this romantic and ethereal depiction. The blazing sunset symbolizes death and the emergence of new steam technology over the sails of the *Temeraire* and the like."

Alexander spoke with a conversational yet professorial air. It was striking to witness. I suddenly remembered all the books in his small apartment, filling the shelves and stacked carefully on the floor. This mysterious man—with more sides than I could count—was obviously intelligent and educated. Despite his unknown upbringing and early life in poverty, he'd cultivated an unmistakable love of learning. I wondered inwardly if Elias Blaidd had encouraged Alexander's inquisitive mind or taught him to read as a child.

Finally, I allowed my smile to gain control of my expression. "So you enjoy the arts?"

His answering grin was mostly shy, but some self-satisfaction found its way through the cracks. "It is one of the topics I take an interest in."

"Will you show me your favorites?"

He nodded, still eyeing me with warm affection. That hopeless feeling swelled again. The one that said heartache was coming for me and there wasn't a damn thing I could do about it. But I beat it back, determined to focus on the journey and not the inescapable end.

We fell into step and explored the halls and rooms of the gallery. There were very few patrons touring the space at this hour. Our stroll felt intimate and private despite the public nature of our adventure.

Alexander showed me a newly acquired Vermeer and explained the symbolism of love associated with the work. His knowledgeable recitation continued while we explored. I pointed out a Jan van Eyck portrait I particularly enjoyed, and he asked me to make up a story about the couple painted so richly by the artist. Alexander laughed through my ridiculous theorizing before telling me the truth behind the Italian merchant and his wife represented on the wood panel.

While I was clearly ignorant of the history behind the majority of the artwork, Alexander never made me feel ill at ease or self-conscious. He continually asked my opinion while also pointing out notable compositions, engaging portraits, or the remarkable use of color.

"Rembrandt looked very much like my father," I mused in front of the artist's self-portrait in the main collection.

Alexander smiled wide, his expression open and happy and so handsome I had difficulty keeping my hands to myself. I indulged, stepping close in the empty room and slipping my hand in the crook of his arm.

"Truly?" he asked, still grinning down at me.

"Oh, yes! There's a resemblance there about the eyes." I pointed toward the canvas before tapping my chin thoughtfully. "Or perhaps it's the floppy hat."

Alexander's laughter was low and intimate. I wanted to hear that sound in the middle of the night while my teeth scraped across his skin.

"You shouldn't be looking at me like that, Cassandra," he whispered in warning. "We are in a public place and you hide nothing with your gaze."

My grin was devious. "I've never been good at keeping secrets."

Alexander's smile slowly disappeared from view. I cursed inwardly at my misstep and thoughtless comment.

"I didn't mean—" I began before he cut me off.

"No, I know." But he looked away and stepped back, putting more than distance between us.

For as honest as my hungry gaze had been moments ago, I was sure he read the open regret and disappointment in my expression now. "I'm sorry," I said quietly to Alexander as a gentleman entered the room opposite us.

"Don't apologize. You did nothing wrong."

But the space was still there, expanding and devouring the easiness that had been present all morning. His smiles and the joy he'd radiated during our tour of the gallery were tucked neatly away behind self-recrimination and detachment.

Dammit.

I risked a glance at the stranger occupying the other end of the room, but he merely stared forward, paying us no mind. "Can we go somewhere and discuss this?" I asked quietly.

Alexander's focus remained on the artwork when he replied, "We should go, actually. The gallery will grow busy soon. We wouldn't want to be seen or recognized."

Irritated with his behavior, I didn't bother whispering any longer. "I don't care if we're seen or recognized."

The gentleman behind us turned and Alexander shot me a frustrated look.

Good. We could both be cross.

I bustled out of the viewing room of the main collection and toward the exit. If Alexander did not follow me to my carriage to resume our conversation, I would come back and drag him out.

Quiet footsteps sounded behind me after a moment, but I kept my pace.

When we finally reached my carriage—free from chaperones at such an early hour—I instructed Landers to simply drive until further notice. Alexander slipped in behind me unnoticed by the coachman and shut the door just before the conveyance trundled into motion.

He sat across from me, looking disgruntled. "You shouldn't be so careless."

"And you shouldn't punish me when I make a mistake."

"I wasn't punishing you. Sometimes, Cassandra, I need a moment to breathe. I know you want the truth. But I'm not keeping you in the dark for selfish reasons—it's not punishment. It's what is necessary to maintain any sort of relationship with you, to keep you safe. I'm sorry if that makes you upset."

I considered his phrasing. "But you're not sorry for keeping your secrets, are you?"

He blew out an exasperated breath. "I'm sorry it bothers you."

Disappointment settled uneasily and I narrowed my eyes. "That is what I thought."

Alexander leaned forward, legs open wide on either side of my skirts. He shrugged out of his jacket impatiently and tossed it on the bench beside him before balancing his forearms on his spread thighs. I was annoyed with myself for noticing the breadth and width of him—how utterly alluring he looked poised across from me.

"I am going to tell you who we are dealing with. Why all of this secrecy is necessary."

If I thought Alexander was giving anything away with this little speech, I would have been wrong. There was no concession in his tone, no compromise. He was teaching me a lesson.

"Remember when you asked about my scar?" He indicated the long-healed line along his jaw. I frowned at the change of subject but nodded my acknowledgement. "I told you I was threatened by criminals when I was young. And while that is true, this is the rest of the story. I had thoughtlessly picked the wrong individuals to practice on. I'd been nicking purses in crowds for long enough at that point that I should have known better, but the man who caught me trying to pick his pocket was rougher than I realized. He would have slit my throat that day on the South Bank if Blaidd hadn't been watching and stopped him before the knife cut too deeply. And while Blaidd came to my aid with the man I'd been targeting, he punished me for getting caught."

I swallowed uncomfortably but didn't speak. This tale was long since over. The proof was healed on Alexander's shadowed jaw, but his impassive recitation brought with it fear and dread in learning the truth of it now.

"He punished me," Alexander repeated. "He withheld food and medical attention, left me to fend for myself for days. He is cold, callous, and calculating. And he will never change. *That* is the danger you face. I will not allow our arrangement to harm you or diminish you in any way. That is why I demand your ignorance. That is why I demand secrecy."

"How did you survive?" I asked, my voice small and wounded, desperate to reach out and touch him—to make sure he was whole and healthy.

"That time? Another child in his network of little urchins and miscreants found me. Brought me food in secret and sewed me up. That's why it looks the way it does." The admission cost him something. Alexander looked away from me and instead stared unseeingly out the carriage window. He'd made his point. He no longer needed to scare me into my best behavior.

"Perhaps there is a way to—"

"There's not," he cut in, meeting my eyes. "I've been distancing myself from him for years. Our contact is minimal now—finally—but Blaidd'll never let me go entirely. I will owe him for the rest of my life for taking me in the way he did. I'll be repaying that debt and keeping his secrets until the day I die. And don't forget, Blaidd has already seen you. If he has someone watching me or my apartment, he might see you again. That is why we must stop this foolishness. The longer we continue, the more you are at risk from his notice and attention."

"But, what if—"

"Cassandra," he interrupted, voice resigned. "There is nothing temporary about the way I want you. But this"—he gestured a hand between us as if he could hope to encompass all the attraction, the complications, and hunger—"has to reach an end. The sooner, the better. It's the only way to ensure your safety. You know as well as I. There is no future here regardless, Blaidd or no."

"I don't believe that," I rushed out without consideration, determined to be heard this time. "We— We— We are well matched."

Alexander regarded me as if I had gone mad. "How can you possibly say that? You are a lady."

He said it simply, as a fact. And it was, but my heart felt the blow as if it was an insult.

"I am a fraud. You likely have a volume in your library chronicling your relations back hundreds of years. I have no history, no family, no past. I am no one. Dressed up and pretending to be a gentleman just so I can be seen near you." He picked up the jacket at his side as he spoke and cast it back down in disgust.

"That's just clothing, Alexander. A tailored jacket and a patterned waistcoat," I argued. "It's who you are that matters." I reached forward, placing my hand on his chest, directly over his beating heart. "We balance each other. You are locked up so very tight. And I am an open book. Perhaps together, I can oil your hinges and you can harness my wildness. We are good for one another. You feel it; I know it." His eyes were unreadable and neither did he speak. "We have time. You promised me weeks. You promised me *more*. You gave your word."

His smile was sad. "And what good is the word of a thief?"

I shook my head, tears threatening. This beautiful day, ruined. Reality had intruded once more. And with his admission I finally had an answer to a question I'd long been asking. But the confirmation didn't feel noteworthy. There was no triumph now.

His hand slipped over mine where it still rested on his firm chest. He took it gently and moved to place a soft kiss on the center of my gloved palm. "What a pair we make. A lady and a criminal."

"You're not a criminal," I argued reflexively, watching his sympathetic expression. I realized suddenly that he was waiting for me to accept reality, and he was…sad *for* me, as if I were a child who could not bear the truth and instead believed in fairy tales. "You're not," I asserted, doing nothing to dispel his look with my stubborn, juvenile response.

But then I took a moment and considered this Blaidd person and how Alexander had been under his care from a young age. Someone had taught him to pick pockets, and there were other children under this blackguard's purview. Alexander had mentioned a network of little urchins and miscreants.

Realization dawned, and with it a theory. I voiced it aloud. "He was your keeper and your instructor. *That* is who Blaidd is to you. Not just a looming threat. You know his methods and his crimes. And for that reason alone he'll keep you in his sights. You never stole anything for yourself, did you? All the purses, all the heirlooms and jewels from homes in Mayfair. They were never yours to keep, were they?"

Alexander's blue gaze was intent, but beneath it was panic—pure and unadulterated. He said nothing, no confirmation nor denial.

I was right.

Blaidd was the mastermind. The puppeteer holding all the strings. Alexander had never been given a choice—taken in as he was, molded from a young age to do this horrible man's bidding. "That is what you were attempting in my father's study the night we met. Stealing for Blaidd. Because of the hold he has on you. The threat he maintains."

"Cassandra," he breathed, the words pained and beseeching. He shook his head and released my hand from his grasp. Irritation flared at my accusation. He no longer appeared resigned, but angry. "Yes, I should have been there, doing the job I was sent to do. But I was distracted and preoccupied. Do you know what it felt like to be alone with you in that room?"

I was not given a chance to answer.

"To be caught by you? Outsmarted and bested. To do battle after a year of watching you steal hearts in ballrooms all across Mayfair? My blood was singing in my veins. Warnings blared with every frantic beat of my savage heart. I needed to get away. I had to run from you and everything you threatened to undo."

He'd been angry when he started speaking, but the fury had dissolved as something far more dangerous crept into his tone. I could fight his irritation and battle a livid beast, but the resignation that had settled with every word spoken was not something my heart could bear. So there were tears now, dripping silently down my face.

Alexander leaned forward and cupped my cheeks, swiping the moisture beneath my eyes and watching me solemnly. "I wanted—no, needed you to be the woman I expected…an empty-headed aristocrat, no deeper than your own shadow. A princess high in your tower. But you aren't those things. Instead you are kind and warm, with a foul sense of humor that surprises me every time." He was smiling softly at me now while I cried into his palms. "You draw everyone into your orbit, myself included. I wanted to hate you for your wealth and position in society because it was the first time I was ever truly sorry for who I am— who I turned out to be."

His thumbs were still stroking my skin. I reached up and pulled his hands away and into my lap, linking our fingers together. I could no longer contain my quiet tears after hearing how he thought of me—how he thought of us. Leaning over, I wept into our joined hands, breaths heaving and body quaking.

I felt him press a kiss to my hair before untangling our limbs and hauling me into a desperate embrace.

His voice was muffled as I pressed myself deeper and closer, clinging to him with all my might. "And here we are. Breaking each other's hearts a little bit at a time. Through time and distance and secrets and circumstance. I don't know how to change that, Cassandra. We will ruin each other and there is nothing I can do about it."

I pulled back on a ragged inhale to meet his eyes. "So…what are you saying? This is the end?"

His eyes searched mine, impossibly blue. "I think it should be. What is the alternative? You were a dream. And I was the fool with my eyes closed."

Fourteen

Expectations were fascinating. They could grow and expand while also caging you quite thoroughly.

The expectations placed upon my shoulders often fluctuated depending on the people doing the anticipating. My family had grown to expect a kind and loving daughter. The members of the *ton* maintained that I was outlandish and entertaining. I laughed too loudly or flirted boldly at times, and so I had been labeled thus early on. Deviating from those expectations would confuse my peers. My close friends—my embroidery circle often expected me to play a certain role as well. Through habit and history I was typically the peacemaker of our group. I redirected attention onto myself and away from difficult topics. However, I had also been known to distract with humor and I sought to entertain my friends in an effort to create a jovial air at our gatherings.

But these were all versions of myself—or at the very least parts of myself that I accentuated or emphasized at appropriate times. I was a loving daughter while also being an outrageous, entertaining flirt. That did not exclude me from being a fiercely supportive and loyal friend. These were all parts of me. Depending on the audience, how I was perceived could change and often did.

Soon after my final encounter with Alexander, I considered his expectations and how I had behaved in his presence as a result. It hadn't taken long for me to reach a conclusion. Truly it was only a few hours after he'd unwrapped himself from my emotional embrace, kissed me on the forehead, and rapped sharply on the roof of the carriage. I'd been too upset to comprehend it in the moment. I hadn't been able to see past my own hurt and rejection as he'd stepped down from the conveyance and walked out of my life. But after several hours of self-reflection that very same day, I'd realized something.

My behavior with Alexander—for the most part—was atypical. I'd been so very cautious with him, tiptoeing around his secrets and lies. A meek and mild observer I had become.

Typically, I did not wait for people to order me about. I was a woman who wielded her authority and influence.

But I'd been so afraid of scaring him off with my questions and interest that I'd clipped my own wings in the process. I'd become someone unknowable—a stranger to my own self—all because of Alexander's expectations. He'd wanted me to accept his half-truths. He'd expected me to be complicit in my own ignorance. And now he presumed I would agree to this forced separation because that was his expectation of me.

Not once in our conversation did Alexander ask what I wanted. He'd voiced his concerns and made a decision without compromise or any sort of input from me. I didn't begrudge him his highhandedness. I could understand his inclination to wish to protect me. When men were fearful, they often did desperate, idiotic things.

And it was equally likely that Alexander's past had never facilitated compromise.

However, I decided it was time I voiced my opinion. Following the events at the National Gallery, I managed to shed my melancholy. I spent the remainder of the day reflecting and plotting. I would be a silent partner no longer.

So it was on the wings of reckless indignation that I found myself at the back entrance to the Baker Street Coffee House that night, attempting to pick the lock.

"Dammit," I muttered around the hairpin in my mouth as the tumblers refused to engage. My fingers slipped and my knuckles collided painfully with the door, rattling it a bit upon impact.

I removed my gloves and dropped them on the stair beside me. Then I reached back beneath my dark hood to liberate two more pins from my coiffure before twisting them around each other. I needed the metal to be stronger and reinforced. The pins kept bending within the gears and causing my hand to lose purchase.

One of the hair prongs dropped and I cursed again. Before I could reach for it, the door flew open and I froze in my crouched position.

"Jesus, Cassandra," came the hissed reprimand just before Alexander reached down and hauled me to my feet. He quickly scanned the alley behind me and presumably spotted my carriage before sighing and pulling me inside. He didn't bother looking my way, just linked his bare fingers through mine and led me through the Patels' storage room and up the staircase to his apartment.

I hadn't picked the lock, but I was in the building. That was the important part.

Alexander paced into the room I'd been in only once before, his stride stiff and angry. I calmly shut the door as he turned to face me, hands on hips.

His mouth opened, but before he could scold me I blurted, "You're wearing spectacles!"

He blinked. "Yes, well, I was reading," he said incredulously, waving a hand toward the armchair and oil lamp sitting atop a stack of books, illuminating the space. "But I was interrupted by someone scraping away on the back door. Were you really trying to pick the lock with your hairpins, Cassandra? Truly? Are you mad?"

I forced myself to focus on the conversation and not the way Alexander looked in spectacles and shirtsleeves rolled up past strong forearms. And, God help me, bare feet. "No," I managed with a sniff. "But I am quite angry."

"You're angry?" he demanded in a rush.

"Yes! I'm angry. You didn't give me a chance to argue with you. And you refused to compromise or discuss anything at all. You never once asked me what I wanted, Alexander. You made the decision all on your own. You expected me to be the submissive little mouse. And that is not who I am!" My breathing was heavy and I'd lost my composure, but that was something he simply needed to get used to. I was an emotional creature. There was nothing shameful about it.

He sighed. "I don't want to rehash everything. You are still a lady and I am still a gutter rat. Nothing has changed. Blaidd still poses a threat to you."

I stepped closer. "We can figure this out. I know we can."

"You do not understand, Cassandra. You're being foolishly optimistic or willfully ignorant. Perhaps both. You have been privileged your entire life and you can afford to believe in a fantasy." His blue gaze searched my face before he admitted quietly, "I didn't even know how to dream of more until I met you. The only lasting relationship we could possibly have is one where I serve you drinks."

I was already shaking my head, but he continued.

"Seeing you in ballrooms—so animated and charming—was torture. You had men eating out of your hand. I used to think I hated you, but then I realized I was just jealous. I was desperate to talk to you, touch you, and dance with you—though I cannot even dance. That's how pathetic the illusion was, how out of control I had become. Seeing you with those men made me furious. They had freedom I would never possess all because of their birth."

"You said you weren't punishing me for being a lady, but you are. The circumstances of my birth are not my fault and neither are yours. Stop using that as an excuse," I argued. "Tell me something real, Alexander. Be honest with me for once. Tell me what you truly want. There has to be a way."

"Why?" he barked, eyes flashing. "Why torture ourselves?"

I let my angry glare be my only response.

"Fine," Alexander snapped, stalking close. "You want to hear how I crave the taste of your skin? How all my thoughts center on you and the sounds you'll make when I'm touching you? Is that honest enough for you?"

My blood was hot in my veins, enough to flush my delicate cheeks and fight the chill in this lonely apartment. "I'm not untouchable!" Reaching forward I grabbed his hand and placed it in the center of my chest over my bodice and under my cloak. "Feel my heart and how it beats for you. I want you. I want to be with you. The only torture is in admitting defeat and denying ourselves."

Alexander's gaze was covetous, a man pushed to his limits. He watched the progression of his hand as it slid up my chest and over my collarbones. My breath was ragged as the warm weight settled lightly on the column of my throat.

"You make me weak, Cassandra." His voice was violent devastation, rough and choked, barely above a whisper. "For the first time in my life, I want something for myself…even if I can never hope to keep you. Or worse, deserve you."

I waited, breathless with anticipation as his rough palm dragged along my skin before reaching around to the nape of my neck and pulling me to him. Our mouths met, hungry and possessive. I cupped his cheeks and strained on the tips of my boots to get closer, lining our bodies flush with one another.

His eager lips moved with mine, fighting the goodbye he'd so desperately attempted. My answering kiss struggled against the inevitable with teeth and tongue.

Alexander's other arm wrapped around my waist, anchoring me. His nearness eased the urgency I felt in the moment. He was warm and solid. My mind and body slowed from frantic to something manageable—something content. Alexander was here in my arms, not turning me away and telling me goodbye.

I stroked his jaw before threading my fingers in his hair, the dark locks so soft and smooth under my touch.

He broke our connection long enough to gasp out a warning. "You can't come here anymore. It's too dangerous. You could be seen. Promise me you won't."

"If I can't come here, where shall I go?"

"I'll come to you," he said, nipping my bottom lip as if he just couldn't help himself. "Just…promise me," he repeated.

"I promise," I agreed before placing a teasing bite on his lower lip in return. Then I whispered, "Take me to bed."

Alexander pulled back suddenly as if burned. "What?"

"I want to be with you," I admitted, reaching for his hand. "I assumed—"

"I won't ruin you," he interrupted, roughly releasing the hand I'd taken hold of. "For that is truly what it would be—utter ruination. These hands, Cassandra…" Alexander trailed off while staring down at the offending appendages, disgust heavy in his tone. "They've done so many things I'm not proud of, but destroying your future would undeniably be the worst."

I frowned at his assessment. I had assumed if I convinced Alexander to agree to continue our arrangement, eventually our intimacies would progress. I knew what happened between lovers, and I was ready for it. Ready for him.

We'd found pleasure together in the dark of my bedchamber and I wanted more. I longed to light every candle and peel the clothes from his skin. Alexander had been so open and vulnerable and I'd felt powerful as our bodies moved together. Didn't he realize how good it would be?

This fire between us would burn out of control if we let it. I was ready to go up in flames.

But he was still shaking his head, voicing his objections, and holding himself away from me—protecting himself, I realized. "When you come back to your senses and this is all a distant dream, I won't give you more to regret."

The path I'd envisioned for so long seemed too narrow. So much had happened, and I no longer sought that route. The idea of accepting my due as a lady and taking a gentleman husband who was likely to be years, if not decades, my senior—one who might or might not tolerate me, and in all likelihood would never remain true—was unfathomable.

Uncertain and complicated though it might be, I wanted the path that now lay before me. The one with too many secrets and deep blue eyes.

"We can figure it out," I said, stepping closer.

Alexander's eyes narrowed and he retreated a pace. "What does that mean?" Another step. Another retreat.

"It means we don't have to decide right now."

"Cassandra," he groaned, hands returning to his hips.

"Take me to bed," I repeated, stopping before him with a smile ghosting my kiss-swollen lips. "We needn't consummate anything tonight. You can keep your clothes on if you like. But I'm not making any promises regarding mine."

SEVERAL HOURS LATER, I emerged out of the restaurant's rear entrance onto the stone steps and inhaled the chilly night air. My breath rose foggy and warm in the darkness as the autumn temperatures cooled my heated skin.

It had been difficult to dress and leave Alexander's bed. He'd been curled up beside me—clinging and warm—his features relaxed and open in slumber. It seemed fittingly clandestine to dress by firelight as he slept and leave a note for him to find in the morning.

I brought the pads of my fingers to my well-loved lips and fought a shiver. Alexander had remained clothed but I too had been true to my word. With me in nothing but my stockings, he had explored every inch of my body, determining what I liked and then what I *loved*—how to touch and how to tease. My pleasure had been his only driving force as he kissed and laved my breasts with attention. He'd used his clever fingers to stroke my sensitive flesh, bringing me higher and higher until I'd broken and drifted lazily back to my body. *I bet Alexander would have no trouble using his talented hands to pick a lock.*

When I'd reached for him, so hard and eager in his trousers, he'd whispered, "Not yet, Princess," and distracted me in other ways. Methods that involved his hot mouth and searing touch.

Alexander had been willful and determined, devoted solely to my desire. Remembering his rough hands and sinful praise brought a flush to my cheeks, even as I made my way toward my carriage at this late hour. I'd instructed my coachman to remain within, having begged Landers to bring me to Marylebone under the cover of darkness to speak to Alexander earlier in the evening.

But as my heeled boots touched the bottom stair, a figure emerged from the darkened alleyway. The familiar woman met my gaze, surprise lighting her features briefly before she tucked it carefully away.

As Miss Bellamy approached, I steeled myself for whatever warning was to come, and I held tightly to the reins of my curiosity. I refused to give myself or my ignorance away. And vowed inwardly that I would be speaking to Alexander about Ember Bellamy very soon.

If my assumptions were correct about Mr. Blaidd and his absolute control over Alexander's life from such a young age, then Ember's involvement must be tied to Blaidd in some way too. She'd claimed during our prior conversation to have been foisted upon Alexander—that their relationship had been one of circumstance. But that didn't explain her presence here and now. Perhaps she was a jealous acquaintance or a former lover. Or she was as much a victim of Mr. Blaidd and his nefarious gang as Alexander was.

"Good evening, Lady Cassandra."

"Good evening, Miss Bellamy."

Her stare was steady and even, dark eyes assessing. She was dressed in men's trousers and a long dark coat that concealed her figure, but her comely face was easily recognizable despite the cap sitting low on her forehead and her brown hair tucked neatly underneath.

"I had hoped I'd gotten through to you, but I can see from the state of your hair and the flush on your cheeks that perhaps I was mistaken."

I measured my words carefully before I spoke. "I appreciate your concern for…the state of my hair, but I assure you, it's not necessary."

"You are intelligent, my lady. You must know that whatever this is will end badly, despite any fanciful and romantic notions you're clinging to. And believe me, I know how handsome and enticing he is." Her smile was catlike. "He exemplifies the strong, silent type. Not to mention how good he is with his hands."

Hadn't I been reflecting on Alexander's skill with his hands just moments ago? I bristled inwardly at her suggestive remarks, and fought any inclination toward jealousy. I didn't know who this woman was—not really. But she hadn't been in Alexander's bed an hour ago. That had been *me*. "Forgive me, Miss Bellamy, but it is quite late and I don't see how it is any of your business."

Her eyes narrowed just a bit—but enough. "Alexander is my business."

"Because of Mr. Blaidd," I hedged.

Ember smiled knowingly through my bluff. "Alexander will never leave us. His leash has lengthened, but that is all."

"He has a life," I argued. "One that is separate. Honest employment. You don't own him. Not anymore."

She continued as if I hadn't spoken at all. "His life is a dangerous one. Not for rich young ladies."

I tugged my gloves on in obvious dismissal and turned in the direction of the carriage. Landers had likely overheard our voices and was now waiting for me with the door held open. "Forgive me for thinking that Mr. Hill should be the one to decide that."

The young woman's eyes lost their harsh edge at that. She looked very nearly saddened by whatever I'd said. "Mr. Hill," she said quietly. "Did you know he didn't even have a name when Blaidd found him alone on the streets with nothing but a letter pinned in his pocket? He didn't speak for a year. Couldn't tell anyone where he came from. Finally, Blaidd started calling him Alexander… after a character in a book he was reading at the time. Hill was simply the name of the street he'd been found on."

I swallowed against the emotion threatening, refusing to show any reaction to the story she told. It was true. I could feel it. And perhaps it was the first honest thing she'd said tonight.

Ember scrutinized my face for a long moment before tipping her hat. "Good night, Lady Cassandra. Be safe on your journey home." She didn't wait for me to respond, simply melted back into the darkness of the alley beyond.

I didn't know if she'd been intent on visiting Alexander this evening. Nor did I know if she'd been a spy sent by Blaidd to report back on his movements.

I had more questions than ever, many of which I considered as I trundled toward Dameron Hall. Ember's subtle warnings were difficult to shake. However, I didn't think she meant me any harm. Her gentle rebuke for considering a future with Alexander struck differently than the disappointment I'd encountered from my own friends.

Miss Bellamy was a part of Alexander's world. They clearly had a long history. But she still viewed my relationship with Alexander just as impossibly from where she was standing.

Our lives could never truly align, but I still refused to give him up. What if we were discovered and my reputation was ruined? Would my family send me away? Would they abandon me?

My heart clenched painfully at the consequences I might face. But when I considered other scenarios, it was less a painful clench and more of a tender spot… What if we married? Would we live in poverty? Would all my friends turn their backs on me for following my heart?

I sighed and braced myself on the bench as the carriage turned down the drive.

The truth was this: the invented circumstances and the agonizing daydreams did not matter. For it was already too late. Those hazy imaginings of a future were no longer quite so indeterminate. The household was still shifting and undecided but the husband had more distinction—a wicked grin and a ragged scar along his jaw. And those imagined children skipping and toddling through my thoughts all had dark hair and indigo eyes.

I'd already decided that the life I'd been leading wasn't enough. *More* was a prayer on my lips and a whisper in my heart. Alexander was that *more*.

And he was mine.

Fifteen

The following Monday, several days later, brought with it dreary gray rain clouds and a suspicious Scottish woman.

My dear friend Miss Ashleigh Winstead was due for tea, and after the recent events on Baker Street, I felt a bit guilty in her presence. Ashleigh had been quite vocal in her disapproval of Alexander and any further contact with him. I was fairly confident she would inquire after any developments on that front. Reminding myself that she was, indeed, one of my closest confidants and only meant well helped soothe the urge to defend myself and my relationship with Alexander.

Friendship didn't always mean harmony. Sometimes it meant thinking the very best of someone even in the face of conflict.

I, along with our butler, greeted Ashleigh in the foyer.

"It's a right dreich mess out there today," my friend remarked as she passed her wet outer layers over to Jansen.

"Well, come in and get warm," I said with a smile as I led her upstairs to the informal drawing room. The fire was fairly roaring and Mrs. Chapman had been kind enough to send up the tea service along with the ham sandwiches I favored as well as Ashleigh's preferred lemon meringues.

We sat and nibbled and made polite conversation for a time. She asked if I'd heard the gossip about Lord Duncan and I asked if she was attending Lady Eugenia's musicale later in the week. Our interaction was not strained so much as it was growing taut the longer we discussed trivialities.

Finally, Ashleigh relinquished her teacup and brushed the crumbs from her velvet skirts before folding her hands primly and prompting, "Well, out with it."

I smiled at her candor. It was one of the things I loved best about her.

"I can tell ye have not abandoned yer pursuit of the footman. There is a sparkle in yer eye that surpasses the typical mischievous gleam."

"Do you truly wish to hear this, Ash? I know your position."

"Aye, of course I do." Her words were enthusiastic but her frown was still firmly in place.

"There have been some developments," I confirmed. "We had an outing to the National Gallery and then he tried to break things off. But I sought him out and…we reached an understanding, I believe."

"He tried to cut ye loose?" Ashleigh's surprise was evident.

"Yes. He is worried for my reputation and my future."

"As he well should be."

It didn't seem prudent to mention the threat of discovery from Mr. Blaidd and the danger therein. So I kept that to myself. "But I realized," I said, ignoring her quip, "I was letting Alexander dictate so much of our relationship, and I wasn't ready to say goodbye. So I asserted myself and what I want. I grew a backbone. Or rather, I found my existing one and used it to stand up for myself."

My friend scrutinized me. "What did ye do at the gallery? He didn't nick anything, did he?"

"Ashleigh!" I scolded.

Her expression was unbothered, but she sighed. "Fine, tell me about yer adventure."

So, I recounted our visit to Trafalgar Square and told her about the art we'd viewed and discussed. "He was so knowledgeable," I elaborated after a few moments. "We spent the morning talking and laughing."

"Has he admitted his secrets? Did ye ask him?"

I swallowed compulsively. "I know some of his history, but he's still doing his utmost to shield me from his life."

Her eyes narrowed questioningly. "And you're satisfied with that?"

"Well, I wouldn't say satisfied," I admitted, picking at the fabric of my gloves.

"But you're allowing it," she countered. "He's still the one in control due to yer sheer ignorance. Ye said ye realized Alexander was dictating to ye, and supposedly you'd found yer backbone. But is that really true?"

I made a frustrated noise in response. I didn't want to admit that I was still bothered by all the secrecy. The encounter with Miss Bellamy had reinforced all that I didn't know. But what could I really do? How could I demand honesty from Alexander when I wasn't able to provide the same in equal measure? The nature of our relationship *was* secrecy. I could not march into a ballroom on his arm. I was hiding my life as much as he was…just in a different way.

"You don't understand," I said in frustration.

"Oh, I dinnae understand?"

"No, you don't," I snapped.

Ashleigh remained quiet a moment, and I looked away.

Finally, she replied calmly, "Why are ye so upset with me, Cassandra? If you're looking only for someone to agree with ye, then save yer pretty speech for the looking glass." My eyes cut back to hers. "I've been around dangerous, selfish men my entire life. I know what signs to look out for. I don't want ye to be diminished so that yer man is all you're able to see. I sincerely hope Alexander is nothing like that. I don't know him. I don't know his intentions. But *ye*. Ye, I do know. You're my friend, and so I will reserve my judgment because it's clear you're addled by love. Yer priorities have shifted. Whereas in our relationship—yers and mine—my worries and concerns are valid because my only priority is ye."

I felt emotion stinging my nose at her words.

Ashleigh's concern and honesty had me reconsidering her questions about Alexander and the intent behind them. I had to remember that she was, in fact, on my side. "I'm not upset with you, Ash."

She laughed lightly at that before regarding me with an indulgent smile. "Oh, yes ye are."

"Fine," I agreed, grinning in return.

Ashleigh shifted in her seat slightly before admitting in a low voice, "I know what it is like for women to make allowances for dangerous men. My mother made the same mistakes, ignored all the signs in favor of a charming smile."

Whatever remaining irritation I had softened at the mention of Ashleigh's family. "I know the pain your father has caused your family, but I do not think Alexander is the same. Charming is not a word I would ever use to describe him. We sniped and argued and antagonized our way into this situation. He's secretive, yes. But not deceptive. He's been quite plain about wanting to keep the truth from me. He has his reasons."

She sighed. "Perhaps I'm being too forthright and meddlesome in my opinions on the matter. But ye are my family, Cassandra. My brothers and I don't see eye to eye. My father is barely a part of my life, thank Christ. And my mother feels so far beyond my reach at times. I see ye as the sister I've always longed for. I only want what is best for ye. Always."

"But what about what I want?" I bit my lip, considering. "I want to be happy."

Ashleigh nodded fervently in response. "And I want yer happiness as well. Ye deserve more than what you would have accepted. Ye would have married any of those gentlemen in yer past. If something hadn't happened to scare them off or embarrass them or drive them away, ye would have accepted that as yer due."

My friend was right. That was how I'd borne four full seasons in London—accepting every suit, saying "please" and "thank you," being a good little girl. But now that I'd experienced true emotion and affection, mutual respect and desire…everything was different. It didn't make hearing about how obedient and accommodating past Cassandra had been any easier though.

"Yet, ye know that women are worth more than how society views them. Ye have more potential than bearing heirs and marrying for status. I would have supported that if it was yer aim just like I will support ye now if a love match is truly what ye desire. Yer happiness is deserved, however ye find it. There will be Fiona's support as well as my own. And Jane's and Mary's and everyone else's. There are those in society who would snub their noses at a marriage like that, at your choice of husband, but you are quite beloved," she said with a smile. "I cannae imagine ye would lose anyone who actually mattered."

Marriage. Husband.

The words aloud were like a blow. I'd only allowed myself to consider them in the privacy of my own heart mere days ago.

If the situation with Alexander had taken place in Mayfair and he'd been a gentleman from an affluent family, there would be no question as to our future. After all we'd done and all we'd proclaimed, the banns would be called and we would be altar bound. But because of the circumstances of his birth, I'd resigned myself to a life lived in secret. I'd hardly allowed myself to consider the alternative. Saying aloud the words *husband* or *marriage* in association with Alexander felt too dangerous and heartbreaking. Hearing Ashleigh utter them so easily now was earth-shattering. My breath hitched in my lungs and my heart raced with possibility.

Ashleigh watched the hope bloom in my eyes, and smiled. "Oh, my little lamb." She reached toward the tray of refreshments and plucked some shortbread before passing it to me. "Have a biscuit and tell me about him. If he's not charming, what is he, then?"

I thought of all the sides of Alexander I'd discovered thus far. His intelligence and his dry wit. The passionate, romantic heart he'd never had the opportunity to use. His fierce loyalty and devotion. The open affection that was only revealed with grasping hands and broken pleas.

But to Ashleigh, I said, "He's a reader."

She paused in her own chewing. "He reads?"

I nodded eagerly. "So many books. You wouldn't believe, Ash."

"Hmm," she replied, considering. "That's a start."

I laughed with my friend as we continued our teatime conversation.

The intensity of our discussion bled away and we settled comfortably into the afternoon. I felt better for having my friend's cautious blessing and her unrivaled support. And I felt buoyant in the knowledge that my secret desires…were given voice and reason.

Marriage. Husband.

It would be later when thoughts intruded and my worries grew.

For all the different parts of Alexander that I'd uncovered, there were still so many sides left unknown. My fear was that he preferred a life cloaked in darkness.

How long could I be expected to drag him into the light?

Despite the chill of the evening in which we'd arrived, the Countess of Langston's music room was positively stifling. I was seated among a group of at least forty individuals in a space that comfortably held twenty-five. But Lady Eugenia's annual recital was a highly fashionable event and drew a crowd every year. The countess's three daughters, all aged between fourteen and twenty-four, were extremely proficient musicians and possessed lovely singing voices as well.

Mrs. Ridley was seated beside me and was looking forward to the evening's festivities. My parents had extended their stay in Hertfordshire once more, and so my helpful chaperone had been called upon to continue her services. Presently she was scanning the space for lemonade from a passing footman and fanning herself.

"Oh, do allow me to retrieve some refreshments for you, Mrs. Ridley," I offered.

"Thank you, m'dear."

Rising smoothly, I proceeded past the rows of chairs until I reached the back of the crowded music room. I knew Alexander would be in attendance. We'd exchanged several letters this week following my unexpected visit to his apartment. He'd indicated he would be serving tonight.

Two footmen entered with trays, both wearing the dark blue Langston livery. I ignored their proffered refreshments and lingered by the doorway. It was getting close to the start of the performance and it seemed all the chairs had been filled because there were several gentlemen and even a few young ladies standing along the back wall.

A flash of dark blue caught my eye and I turned to see Alexander approaching.

He held the tray aloft and uttered a low, "Your Highness."

His voice, so deep and tempting, had my mind drifting far from the proper confines of a society event. I heard instead the sounds he made when his hands grazed my skin. And recalled the quiet groans that vibrated the heated air between us.

Shaking myself out of the inappropriate thoughts, I murmured quietly, "Thank you, sir," as I retrieved two glasses of lemonade.

Alexander's blue eyes lingered on my face before he stepped away toward the other guests.

With a bracing inhale, I returned to Mrs. Ridley, only to find another elderly woman occupying my seat.

"Oh, Cassandra, this is Mrs. George. She is attending to young Lady Josephine," Mrs. Ridley said by way of explanation.

"Good evening, Mrs. George. Here, why don't you ladies take these refreshments and enjoy the musicale. It should be starting soon. I shall join the younger set," I said with a happy smile, indicating those standing for the performance.

After several objections followed by adamant reassurance, I relinquished the glasses and returned to the rear of the space, greeting several acquaintances in attendance along the way. I could no longer see Alexander circulating. It appeared as if all the servants had disembarked as Lady Eugenia's daughters took their places at the front of the room. I swallowed my disappointment that our encounter had been so brief this evening. But I found a place beside a potted fern near the open doorway and planned to enjoy the recital anyway.

As the opening strains of the harp rang out and the melodic sounds from the piano joined, I was distracted by an awareness at my back. With a discreet glance beyond my left shoulder, I saw that Alexander had slid smoothly into the space behind me. Our eyes met briefly before I spun quickly around to face the performers.

With the attention of all the guests focused forward, I felt the awareness of Alexander in close proximity. We had the illusion of privacy. Dangerous because it was merely that—an illusion. We were surrounded by a roomful of people. Alexander wasn't close enough to touch but I could *feel* him—his nearness, the exhilarating prospect of being in each other's orbit for just a little while longer.

The first song came to an end and all those gathered applauded merrily for the girls.

Tension and heat were growing unchecked as Alexander remained just beyond my reach. I heard him release a sigh during a break in the music, and the sound had me straightening. To be this close was torture. As the next song concluded, all eyes were on the performers who now rotated instruments and prepared to begin again. I suddenly felt a strong hold clasp my fingers where they rested at my side. I didn't turn because I knew I should not be obvious in whatever was happening. But I wanted to. In the way flowers sought the sun, I longed to turn my attention to Alexander and the escape he had planned.

A gentle tug had me stepping silently back. A barely there squeeze to my hand had me retreating another pace. Eventually I was out the door and in the corridor with no one the wiser. Alexander still held my hand as I fought an exhilarated grin. Here I was, once again, chasing this mysterious man through hallways in the middle of a society event.

We hadn't gone far when Alexander turned abruptly and opened what appeared to be a small cupboard. The light from the hallway sconces briefly lit the empty interior as I scurried in ahead of Alexander who scanned the corridor before joining me inside.

It was dark and quiet save for our breathing and the absolute frantic beat of my heart. A bit of light sneaked in around the doorframe, but not enough to make out Alexander's features.

"Well, this is cozy," I whispered as his hands settled easily around my waist.

He placed a featherlight kiss to the underside of my jaw that had me arching into his embrace, straining toward the source of his affection.

"I can't tell if you meant to kiss me there, or if you were aiming for my lips and missed your target."

His answering laugh was mostly hot breath against the side of my neck as his lips once again found purchase and journeyed north to the delicate skin beneath my ear. "These lips know exactly what they are doing," he whispered and I shivered.

His proximity in the music room this evening tightened something deep within. The awareness and tension had been palpable. Having leave to touch him now after the strain of resisting made my hands too eager. They snaked beneath his jacket and I raked my nails up his back. His lips faltered briefly in his ministrations as my fingers made the return trip, scoring over the thin fabric of his shirt. "I thought those lips knew exactly what they were doing," I teased.

Alexander's response was to reach down and lift me against him. His hands clutched my thighs firmly as my legs spread and circled his waist, the fabric of my skirts shifting and bunching around us. And then he was bracing my body against the door and kissing me.

My lips parted and all the frustrations of being close but not close enough began to evaporate as we sought one another with teeth and tongues. His hands moved to support my weight beneath my bottom and then he squeezed. The sensation had me gasping against his mouth, but he simply kissed down my chin and the column of my throat, never ceasing his sensual massage of my backside.

The smooth skin of his jaw grazed the tops of my breasts which were plump and round against the neckline of my gown. And I realized suddenly that I could feel the insistent length of his manhood pressed firmly to my core—even through the layers of fabric. He was hard against me, and with his hands supporting me, we could move together. My center stroked deliciously up and down his shaft. I could feel myself growing wet and sensitive beneath my skirts.

This was madness. We were in the cupboard of someone else's home behaving like animals…and I loved it. Alexander was passionate and uninhibited, and *I* had made him this way. We'd made each other lose control. And as I felt my crisis rising swiftly to the surface, I couldn't make myself regret any of it.

Moments later, Alexander's mouth returned to mine as he swallowed down my moan of release. I clutched his shoulders and squeezed my legs tight around his waist. Eventually I pulled my mouth away, breathing hard in the quiet of the small space.

Alexander lowered me to the floor and made sure I was steady before releasing me. I followed on shaky legs, reaching for his manhood that still strained the placket of his trousers quite impressively.

He captured my hands in his. "Not tonight, Princess."

"You always say that," I complained.

"It's always true." He laughed lightly before placing a consoling kiss upon my pursed lips. "I won't ruin you," he said plainly. "But if you start touching me…"

The way his voice trailed off had visions of the pleasurable alternative running through my head. But he resumed his speech before my imagination got too carried away.

"Regardless, this is neither the time nor the place. We should get back before you are missed."

I sighed, knowing he was right. But I couldn't help the sting of rejection and wondered suddenly what other hands had been privy to his pleasure in the past. "I need to tell you something."

Alexander stiffened in my arms.

"Someone you know, I think, approached me. Twice now, to warn me away."

"What?" Alexander snapped suddenly, nearly full volume.

I rose quickly on my toes and placed my hand over his mouth, as if to erase the sound. "Shhh," I said, waiting and listening for voices in the hallway that could have been alerted to our presence.

When none came, I left my fingers against Alexander's full lips and explained, "She introduced herself as Miss Ember Bellamy. I don't believe she means me any harm, but she very clearly expressed her opinion on our continued acquaintance."

He pulled my hand away from his face and instead linked our fingers together. "When was this?"

"Well, she surprised me in the hackney after our outing to Covent Garden. And then I surprised her last week when I left your apartment. She was waiting in the alleyway." When he failed to respond beyond a low curse, I hedged quietly, "Was she waiting for you, Alexander? Were you to meet her?"

"What? No," he said immediately. "It's not like that."

"Will you explain it to me, please?"

He sighed, but to my surprise he began talking. "Ember is Blaidd's daughter."

I couldn't contain my shock. I was only thankful that the dimness of the cupboard hid my gaping mouth.

"Her mother died when she was a young girl, and she'd never met her father before. But she came to live with us…and the others. This little girl in dresses and ribbons from a moderate household, forced into an impossible situation. She taught me to read. I've known her most of my life. Blaidd dotes on her, but he also expects more from her. And so her life has been difficult. There was a time when we were…close to something beyond our shared history. But I knew her loyalty would always lie with Blaidd. She seeks his approval above all else. And ultimately I cannot trust her, so I never allowed anything to grow between us."

I couldn't imagine being in such an impossible predicament, looking for solace in someone else, and still Alexander would not allow it. His distrust overruled nearly everything else in his life, and that made me inexplicably sad.

I didn't begrudge him a stilted romance with Miss Bellamy. I hoped they were able to provide each other a bit of comfort in the hard lives they'd led. But it didn't sound as if that was the case.

Alexander continued while my thoughts tumbled wildly. "Ember has no claim on me, Cassandra. No piece of my heart."

"Oh," I breathed, surprised by his honesty. And then the sting of those words pinched between my ribs. Alexander's heart was unoccupied, but could I say the same? I'd been daydreaming of a future, but would this complicated man, with a life and obligations I could only hope to understand, allow me to claim him as well? If he wouldn't even consider a relationship with someone as close as Ember, how could I possibly hope to win his trust, or more accurately, his heart?

His hands moved up my arms and squeezed my shoulders gently, releasing me from the spiral of my thoughts. "Our contact is minimal, I swear it," he insisted. "She passes communication along and seeks me out when Blaidd will not be deterred. I haven't seen her in some time—since that night at the St. Clair masquerade. Blaidd had given me my target and the job was arranged, but I told him no. The first time I've ever done that. I think he was so surprised, he let it go and sent Ember instead. I attended because I knew you'd be there. It was weakness on my part simply because I wanted more time with you. But truly, I don't know why Ember would approach you now or what she was doing outside my home."

"She's the one who stitched you up, wasn't she?" I didn't know why I focused on that, but the words were out before I could stop them. The image of a scared and bleeding boy called forth. If I was right, Alexander had been tended to by another child after being failed so thoroughly by the adults in his life.

"Yes," Alexander admitted softly.

My hands sought the jagged line along his jaw. I stroked it gently, feeling an ache in my chest. I would be grateful to this complicated woman for showing Alexander kindness even as she risked the wrath of her father.

Footsteps sounded suddenly beyond the cupboard door and I held my breath. They passed quickly, but they brought awareness and rational thought seeping beneath the barrier.

Alexander rested his forehead against mine and my eyes slipped closed. "We need to go," he whispered, reluctant, longing.

"I know."

"I'm sorry about Ember. I never wanted…any of my complications to touch you, Cassandra."

"I know that too."

We said our farewells, and after a sweet kiss to my temple he instructed me to walk out a few minutes ahead of him.

I didn't see Alexander during the intermission nor the remainder of the recital. I felt the pressure of the evening acutely. I needed to retreat and think. Consider the ramifications of what we'd done and also what I'd learned tonight.

He'd apologized for Ember's appearance in my life. But *I* wasn't sorry. My honesty about Ember had necessitated his own. Alexander had been truthful about this aspect of his life. Would he show honesty in the rest?

I wondered desperately if this was the beginning of our direct and open communication. Or would it signal the end of everything with the truth I'd been too afraid to learn?

Sixteen

"Ye could tell the horse was willful and high-spirited but I kept my seat easily enough."

"Of course you did, Ashleigh. You're an excellent rider," Mary complimented.

"Thank ye," Ashleigh acknowledged. "I don't know why Lord Sedgewick assumed my horse needed to be led through the park."

"Probably because he's a highhanded and overbearing pain in the horse's… Well, you can probably guess," Nicolas said with a laugh as the rest of us joined in.

Our Tuesday embroidery salon was a large affair at Randolph House this week. Nicolas finally had availability between his busy theater rehearsals. And even the Earl of Sullivan was in attendance, seated stoically by Jane's side on a settee that didn't quite fit them both. No complaints were issued however as the married couple settled close to one another, Jane hardly touching her embroidery.

"What happened next?" Eliza inquired, blue eyes eager for Ashleigh's particularly ruthless account of her outing with the pompous Sedgewick.

"Well, he insisted on dismounting and leading both horses. But my mare easily pulled the reins from his hands. And every time he bent over to reach for the leather straps, she backed away. This happened no less than six times before he grew frustrated and lunged for the bridle. The mare made to rear but I calmed her before I climbed off and snatched the reins back." Here a wicked gleam and corresponding smile claimed her features. "Then I threatened to tie his hands together with his own reins if he didn't stop interfering with my horse."

We were all in stitches by the time Ashleigh concluded her tale. Nicolas was wiping tears of mirth from beneath his eyes and Kathleen was covering her face with both hands, shoulders quaking in amusement.

The gentlemen of London did not stand a chance where Miss Ashleigh Winstead was concerned.

"Oh, the leather is much too smooth to properly subdue the marquess, Ash," Jane stated matter-of-factly. "You would need natural fiber rope to keep Sedgewick restrained effectively. Preferably one used in shipbuilding or other construction efforts."

We all turned amused looks on Jane's pragmatic approach to the issue at hand.

"It would likely take much more than rope to convince that arrogant idiot that you could outride and outsmart him any day of the week," Fiona murmured with conviction.

"Aye, that's probably true," Ash agreed.

Being with my lovely friends was just what I needed following the evening I'd had with Alexander. I had much to think on, and doubts often made themselves known when they were least welcome.

When the amusement had finally subsided, I looked down and considered my own embroidery project. I'd decided to make a handkerchief for Alexander. The double border was fairly masculine and commonplace in a luminous green thread, but I thought the tiny princess crown in one corner was quite funny, and would perhaps make him smile when he saw it.

I looked up to see Nicolas smile devilishly at Eliza, dimple on display, before he leaned over and whispered in her ear. Her answering grin was radiant before she flushed red and then whacked him on the shoulder. Nicolas caught her hands in his and laughed delightedly at her reaction. And I suddenly felt like an interloper.

Forcing my gaze away from the newlyweds, I added another two stitches before my mind wandered to Alexander. Was he working at the restaurant this afternoon? What would it be like to have him here with me, the way Quinton and Nicolas were accompanying their wives? I couldn't imagine how he would perceive my circle of friends beyond his bone-deep distrust of others.

Being in the presence of these love matches had something envious awakening within. Ashleigh had been right when she said I would have accepted my due. I would have married any one of the men I'd courted in the past despite my heart being perfectly unaffected. But experiencing the other side of that with Alexander—true affection and genuine emotion—made my previous attachments pale in comparison. Bearing witness to the reality of love that Eliza and Jane and Fiona had experienced had never affected me so. Not until Alexander. With his possibility. With the promise of more. I felt rather like a willful horse given a bit of rein. Now that I had a taste of freedom, there was no turning back.

Our discussion continued, and my mood stayed quiet and thoughtful. When I finally rose to depart, Fiona joined me, saying she wished to speak with me for a moment. Kathleen looked on nervously as Fiona and I made for the exit, but Ashleigh leaned forward and engaged her in conversation just as we breached the corridor.

"I wanted to make sure you are all right, Cassandra. You are so quiet and subdued," Fiona said as we walked slowly toward the staircase.

"I am well," I assured her.

"Has anything happened with Alexander since we spoke last? Are you still spending time together?" She didn't sound judgmental or disapproving, merely curious.

"We are still in contact," I confirmed as I slowed to a stop on the balcony overlooking the foyer.

The duchess placed a warm hand on my arm before gentling her already kind voice. "Has he told you the truth about his life? About the dangers that could affect you?"

I thought of the warnings from Mr. Blaidd and my encounters with Miss Bellamy, and all that I'd pieced together from the ragged edges of Alexander's life. "I know a bit more than I did before. Alexander is still determined to withhold some information for my own protection, but I've deduced that he was part of a criminal gang from a very young age. He was manipulated by the man who found him in Covent Garden and raised him. And that relationship has led to all the complications between us. I do not believe I am in danger at present. Our arrangement has been well concealed." I didn't let myself consider the fact that Ember could very easily report back to her father that the daughter of an earl was in a very compromising position outside Alexander's home.

Fiona's dark brows furrowed. "What sort of criminal gang?"

"Picking pockets and general thievery. I believe this Mr. Elias Blaidd trained Alexander and others to steal for him while he withheld food and other necessities unless they performed as instructed." Fiona's hand tightened on my arm, but I rushed to explain. "Alexander hasn't exactly confirmed my suspicions but he hasn't denied them either. He's been able to distance himself over the years and support himself with his work at the restaurant, but I believe the fear lies with the fact that he knows so many of Blaidd's secrets that he'll never be truly free."

Fiona's face had lost much of its color as I spoke. My sweet friend cared so deeply.

I adopted a bright smile and rushed to reassure her. "But we are being careful, Fiona. Do not fret. I will not return to Baker Street to visit Alexander at the restaurant. And I will not be visiting Covent Garden where the majority of Alexander's past resides. And...I don't know what the future holds, but I promise I will come to you if I need your help."

"You must," she insisted, some of the color returning to her cheeks. "No matter what happens with Alexander. Please come to me and I will assist you—both of you—however I can."

I didn't know exactly what sort of hypothetical assistance I would potentially be requesting, but the possibilities made my stomach give a nervous, hopeful leap. Could there truly be a future for Alexander and myself? One in which my friends supported me and offered aid to a scandalous union? The backing of a beloved and respected duchess would be a tremendous benefit should the opportunity arise.

My smile settled into something genuine and true at the thought of Fiona's generosity. "I will come to you, if needed. I swear it."

She nodded, still looking a bit unsteady before finally dropping her hand from my arm and wishing me a good afternoon. "I should get back to Kathleen before she thinks I abandoned her."

I smiled as my friend turned back the way we'd come, her booted feet nearly soundless on the rich carpets.

My introspection continued as I settled in my carriage for the journey home. I joined Mrs. Ridley for a sedate dinner where we discussed the novel she was reading presently. I promised to devote my time upon retiring this evening to perusing the interesting bits she'd indicated so we could compare notes on the morrow.

And that was how Alexander found me several hours later—in my night-gown and reading Mrs. Ridley's recommended romance novel. I started as he pushed open my unlocked balcony door, bringing with him the scent of autumn rain.

His hair was damp from the weather. He wore no hat and just a simple jacket over his shirtsleeves and trousers. Alexander had to be freezing. But he remained just inside the doorway, motionless and watchful.

I set my book aside and rose from my place by the fire, searching his face. We hadn't planned a rendezvous. I'd intended to write to him in the morning.

"Alexander?" The question in my voice elicited no response. I couldn't read his expression beyond the intensity in his eyes and the general feeling of something being not quite right. "What's happened?" I asked when he was close enough to touch.

I slid my arms up his shoulders and cupped his pink cheeks. The chill of the night air hovered over his skin.

"Come," I urged, reaching for his ungloved hands and tugging him toward the fireplace. "Let's get you warmed up."

I led Alexander to the armchair I'd vacated upon his arrival before slipping smoothly onto his lap. I could feel the cold seep through the thin fabric of my nightgown as I began rubbing his shoulders and smoothing his hair.

I'd just started massaging warmth back into his fingers when he finally spoke. "I need to tell you something, Cassandra."

I glanced away from his hands to meet his hesitant blue gaze. "All right."

Nerves tightened my throat, and I grew suddenly very worried. Alexander never offered up information or explanations. I feared something dire must have happened to instigate this visit. He was so unlike himself just now, and I didn't know what that meant.

"I went to Blaidd tonight and told him I was done. I asked him what it would take for him to let me go, to release me entirely. To be free of him and my past."

"What did he say?" I whispered, fearful of the answer.

Alexander glanced toward the fire. "He seemed offended, feigned hurt and injury. Said he always thought of me as a son, his heir." A bitter laugh escaped before he controlled it. "Funny, that was the first I'd ever heard of it. Fathers don't force their sons to steal to cover their gambling debts and build their empires. Fathers don't starve their children for mistakes they make. Fathers don't manipulate sons and daughters to fight to earn their place. The good fathers, anyway. I wouldn't really know. I can't imagine being anyone's son. I was never allowed to be a child. I only ever thought of Blaidd as my employer—my master. And then his protégé, his secret-keeper. But I never wanted it. I didn't want to steal from people."

Alexander's resigned gaze returned to mine.

"Even the rich toffs who have more money than God—I stole jewelry and money, documents and artwork, anything Blaidd sent me to fetch. It was a job…one that I'd been molded for and was good at. There were times when being in the gang felt like having a family—or what I always imagined a family would be like. But as we grew, Blaidd sold off some of the others to workhouses and the like until it was only Ember and me. I was so scared of being turned out and left to fend for myself that I did whatever he asked. When I grew old enough, I realized there were other options. He let me move to Marylebone and work at the restaurant because he and Ember had moved on to art forgeries and fencing and other enterprises. But he still needed me for thieving. I could get in and out of places much easier than Ember. He'd educated me to float among the aristocracy. And I agreed to the jobs as they came fewer and farther between. I thought I could survive like that. Pulling one job every few months, and pretending to be someone else for all the rest. Until I met you."

The tightness in my throat had gone nowhere. I didn't know what it meant that Alexander was confiding in me now. Was this the final act of a desperate man? What had Blaidd demanded for Alexander's freedom? I was afraid to ask again. So instead I considered what he'd admitted to me. It was as I suspected. Alexander had been used cruelly by the only adult he'd ever had in his life. His crimes were not his own, and Alexander was only guilty of the circumstances of his birth. I thought back to his knowledge of the artwork we'd viewed at the National Gallery—the compositions and the textures and colors. He'd stolen paintings from high-society homes for forgeries. His mastery was due to necessity and likely as a result of his trade.

"Until I met you," he repeated, "I didn't consider the future. I was simply existing. Putting one boot in front of the other. But now I'm like you, Cassandra. I want more."

My chin wobbled and I fought to firm it up—to fortify my tender heart.

But Alexander smiled gently and ran his thumb over my quivering skin before saying softly, "I will protect you, I swear it. Nothing from my life before will ever touch you. I won't allow it. I know I don't deserve you. I will never be good enough."

I made to protest, but his thumb moved from my chin to press against my lips where he stroked gently.

"And not just because you're a lady. But because of how good you are. You're kind and honest and so fiercely loyal. I've never loved anything before, but I know I love you, Princess. I've never asked for anything for myself either, but I'm asking for you. If you'll have me. For as little or as long as we have."

I felt his admission of love echo somewhere deep within before igniting. His declaration—so passionate and raw—balanced on the edge of our uncertain future. The unfairness and the joy melded together, tightening my throat and making speech impossible.

Did I want this moment—here and now—with Alexander? The question was inherent in his declaration.

I did. Of course I did.

For as little or as long as we have.

In answer, I rose from his lap and admitted, "I'm yours."

The spark became a slow, steady burn as I reached down with shaky hands and gathered my nightgown, lifting it up and over my head. Alexander's gaze followed the progress of the garment until his brilliant eyes caught on mine. He didn't immediately examine my naked body, but instead scrutinized my face.

If he was looking for fear or hesitancy, he would find none. I might be nervous to share my body with him, but I wanted it—wanted him.

Finally—*finally*—Alexander's attention dropped lower. His eyes traced the curves of my breasts and the buds of my rosy nipples before drifting along the line of my torso until he focused on my core. His perusal continued as he took in the length of my bare legs.

I shifted restlessly as the fire warmed my side. Sliding one leg forward, I stood within touching distance and Alexander raised a callused hand between my legs to the inside of one knee. His fingers skimmed up and down a few degrees, as if to savor the feel, before reaching back to smooth along the back of my leg. His touch rose higher before I felt his blunt nails score lightly back down the length of my thigh.

My eyes closed at the sensation—calming and rousing all at once. I wanted to experience that all over my body. I brought my hands to Alexander's shoulders to steady myself and he moved closer, his forehead nuzzling my stomach. Turning, he pressed slow, wet kisses, lingering deliciously over the sensitive skin there.

I fought the urge to squirm, to hurry our pace. Instead I focused on the feel of his soft lips—so welcome on my exposed body—and the warm heat of his mouth. Those strong fingers were still working their way up and down my legs, stroking me over and over. My hands tightened on his shoulders as he lifted higher to place kisses along my ribs. The area was surprisingly sensitive, and his mouth felt decadent. I ran my fingers through his hair as I breathed in a gasp at the feeling.

Alexander paused. "Did you like that?" His words, so rough and low, breathed across my skin and had my eyes closing again.

"Y-yes," I admitted.

He shifted to my other side and followed the bottom edge of my rib cage before retracing his path with the firm line of his tongue.

I made an indistinct sound of approval from somewhere in my throat and then I felt the curve of his smile searing against my skin, warm and wicked.

"Cassandra," Alexander whispered after a moment, face tilted as he stared up the line of my body to watch my face. "Will you tell me what else you like?"

I paused, considering. "May I show you?"

Heat flared in Alexander's eyes as he watched my hand move away from my side to skim across my torso. With his fingers still stroking the back of my knee, he leaned away to create space as my hand continued its journey to my center. Using two fingers, I parted my sensitive flesh. I felt the drag of my fingers along my skin, slick with arousal. Alexander watched my ministrations, an eager observer as I touched myself.

Embarrassment came unbidden as I widened my stance and sought the pleasure I so often reached for under the covers in my bedchamber. But the awkwardness eased as the intensity grew. Alexander looked on in wonder, learning all the ways I could make my body sing. When I reached down and pressed a finger within, his lips parted on a ragged exhale. His impatient fingers stilled on the back of my leg before they drifted slowly up my inner thigh.

"Can I?" he asked, voice rough.

Biting my lip—knowing I was close—I nodded and called out a broken "Yes."

He used the pads of two of his fingers, just as I'd shown him, and began massaging circles around my most sensitive flesh. Alexander varied the pressure and speed until I made sounds of encouragement. My breathy moans spurred him on, and instead of watching his clever fingers at work, he took in my face, monitoring my pleasure and fixing his stare.

I was his sole focus. His driving need to be the source of my desire was intoxicating and powerful. This dark soul, bowed before me, touched me with urgency and need. And I'd never felt more wanted.

I could feel my body tightening and preparing for release. "Slow just a bit," I instructed, knowing what it took to get me to the top of the cliff, just before falling over.

"Wait," he said, as if waking from a dream. "I wanted to try this." And then he removed his fingers and shifted forward, pressing his lips to my core.

The shock of it—the overwhelming sensation—had my own hand falling away and my crisis striking hard and fast. I braced a hand once more on Alexander's shoulder for balance and support and just to generally keep myself from tumbling to the ground in overwrought ecstasy. He sucked at my skin and brought his hands up to support my bottom, bringing my center closer to his mouth.

The waves of pleasure went on and on, and finally I had to push his eager lips away when the last contraction signaled I was too sensitive to take any more.

Alexander continued massaging the flesh of my backside while I caught my breath, his attention never leaving my face. Finally, after a few deep inhales, I leaned forward and pressed my lips to his in a filthy kiss. I could taste the salty tang of my arousal as I cupped his cheeks and pushed my tongue into his mouth.

Standing slowly, he matched my movements, kissing me with intent. His hands smoothed up my back as he clutched me tighter. The feel of his body—still clothed—created delicious friction, and when his manhood pressed against my middle, so firm and insistent, I felt the stirrings of desire once more.

Pulling away, I tugged his arms in the direction of my bed. In the brightness of my bedchamber—lit by the fire and oil lamps—I could see Alexander's flushed cheeks and sudden concern.

"Yes, I'm sure," I said before he could voice the doubts written clearly across his handsome face. "I want you. I want to share my body with you. For as little or as long as we have," I repeated.

Together we worked to remove his garments until we both stood naked.

I wanted to calmly examine his form—the way he'd done to mine. But instead I stared below his waist and blurted, "That's not going to fit."

Alexander's cheeks darkened as he looked to the ceiling, biting his bottom lip.

"What?" I demanded. "It's not. I can't believe you walk around all day with that in your trousers. Good God, Alexander."

His gaze returned to mine as his shoulders shook with laughter. "Stop it," he choked out, color still high.

I fought the urge to grin as well, but I did indulge in the warmth that always came when I made Alexander laugh. "I suppose we can try," I stated magnanimously. "I doubt I'll be able to walk tomorrow—"

I cut off when he lunged forward and lifted me into his arms, amusement and embarrassment still illuminating his features. "All right, that's enough of that."

Finally, I allowed the smile I'd been fighting and peppered delighted kisses all over his pink-tinged face. The warm, decadent press of our nude bodies quickly shifted our manner from playful to something else.

Alexander laid me gently on the coverlet with his large body poised above me. His touch became slow and reverent as he kissed a path from my lips down the column of my throat to pay careful attention to my breasts. His hands traced my curves while the wet heat of his tongue stroked my straining nipples.

I spread my thighs wide so he could settle into the cradle of my hips. Our bodies sought friction and heat, and the feel of him just *there* had me squirming beneath him.

Alexander was warm and firm all over. I smoothed my hands from his wide shoulders to his lean waist and then around to grab the taut globes of his backside. The impatience of my grasping had him lifting up to kiss my lips once more before he made an experimental thrust against my core. My eyes rolled back and an embarrassingly eager sound emerged, raw and wanting, from my throat. He was so very hard against me, sliding easily through my wetness.

"That feels so good," I encouraged as my breaths grew ragged.

His face was buried in my neck as he reached around to grasp my thigh and pull it high on his side. The movement widened my legs farther for his continued ministrations, and a low moan escaped us both.

"Yes," I chanted as my crisis grew nearer. The feel of him—surrounding me, clutching me, loving me...

I fell over the edge with that last thought filling me up within.

I came back to myself moments later with Alexander stroking the hair away from my face. He was once again singularly focused on my features, reading my every expression for signs of pleasure and approval.

Leaning forward, I took his lips with my own as my hand reached between us to grasp his firm length. I feared he wouldn't take this final step and erase the only remaining barrier between us without my pointed encouragement. He'd been so vehement in his insistence that he wouldn't ruin me, determined to keep my virginity intact. Whatever had happened with Blaidd tonight had obviously changed that, but I feared it wouldn't be enough to banish Alexander's hesitancy in this act.

But he was mine, and I was his. And this was the beginning. Not the end, as I imagined he feared.

"I want you," I whispered against his lips.

I knew he wanted me too. I could feel it in so many ways. His heart pounding a frantic beat against my chest. His body vibrating with restraint. The covetous ways he clutched me to him.

Positioning him at my entrance, I wrapped my thighs around his waist as Alexander raised up on his hands, hovering above me.

Finally, with focus and patience, he pressed forward—a steady pressure that had his eyes falling closed on a desperate moan. I felt the pinch of his progress and a dull sort of ache as he worked to seat himself fully.

"I was right. You're enormous. This will never work."

Alexander's eyes snapped open to see the teasing grin on my face. His answering smile was all lightness and love. I fought the urge to weep at the beautiful sight.

A short while later, when he'd pulled me close and found his rhythm, I clutched him back just as wildly—pouring every ounce of my affection into the embrace.

I needed Alexander to know that this was true and real. This was our future, whether he believed it or not.

As his movements faltered and his thrusts grew inelegant, I ran my nails down the wide expanse of his back.

He groaned low and long into the skin of my neck as his release claimed him.

And feeling the closeness and connection we shared just then banished the heartache and the worry. I didn't think about the unknown future before us. Nor did I consider Alexander's complicated past. I only felt the heat of his skin and the gentle kiss he pressed to my temple that spoke of love and adoration and the undeniable truth in his touch.

Alexander was nothing if not a thief. Stealing pieces of me until he'd claimed everything—heart, body, and soul.

Seventeen

I t was a long time before we fell victim to exhaustion.

I took my turn exploring every inch of Alexander, learning what he liked and having him show me as well. In a rare display of indulgence he allowed me to kiss and soothe every mark upon him. All the scars and wounds that signaled a life hard-earned. I chased the hurt with sweetness and layered love upon the years of torment and strife.

Finally we locked the door to keep out the servants, and turned down the lamps. I pulled the sheets up and over our heads as the waning fire caused the bed linens to glow.

Alexander's hands had hardly left my body. We remained unclothed and he seemed spellbound by my form. I would turn or shift and he would reverently trace whatever new line had been revealed.

I was pressing my thumb to the divot in his chin when he admitted, "I know it's wrong, but I'm glad we were intimate. I am terrified of hoping but I am equally desperate to keep you. Part of me thinks you could be with child from our joining tonight. And while that is alarming to someone who has no idea how to be a father…part of me relishes the fact that you could be tied to me as a result."

The confession should have frightened me or should have at least caused bells of warning to ring insistently in my ears. Instead, I smoothed my thumb back and forth along his jaw and asked, "Do you want children someday, do you think?"

He shook his head and my heart dropped, but then he smiled ruefully and said, "You never react how I think you should. How any normal person would."

I grinned at his assessment. Being predictable was boring.

But then he sobered. "I truly would not know how to be a good father, Cassandra. Whether I wanted a child or not. I have no experience to draw from nor role models to call upon."

"That's not true. You've known Mr. Patel for years. And besides that, I think the most important part of being a parent is simply loving." My hand smoothed down his stubbled throat to rest over his heart. "You have been waiting for a very long time to share your love with someone. To know safety and trust. A child is the purest form of that. I should think you'll know exactly how to be a good father."

In the unearthly glow of the bed linens and the little cocoon we'd created, Alexander's eager heart was shining through his dark eyes. He wanted a family. I could see he'd considered it and been too fearful to allow the daydream to form. But here, in my darkening bedchamber, he could imagine it and let it take shape in his heart.

He didn't answer or agree, but he shifted to his back and pulled me to him. Lowering the covers, I settled across his chest and together we watched the fire burn low. I could feel my eyes drifting closed, exhaustion taking hold after hours of lovemaking and exploration. But before I drifted away completely, I laced my fingers through Alexander's opposite hand and whispered, "Don't leave in the morning. Be here when I wake." When sleep tugged insistently once more, I squeezed his hand. "Alexander, did you hear me?"

"Yes," he murmured, sounding more alert than I expected.

"Will you stay?"

"Yes, I'll stay until you wake."

My eyes closed reluctantly. "Do you have work at the restaurant tomorrow?"

"No. Not tomorrow."

"Then I'll come with you. We'll spend the day together. We shall try out the bed in your home."

He snorted a laugh, and I felt the shot of warmth delivered straight to my heart.

"Stay with me," I urged, in a final attempt.

I caught the end of Alexander's reply, more breath than voice before I was pulled under. "Always."

PERHAPS IT WAS my fear that he'd disappear in the night, or the panic that everything that had transpired had been a dream, but my worry woke both body and mind early the next morning. The room was chilled and the sun was but a thin gray line on a yawning dark blue horizon. And still Alexander breathed deep and even at my side.

My relief came tinged with emotion and I felt the sudden burn of tears behind my eyes.

He'd stayed. He was here. And everything had changed.

Alexander had demanded his freedom from Mr. Blaidd. He'd confronted the near-constant tyrant in his life…for me. He'd said he wanted *more*. His devotion was a real and tangible thing beyond the surprising declaration of love and his reverent touch.

What had I done to ensure the future I knew I wanted? A future with Alexander.

I didn't know what *more* looked like moving forward. How did I take my carefully crafted future and burn it to the ground?

It wasn't true if it wasn't brave.

Alexander had shown his courage and his mettle. He might not believe our future was forever but how could he? What proof had I given him? How had I encouraged our unconventional match? He'd told me he loved me, and I'd said nothing.

It was time I considered how to make this dream a reality.

There were risks involved for both of us. My proper future would look vastly different than what I'd expected. In the middle of the night, with our whispered promises drying like the sweat on our skin, I'd thought of nothing but spending my life with Alexander. In the light of day, turning those words into actions was a frightening concept.

I had to consider the practical application of profound upheaval. If I chose Alexander, I would lose my place in society. Acquaintances and popularity would be sacrificed as well as my status. But what Ashleigh had said was likely true. I wouldn't lose anyone who mattered. My friends—my true friends—would support me. I'd be accepted at their tables, and more importantly, they would fold Alexander into our group with loving arms. Nicolas and Eliza's marriage had layers of scandal and complication as well, yet the famous stage performer and the brilliant physician had made it work. I had strong friendships with influential people. Things would change but all would not be lost. They wouldn't allow it.

And my family...well, they'd always been indulgent. I was blessed with a loving mother and father. They wished for my happiness. They would never disown me. Even if my attachment with Alexander cost them connections and associations, they prized family over invitations. They would love me through anything. And I truly believed they could accept and care for Alexander as well. I would speak to them upon their return to London and solidify my plans for the future.

I stared at Alexander's profile as gray light slowly filtered into the room, and I thought...this could be real. I would marry this man and wake up with him every morning.

He shifted slightly. Perhaps awareness was coming with the rising sun. I held my breath as his eyes blinked open. He stared at the canopy above for a long moment before his gaze found mine perched nearby.

"Good morning," I said. "You stayed."

He rolled onto his side to face me. "I did. You threatened my person should I leave in the middle of the night." I smiled at his jest. "So I thought it best to remain."

Alexander's hand came up and touched my face. He brushed my hair back lightly before stroking the skin across my cheekbone. The love in his gaze was humbling and weighty. I felt his admiration strike an answering chord deep within. The delicate new experience between us—waking up together from a night of lovemaking—was precious and awe-inspiring. I was glad it was him. The thought of my prescribed future, the one with an earl or a baron or whichever faceless gentleman who only wanted my dowry or the connection to my family's estate, had my chest lightening with sudden relief.

But this—this was right. This was love.

Therefore it was with heightened emotions and little forethought that I blurted, "I'm glad it was you."

Alexander's dark brows furrowed in confusion.

"I'm glad I made love with you. I have no regrets. I wanted you to know that. I've never felt more cherished and cared for in my life. I am glad it was you."

He smiled, small and relieved. "I'm glad it was you too."

It was my turn to frown.

The very naked man in my bed looked suddenly uncomfortable with his confession. He pushed a final strand of hair behind my ear before retracting his hand and tucking it beneath his cheek. "I've never…before last night…before you."

I didn't allow my surprise at his admission to show. I simply waited. But on the inside, my feminine pride was doing a smug little quadrille.

"You know that I don't trust easily. Opening myself up to someone—even physically—seemed more than I could tolerate. And things with Ember ended nearly as soon as they began. I knew where her loyalties lay, and I couldn't ignore my instincts where she was concerned."

"I see," I said easily, reaching over to smooth away the frown that had developed as he spoke. "I am outrageously glad it was me." Before our matching smiles could drift away, I said, "I'm going to leave a note for my chaperone, grab us breakfast from the kitchens, and then sneak out the window with you."

Alexander's brows rose again. "And where are we going?"

I threw back the bed linens and made my way over to my wardrobe. While shrugging into my dressing gown, I turned back to find Alexander stretched out on my bed. His hands were crossed beneath his head and he watched my movements with an attentiveness that had a zing of arousal shooting straight to my core. "Well, we could go to yours, I suppose. Whatever you want."

"Whatever I want," he echoed, voice deep and enticing.

I nodded even though it had not been a question.

Alexander rose smoothly from the nest of blankets, unconcerned with his nudity. He approached and stopped my attempt to tie the sash of my dressing gown. His warm hands snaked around my waist as he enveloped me. With the hot press of his mouth, he made his way over my collarbones and along my throat until his mouth fit itself neatly over mine.

We kissed until my lips were sore and his erection prodded insistently against my stomach. Alexander pulled back on a ragged breath before saying, "Go, before we're caught here or someone hears how irresistible you are."

I stroked my hand over his firm length and gave a little squeeze. He grunted against my hair before stepping away and closing my dressing gown himself. I watched in amusement as Alexander secured the fabric nearly up to my neck before tying the sash deftly. He pressed a quick kiss to my lips before turning me toward the doorway.

With a firm pat to my behind and an "Off you go," he ran frustrated hands down his face and collapsed on the bed as I watched.

My laughter had mostly faded by the time I removed the key from the lock. Before opening the door and quitting the room, I whispered over my shoulder, "Don't worry, I'll bring back a full tray. We'll need to keep up our strength."

~

WE DID, indeed, eat a hearty breakfast in my bedchamber before dressing and stealing away. Alexander guided my climb down the trellis and I landed in the back garden with an enormous smile on my face. We scurried along the perimeter and exited using the same path we'd taken on the morning of our visit to the Covent Garden Market. Had that really been but a few weeks ago? It felt as if so much had changed since then.

Alexander felt comfortable taking me back to Baker Street in the light of day. So he hired a hack and we traveled to his apartment where we spent the morning in and out of bed. There was no hiding our emotions, no ignoring the intensity between us. I didn't miss the romantic candlelight when instead I could read every expression that crossed Alexander's face while he was poised above me, losing himself to the love we were creating.

While I cleaned up a bit, Alexander went down to the restaurant to acquire more nourishment. And since the day was surprisingly mild for mid-October, we decided on a stroll and a picnic in nearby Regent's Park. Alexander said he had a favored spot—secluded, without foot traffic—and we wouldn't be bothered by the crowds I was typically used to in Hyde Park. He assured me my reputation would be safe, and I trusted him.

I picked a few books from Alexander's vast collection to accompany us on our adventure, and after we'd eaten, we lounged and read in the dappled light beneath an ash tree. I would occasionally comment on a passage in the book or ask a question or an opinion of Alexander, but for the most part we passed the afternoon in companionable isolation from the outside world. It was both thrilling and as comforting as a warm blanket, all at once.

The simple act of spending the day together—eating, conversing, loving—fueled my daydreams for a future. I knew better than to speak to Alexander of my wistful imaginings. He was still so unsettled regarding Blaidd and his ability to free himself from his past to even consider his future—much less a future with someone like me. But I was planning and plotting how to turn the simple domesticity of today into forever.

It wasn't until we were packing up our supplies that reality intruded on our time together. Ember emerged from someplace unknown and Alexander became a version of himself that I hadn't seen in a long time—rigid and impenetrable.

He rose to intercept her even as she continued her approach. I set the books and hamper aside and stood as well.

"What are you doing here?" Alexander's words were low and angry.

She was dressed in her subtle workman's attire again—domed hat, trousers, and large, form-hiding dark coat. Her boots were soundless on the grass. "I mean no harm to you or Lady Cassandra." She raised her hands in a show of peace. "I just have a message and I'll be on my way."

"Well, out with it, then," Alexander said impatiently.

Ember's gaze flicked to mine briefly before she responded. "He wants to see you." And then on a sigh, "You can't just run away, Alexander. He will never allow it. If it were up to me… I've tried talking to my father, believe me." Her expression fluctuated between apologetic and pitying.

Alexander cut off whatever reassurances or platitudes she'd been prepared to say. "Message received. I'll come to him."

"He gave you a fortnight." The scale leaned more heavily toward apology now.

"Generous," Alexander said flatly before turning his back on Ember Bellamy and dismissing her soundly.

We regarded each other—this woman and I.

I didn't have any ill will toward her. She wasn't to blame for the life she'd been born into. And Ember, while secretive and theatrical in her ways, had never truly meant me any harm. I imagined she'd been Alexander's only ally for a very long time, and for that I was grateful. But she hadn't been someone he could trust—someone who would put him above all others.

Everyone needed a champion. Someone to love you more than you loved yourself. A fiercely loyal presence to be the blade at your side and the voice of reason in your head.

Alexander needed someone to love him with their whole heart, not just pieces. I felt buoyed by the knowledge that I would be that person.

With a tip of her hat, Ember backed away and left us to a tense and pervasive silence.

After a moment, Alexander said, "It's getting late. You should return home."

I ignored the suggestion and the brush-off. "Can we talk about this?" I said, refusing to be either tentative or timid. I'd learned my lesson on that front.

Alexander was still crouched on the blanket, packing our things. But he paused and looked up at me with a resigned sort of expression.

I slowly lowered myself to join him. "What happened when you talked to Blaidd?"

With a sigh, he answered. "He told me how disappointed he was in me and how I was like family to him." Alexander rolled his eyes before continuing. "Then he said he needed time to think. I guess…he's had the time he needed."

"Will you go to him soon?" I fought to keep the worry out of my tone, but he must have heard it because his face softened and he reached for my hand.

"He's given me a fortnight. I won't rush into anything. Besides, I'm busy at the restaurant for the rest of the week."

I nodded. But despite his assurance I felt suddenly panicked that something would happen—that he wouldn't know what he meant to me. I fought the urge to blurt out that I loved him and he couldn't go to war with Blaidd because we were going to have a life together. But I forced my tongue under control and asked reasonably, "When can I see you again?"

"What are your upcoming engagements?"

I thought for a moment. "I have a visit to the children at the Home tomorrow, then a ball at Lady Crestleigh's home in two days' time, and my parents return early next week. They're attending Jane's garden party with me one week from today."

"I shall see you at Lady Crestleigh's event and perhaps I could pay you a visit afterward?"

I smiled. "I am amenable to that." But then my amusement dissipated. "And you won't go to Covent Garden?"

Alexander squeezed my hands once more and promised, "I won't."

Despite his reassurance, the worry—useless and adrift though it might be— refused to leave me.

Eighteen

Spirits were high in the Earl and Countess of Crestleigh's ballroom. My mother had accepted the invitation on our behalf weeks ago, otherwise I likely would not have attended. None of my close friends would be here tonight, and the countess, while friendly with my mother, was not terribly pleasant. She frowned mightily when Mrs. Ridley and I entered without the accompaniment of my mother.

Nevertheless, I smiled my brightest, most winsome smile and passed along Mama's regrets. I threw in a compliment or two for the floral arrangements and general beauty of her gathering. Couldn't hurt, after all.

Mrs. Ridley had already tottered away to find a quiet space, and I was busy scanning the area for footmen. When a particular footman—tall and strapping with dark hair—did not immediately appear in my vicinity, I moved toward the refreshments table.

Just as I approached, a gentleman turned—glass in hand—and froze at the sight of me. Amusement threatened, but instead of the startled laughter that desperately wanted to escape, I instead aimed a polite smile at Carlton Barrington, Lord Bunsen, ingestor of citrus fruit.

The man finally managed a hard swallow and resumed motion.

"Good evening, my lord. How do you do?"

He lowered the small glass in front of him, rather like a pitiful shield, before bowing slightly. "Good evening, Lady Cassandra. I am well. No garnishes for me this evening." Lord Bunsen's cheeks pinkened just a bit at his self-deprecation but I liked him all the more for it.

"I am relieved to hear it." His companionable smile mirrored my own. "I was also quite happy to hear of your recent betrothal to Miss Whitmoore. Felicitations to you both."

"Oh, yes. Well. Thank you, Lady Cassandra." His voice lowered slightly as he continued. "I am comforted to know that you are not upset."

Despite being a master of my expressions, I feared I could not keep the confusion from my face. Lord Bunsen and I shared but one dance at an event earlier in the season where he proceeded to choke on a lemon rind and then never speak to me again. I could not imagine a scenario in which I became upset that this man planned to wed someone else.

Lord Bunsen cast a discreet glance about us before indicating a less crowded space along a nearby wall. "Might we speak for a moment?"

"Of course," I agreed and followed.

With our relative privacy, the gentleman turned earnest brown eyes my way. "I wanted to apologize for the way I fled our last encounter. It was cowardly, of course. But I found myself overwhelmingly humiliated...by the incident at Dameron Hall, and then Miss Whitmoore was kind enough to ensure I was well. We conversed easily and I became distracted. I should have returned and explained."

"My lord," I rushed to assuage his worry, "no apology is necessary, I assure you. I was relieved you were well and I am grateful that the whole occurrence became a blessing in disguise. I hope you and Miss Whitmoore will be very happy together."

Lord Bunsen smiled. "Thank you. I do believe we shall be."

I thought suddenly, while I had one of my former suitors here—and one who seemed genuine and open to making amends—perhaps I should settle something. "Lord Bunsen, might I ask you for a truthful response to an odd question?"

He hesitated, but finally nodded solemnly.

"Did you dance with me in order to find your true match, so to speak?" My words did not trigger any recognition. Carlton appeared confused. "Was it because of the"—I lowered my voice to a whisper—"curse...that you wanted to dance with me?"

That had his dark brows lifting. "The curse?"

Good Lord, this was awkward. "The legend, rather, that is circulating about me. If a gentleman survives a disaster in my presence, then he'll meet his future wife immediately after." I had to admit, saying it out loud in front of one such gentleman was a bit ridiculous. But then again, I hadn't known the circumstances surrounding his relationship with Belinda Whitmoore. The curse was particularly fast-acting in their case.

But to my surprise, the man started laughing. "No, of course not. Lady Cassandra, that superstition is utter rubbish. I didn't consider it for even a moment. And I don't know anyone else who puts stock in that bit of gossip either. I assure you, I asked you to dance because I bucked up enough courage to finally do so. You are beloved, my lady. You must know this. I felt honored to be your dance partner. I did hope that something more would develop between us, but like I said, the run-in with Miss Whitmoore was fairly unexpected and I'm afraid it changed our course more so than any disaster—or citrus fruit—could have done."

His smile was gentle, as if he was letting me down easy. I supposed that scenario was slightly less humiliating than believing a ridiculous legend about oneself.

"I appreciate your candor, my lord. Now, I've kept you for far too long. I am sure your betrothed would appreciate a turn on the dance floor."

Lord Bunsen bid me a fond farewell, and as we parted I reflected on the validation I'd received this evening. I'd perhaps placed too much importance on gossip and hearsay. But I couldn't very well regret the path I was now on. Allowing myself to be manipulated by such irrationality had given me the courage to question what I really wanted.

And what I really wanted was standing across the room in dark trousers and an absurd white wig, watching me with a curious expression on his face.

I did not think. I simply started for him, a pleased grin tugging my cheeks.

Alexander looked alarmed and it reminded me so much of the night I'd chased him through my home and caught him in my father's study that a huff of unexpected laughter escaped.

He didn't run, but he did move away from the crowd and held his tray before him like a shield against my approach.

"Good evening," I greeted.

He swallowed visibly. "Good evening, my lady."

I plucked a champagne flute from the serving platter and brought it to my lips, my smile firmly in place and curving against the delicate rim.

"Is everything all right?" Alexander whispered, eyes scanning those nearby before taking in what was sure to be my maniacal radiance.

"Everything is perfect." I finished the champagne as an excuse to remain in his presence. His deep blue eyes widened fractionally. Placing the flute carefully back on his tray, I said in a low voice, "I'll see you tonight."

Alexander nodded carefully before turning away.

I felt my worries lighten like the bubbles in my glass. The fears for my future —the one I wanted with Alexander—were dissolving like the sweetness on my tongue. Hearing the truth tonight from Lord Bunsen had given me a sort of freedom I could not pinpoint. Knowing that the way forward was one of choice and not circumstance made all the pieces fall into place within. My confidence grew along with the knowledge. The *more* I sought wasn't simply a notion or a whim. And neither was it the reaction of a spoiled princess who'd grown weary of her constant admirers. It was necessity. The same way Alexander had become essential.

Buoyed by my realization, I spent the remainder of the evening in high spirits. I mingled with acquaintances, and I laughed loudly and often. I danced and I made merry. I didn't fear the authenticity of every encounter, nor did I allow fluttering fans and gossip to threaten my jubilant mood.

I loved Alexander, and we would have our future together. Determination and dedication were firmly within my vocabulary. Alexander would be mine and we would be happy. I'd make it so.

That did not mean the path would be easy. We would certainly face obstacles and challenges, but my confidence lay in knowing that there were a multitude of routes before me. And the one I sought was the one with Alexander by my side.

Unfortunately, Alexander was not aware of my realization. Nor did he share my triumphant mood.

He entered my room through the balcony with a stony expression and a grunt of greeting.

Undeterred, I smiled brightly, planning on confessing my affections and the truth of my love. I wanted him to know that I'd chosen him. I'd chosen us. He still didn't believe. It was in his hesitancy with me and the intensity of his stare. He thought our every encounter could potentially be our last. I didn't know if Alexander was capable of having faith in anything, much less a future with me. But I was done kissing him as if it was constantly goodbye.

"Well, you're in a state, I see."

His expression remained thunderous as he stalked toward me.

I did not rise from where I sat. We'd discussed that he would pay me a visit following tonight's event. I'd been propped up in bed, knitting socks for the children of the Home, comfortable beneath my blankets as I awaited Alexander's arrival. The fire was burning, lighting the room golden as it fought the autumn chill.

I'd left my long red hair loose, forgoing my evening plait, and I could see Alexander cataloguing the change. And admittedly, knowing he'd be in my bedchamber later, I was not wearing much beneath this coverlet. But he didn't know that yet. Perhaps he'd abandon this foul mood and lose himself in the spirit of discovery.

Shrugging out of his great coat, Alexander approached my bedside.

I calmly laid down my knitting needles and moved my project to the bedside table where two candles were lit. He did not speak, simply loomed with a grumpy expression, but I saw his eyes flicker to the progress I'd made on the left sock. His inherent curiosity—even in the face of his bad temper—had me fighting a smile. Instead, I smoothed my hands over the crease in the bed linens before lacing my fingers and placing them demurely on my lap.

"Would you care to join me?" My cheerful attitude seemed to irritate him further, his glorious frown deepening to bracket his wide mouth. I didn't know why he was so grouchy, but I could wager a guess.

"Would I care to join you?" he echoed back, voice firm. "After tonight? All season I've only continued accepting work as a footman to see you and be near you. But tonight I had to watch you, smiling and laughing and dancing. When I couldn't touch you or speak to you or claim any of your attention for my own."

I smiled sweetly. "We shall have to work on your sharing ability."

"I don't want to share you," he growled.

I patted the top of the bed near my hip and indicated he should sit. He did, but he didn't look happy about it. Alexander turned toward me and braced one arm over my legs.

"I know you don't wish to share, but you are going to have to. I have friends, Alexander. And a family. Philanthropy work that is important to me. Devoting all my time to you would mean neglecting all my other relationships and responsibilities. That is not healthy or wise. But I see your point about this evening, and specifically the dancing. I found myself to be in high spirits and could not help expressing it."

His blue gaze was scrutinizing as he considered my response. "Why were you in high spirits?"

Abandoning all teasing, I met his stare with equal intensity. "For the first time in my life, I feel like I'm finally in control. And that seemed like cause for celebration. I apologize if my happiness came at a detriment to your own. That would never be my wish." I leaned forward and cupped his cheek, smoothing my thumb across his dark stubble.

Alexander searched my face, eyes glancing between my own before he seemed to reach a conclusion. "You wish to be in control?"

"Doesn't everyone want to be in charge of their own destiny? To feel purposeful and powerful?"

His attention wandered to my lips. "You can be in control now. Here. With me." The words were low and seductive. "Take whatever you want. You're in charge."

I remembered the frustration on his face when he'd arrived, the anger and irritation. But after hearing the cause, I realized all those surface emotions covered the hurt Alexander had likely been feeling. He'd been forced to watch me from across the ballroom. It was how our interactions had all started. Him in the role of servant, and me, the charming but untouchable princess. He'd told me before—he'd thought he hated me, but in truth he was jealous. Tonight had done nothing but reinforce those ideas, irritated those old wounds.

I could do more than tell him how I loved him. I would show him.

Slowly dragging my hand along his jaw, I began loosening and unwinding his cravat. Once the pale, wrinkled fabric littered my floor, I focused on the buttons of his white waistcoat. Slowly, piece by piece, his uniform from this evening—the painful reminder of our separation—was discarded.

I finally urged a nude Alexander across my bed and rose onto my knees. Gathering my shift in my hands, I lifted it up and over my head.

Alexander was watchful and silent. He was ceding control, giving me the space to assert my authority. And I was doing my utmost to assuage his fears, to show him that I was his—body and soul.

Straddling his hips, I lowered my center to meet his.

He swallowed at the contact and made to reach for me before catching himself and dropping his desperate hands back to the bed. I smiled and leaned forward, pressing a kiss laced with gratitude for his restraint to his perfect lips before grabbing his hands and bringing them to my hips. A reward for his self-control, while I was equally desperate for his touch. The movement made the tip of his erection slot teasingly into place. So I leaned back and eased myself onto his hard length, joining our bodies in a steady descent.

Alexander was still large, and this position—with me above—didn't diminish his overwhelming size, not one bit. But soon my body adjusted, softened to his invasion. And before long I was shifting restlessly atop him.

I smoothed my hands along his firm chest and the smattering of dark hair in the center. Bracing myself, I began a steady push and pull, raising and lowering my body, rolling my hips and experimenting with my movements. Alexander's eager fingers tightened in response and I soon figured out what he liked. Using one hand for leverage, I brought the other to my center, just above where we were slick and straining.

Alexander tracked the movement, watching me touch myself as I continued moving above him. His groan vibrated beneath my palm and I watched as he fought the urge to react—to touch, to grasp, to take possession.

I didn't want this love between us to be a battle. I didn't want a fight for dominance—for one person to be in control over the other. I longed for a partner, ached for someone who could love me equally.

"Touch me," I gasped out on a breath.

Alexander met my eyes but his remembered promise seized his limbs.

"I want you to be with me," I begged. "For us to be…together." My crisis was growing nearer. I didn't want to lose myself to this struggle for control.

Finally—*finally*—Alexander's hands slid from my hips to grasp my backside. He guided my movements before the fingers on his right hand came back to my front, taking the place of my own as he claimed my pleasure.

Soon we were frantic, inelegantly chasing our shared desire. I was close, so close. But I wanted Alexander with me.

I leaned forward and brought my mouth to his, pouring forth all my yearning in a kiss that melded our hearts together. Alexander's knees bent. He thrust up from beneath as our desperate kiss went on and on—until we lost ourselves to the need roaring between us.

I gasped as my crisis hit, and Alexander groaned low against my mouth as we found our release, together.

I collapsed boneless against his chest, my breathing ragged. But I was gratified that we'd reached this point together—giving nothing away at the expense of the other. No wins, no losses, and no score to be kept.

I sighed deeply, free in the knowledge that where one would lead, the other would always follow.

"WHAT DO YOU NEED, JANE?" Fiona's voice had a stabilizing effect on the ladies gathered in the front room of Randolph House.

We'd been summoned midmorning to help Jane with her afternoon event. The weather hadn't held, and autumn in London was dreary and gray with mild, golden days a distant memory. Jane's garden party had to be moved indoors, and the staff was in disarray with reinforcements being summoned and Mrs. Hooper —Jane and Quinton's housekeeper—organizing all available hands with the skill of a seasoned general.

Jane was hosting an intimate gathering of close friends to welcome the Duke and Duchess of Benton—Quinton's parents—back to London. I wasn't sure of the details but Sullivan and his family had been estranged for some time until Jane began communicating with them via letter following their marriage last winter. After some cajoling on her part, Quinton agreed to see them. The duke and duchess had their own home in Mayfair, of course, but it mainly went unused as they preferred to remain at their country estate year-round. Jane had mentioned during our recent embroidery circle that she would be putting together this hasty gathering with the duke and duchess's close friends, and could we please all attend and help with conversation and prevent any awkward silences. In true Jane fashion, she'd even provided a list of potential topics to avoid.

As the English weather necessitated adjustments to the event, I'd been called away during breakfast with my parents, who'd recently returned from London. The conversation regarding Alexander and our future had to be postponed as a result.

Jane's nervous, darting gaze finally focused on the duchess before she took a deep breath. "Right. The ballroom is currently being set up with tables for mingling and conversation. Refreshments will be served within, and musicians were summoned to provide entertainment since we can't use the garden. Really, I don't know what I was thinking by attempting a garden party in late October. It was madness. Who would have—"

Fiona disrupted Jane's self-recrimination. "You were thinking that an informal garden party would be more appropriate for Quinton and his visiting family. And you thoughtfully recalled how much the Duchess of Benton loves the outdoor air and gardens of London while she has to be away from her beloved country estate."

Jane nodded around a strained smile. "I suppose…I just want everything to be perfect. I want Q to have his family back, and I don't want anything to ruin this day."

"Jane," I said softly, a sympathetic smile hovering on my lips, "you are doing a wonderful thing for Quinton and the duke and duchess. And nothing will ruin this day. We won't allow it."

The other ladies nodded their agreement.

"Give us tasks, Jane. Tell us what needs to be done and where we can best focus our energies." Eliza stepped forward and clasped her friend's hands firmly.

"Aye," Ashleigh agreed.

Jane wavered for a moment before issuing orders. "Mary, the duchess invited more of her friends than I was anticipating. If you and Cassandra can circulate and make conversation prior to luncheon being served, that would ease my worries."

"Done," Mary chimed in.

"And done," I echoed.

Satisfied, Jane continued. "Fiona, could you stay close to Q? You are a calming presence and you'll know how to smooth any lingering awkwardness between us and his family."

"Of course," Fiona agreed. "I'll be wherever you need me."

"Thank you all so much for rushing to my aid," Jane said. "Guests will be arriving shortly. Should we relocate to the ballroom?"

"Jane, have you eaten today?" Eliza asked as we all started to turn toward the doorway.

Jane blinked, and hesitated before responding, "You know, I don't believe I have. In all the commotion this morning, I overlooked breakfast."

"Well, you ladies accompany Jane to the ballroom," Eliza said firmly to the rest of us. "I'm off to the kitchens to get her something to eat. No swooning on this very important day," she said with a teasing wink for Jane who rolled her eyes heavenward.

With our orders very much in place, the afternoon progressed beautifully. Mary and I met and conversed with many of Quinton's mother's friends and acquaintances. They were eager for her notice and attention after so many years away from London. But to allow Q time to speak with his parents unencumbered, we made ourselves charming and delightful so that they did not miss their time away from the duchess.

Extra tables had been brought in for the unexpected growth of the guest list, and luncheon was served. The general atmosphere was welcoming and celebratory, and I dare say no one regretted the change of venue in the slightest.

At one point, Fiona and I passed close to one another and the duchess whispered, "I have something I wish to discuss. Let's make time before you depart today."

Somewhat confused, I'd simply nodded in response as Fiona moved in the opposite direction. I was soon distracted from my curious state and continued mingling among the guests.

I detected smiles from Jane and the Duchess of Benton. And I could see that Quinton had inherited his stoic regard from the current duke, but everyone appeared at ease and comfortable.

The musicians were playing and the lady of the hour was finally circulating among her own set when I caught an unexpected flash of movement by the open ballroom doors. Servants had been coming and going, removing the remnants of the midday meal as the musicians played and guests chattered happily.

But something had me turning at that exact moment and seeing a familiar profile move quickly beyond the doorframe.

I mumbled a distracted "Excuse me" to my mother and father who—despite their recent journey—had attended today in support of Jane and Sullivan, before standing and walking quickly toward the exit. I distantly heard Fiona call my name, but my mind was spinning and I had to see with my own eyes that the footman who'd shuffled by the ballroom had not been Alexander.

Once I was out of sight of the guests, I picked up my skirts and moved quickly. I peered around corners and continued down the hallway toward the interior of the residence, searching for a tall form with strong, broad shoulders and a body I would recognize anywhere.

I passed Mr. Daniel O'Connor, Quinton's trusted friend and business associate, at some point. He called after me, asking where the fire was and chuckling to himself.

It was somewhat of a jest between us, and I told him quickly, hardly slowing in my mindless pursuit, "Oh, you know me, Mr. O'Connor. Always in a hurry."

I'd just breezed by a corridor to my right when a dark coat caught my attention. My mind was thrown backward in time as I remembered spying Alexander in my own home in a similar manner. But this time I didn't plan my attack. I didn't ease back behind the corner to regroup. I simply changed direction and took off after him.

I had no idea what he was doing here. I'd told him specifically about this event and my plans to attend. He hadn't said he'd be working. Alexander knew Jane and Quinton were my friends. *I'd told him.*

Some fearful part of me whispered doubts, told hurtful truths about Alexander's nefarious past. But he would never do that now. He was not here to steal. I had to believe that.

What if he'd gone to Blaidd? What if this—a final job—was the payment for his freedom? What would I do then? Maybe he—perhaps…

I shook my head, refusing to allow fruitless worry and aimless conjecture to derail me. I did not have answers, merely more questions. That was why I needed to speak to him.

We hadn't seen each other since the night of the Crestleigh ball, days ago. He'd left my bedchamber at some point in the night and I'd woken up to a note instead of his warmth at my side. Alexander had been busy with the restaurant on Baker Street and was entrusted with opening the Coffee House for Mr. Patel for much of the week. And my parents had since returned to London. It was no longer safe for him to visit Dameron Hall in secret with my mother and father back in the family wing. We'd exchanged a few letters in the five days since our last meeting. Nothing was amiss.

Why hadn't he told me he'd be here?

Before I could get close enough to call out, Alexander quickly ducked through a doorway midway down the corridor. I followed, breaths straining against my undergarments. With a hasty look over my shoulder, I entered the room and shut the door behind me.

Alexander spun from his position on the adjacent wall. He'd been examining a landscape painting hung behind a large oak desk. This was a study—Quinton's study, if I had to hazard a guess.

"Cassandra!" Alexander hissed, taking a step toward me at the same time I whispered, "Alexander!"

"I can explain," he said, rushing closer, clearly attired in footman's garb.

"What are you doing here?" I said, speaking over him.

"I'm not taking anything," he insisted.

"I know that!" My whispered exclamation sounded unhinged.

He startled a bit. "You do?"

I frowned, intent. "Of course I do. These are my friends. You would never do that."

And then his face fell, guilt lining every one of his features. The defiant young man who so often glared back at the world wilted entirely in on himself.

I balked before stepping close to him, holding his cheeks and forcing his broken gaze to me. "You wouldn't, Alexander," I insisted. "Tell me what is going on."

But before he could open his mouth and ease my fears and his misplaced guilt, the door opened and three familiar figures filled the doorway.

It seemed all the risks we'd taken in compromising situations had finally caught up with us. The threat of discovery was no longer merely a threat.

We were caught.

Nineteen

The three newcomers quickly entered the room and shut the door behind them.

I released Alexander but didn't step away. I clutched his hand and stood by his side to face whatever was coming. His gloved hand squeezed mine in turn.

"Does someone want to tell us what's going on?" Daniel O'Connor said with marked patience.

I looked from Mr. O'Connor to Quinton to Fiona, where my pleading gaze remained.

"Cassandra?" Fiona's voice was utterly calm despite the circumstances.

I wasn't given a chance to speak. Alexander stood straight and admitted in a rush, "I took something from you."

I looked on in horror as Alexander stared resolutely at the Earl of Sullivan.

"He didn't," I asserted. "I was here the whole time!"

Quinton didn't appear angry, simply resigned. "Why don't you start at the beginning?"

Alexander took a breath. "At your event in the spring. The first ball hosted by Lady Sullivan. I was tasked with retrieving something from your safe." He glanced back over his shoulder to the landscape on the wall.

We all followed his gaze to what I assumed was hidden behind the rather lovely and atmospheric depiction of the English countryside.

"But that was before," Alexander continued with another press against my palm. "I tracked your property down over the summer. It changed hands and took me some time. But I recovered your possession. I came here today to return what I'd taken."

I was staring at Alexander as he explained his presence here to Quinton. "But why today?" I asked, not understanding what could prompt his return now, during an event.

Alexander finally looked at me. "I'd attempted to get in several times in the last few months, but the security here is unmatched. I could never find a way in without being noticed. Today's gathering was the first since the ball in the spring. I knew there would be more staff on site and more guests milling about. So I took the opportunity. I steered clear of the ballroom."

Steered clear of me, I clarified with my glare. His answering sigh said he'd read the accusation accurately in my expression.

Alexander hadn't wanted me to know. He thought he'd simply return whatever mystery item he'd stolen and that would be done.

"You were going to put it back in the safe, then?" Quinton's voice broke our staring match.

"Yes."

Quinton eyed him with a smirk threatening to curl the corner of his upper lip. Daniel wiped a hand across his mouth, brown eyes bright and dancing.

"What?" I asked, not comprehending.

Alexander looked between the two men before he breathed out a curse. "It's fake. The necklace is fake."

Daniel finally released the chuckle he'd been withholding.

Crossing his arms over his chest, Quinton said simply, "Do you honestly think I just leave valuables lying around?"

With cheeks an alarming shade of pink, Alexander accused, "Who keeps decoy jewels inside an exceedingly hard-to-crack safe?"

Quinton simply stared, lips now in smug smirking territory.

"That's not the actual safe, is it?" Alexander stated flatly.

Q's expression changed not at all. Neither did Daniel's laughter.

My exasperation, however, had reached new heights. "Well, as amusing and enlightening as this has apparently been, I would really like to—"

"I think we should talk, Cassandra." Fiona's interruption had me frowning. She didn't seem particularly surprised or distraught by what had been revealed just now. "We are aware of Alexander's situation."

The attention of the man in question shifted to my friend.

"Mr. Blaidd is a known entity," she offered. "And before you erupt with questions, Cassandra, I simply want to help. Blaidd is known to myself and to Quinton. We've been aware of him for some time, as have Q's men at Piker House. Alexander has been widely regarded as Blaidd's protégé and successor, and we are interested to know if that assessment is correct."

I could not, for the life of me, understand what was happening right now. How did Fiona—a duchess and mother of two—know anything about the criminal element I'd mentioned briefly in passing? I knew Sullivan oversaw Piker House, a profitable gaming hell, but didn't understand why his interests extended beyond the gamblers on St. James's.

"It's no longer accurate," Alexander admitted. His expression was entirely closed off and distrustful.

"That's good to hear," Fiona said with a small smile.

Impatient, I said, "Would someone mind telling me what in the bloody hell is going on?"

Both Fiona and Daniel looked to Quinton who turned his assessing blue gaze my way. "Piker House supports a network of informants. I have certain… personal interests in the criminals of London. Their known associates and how and where they operate. The duchess"—he indicated Fiona with a tilt of his head—"has a vested interest as well." My mouth dropped open. "Blaidd and his criminal operation have been a particular thorn in the side of many, and information on his mysterious protégé has been hard to come by. It seems you've stumbled quite blindly into all of this, Cassandra. But we do believe there is a way out. For both of you, if you want it."

"What does that mean?" Alexander's suspicion lived and breathed on the surface of his skin. "I'm handling Blaidd myself. Why would you possibly have any stake in the outcome—"

"We would," Fiona cut him off, voice clear and unyielding. And I suddenly recalled her whispered words in the ballroom, saying she had something to discuss with me. "Cassandra is part of this now, no matter how careful you think you've been. We can help you. I have clout and standing in society, as does Sullivan. With his connections and information, you could leave your circumstances behind. There are things you do not know."

The silence stretched. Alexander did not inquire after these mysterious, unknown things. He was as still as a statue at my side.

"The necklace. Was it the only thing Blaidd asked you to retrieve from my home?" Quinton asked evenly.

Alexander frowned. "No. He asked for any correspondence I could locate from a solicitor—a Mr. Carl Davis. I found nothing and Blaidd didn't bring it up again. I assumed the necklace was the true prize."

The silence was pronounced.

"What is it?" I urged, frustrated by Alexander's nonresponse. But, I supposed, when you lived the life he had, information had a price. Perhaps he feared the cost of what Quinton offered.

Quinton took a breath and then explained. "Elias Blaidd owes me a great deal of money. Gambling is one of his many vices, and fortunately for Piker House he does it quite poorly. When his debts came due at the beginning of the season, he told me he'd have my money by the end of the year, once his ward came of age." Quinton paused to let the statement sink in.

It didn't make any sense. Ember was his daughter. And he used Alexander, considered him an employee. Or in the best light, a protégé. But a ward? That seemed incongruous with all I'd witnessed and been told. My heart still beat in my throat despite the threat of discovery having long since passed us by.

"I didn't trust him—I don't trust anyone," Sullivan continued. "So I used my contacts to find out about this mysterious ward and Blaidd's imminent windfall. I tracked down a solicitor—Mr. Carl Davis. He's actually a colleague of my own solicitor, Mr. Stevens. After some…persuasion, Davis confirmed Blaidd's claims —that his ward would reach one and twenty within a few months and his birthright would become accessible to him. I assumed I'd have my money at that time. So I waited."

I looked between Alexander and Quinton and could not for the life of me figure out what was going on.

Once, when I was but an adolescent—and an exceedingly foolish girl at that —I was being foolhardy on the back of a horse and lost my seat. The resulting fall and knock to my head had made things muddled for a few hours. Words and sounds had been confusing. Merely standing had been a challenge.

I felt that way now. As if I'd taken an unfortunate fall from a great height and nothing made sense to my poor, addled brain. "His birthright? What does that mean?" I asked, confusion saturating my tone.

Quinton's eyes came to mine and he looked almost apologetic. "It means that when he comes of age, he'll receive the inheritance left to him by his father, Robert Greene, the former Baron of Hackstone. And all the documentation to petition the Crown and prove himself the rightful heir and current baron."

Alexander was already shaking his head and my brain was still misfiring. "But what does this mean? What does it have to do with Alexander?"

"Cassandra," Fiona said gently, "it's Alexander. He's Hackstone's son. Blaidd knew all of this. He's known it since he found Alexander."

My gaze swung to the man in question, thoughts struggling against the tide of disbelief. Alexander broke away from our tense standoff and paced to the window, giving us his back.

"You were found with papers in Covent Garden, isn't that right?" Quinton's words were likely as gently inquiring as he could make them.

I knew he was right. Alexander had told me about the letter in passing, as had Ember Bellamy. He didn't need to respond. Quinton already knew.

"The letter was from your mother, Jacqueline Tremaine. It explained everything. How she—the daughter of a shopkeeper on Bond Street—met Robert Greene at eighteen. They fell in love, and when she got with child, Hackstone took her to Gretna Green and married her in secret. He thought that would be enough. But his father refused to acknowledge the union, said he'd cut Robert off and disinherit him, that they would never support your mother nor her child. While they could never withhold Robert's future claim on the title nor any entailed property, they could force him to live in poverty until his father died. Robert wouldn't go against their wishes, but offered to give Jacqueline money and a home in the country to raise the child. She refused, saying she'd rather live on the streets than accept any help from him, and vowed she'd never forgive him. The old baron and his wife died from illness shortly thereafter. Robert became baron and made arrangements with his solicitor to set up a trust for a child he'd never met, not knowing that Jacqueline's religious family had turned her out after discovering she was with child. Robert died unexpectedly the following year in a hunting accident."

Quinton paused briefly, but Alexander made no move to turn, to face these horrible truths.

Eventually, the earl continued. "The solicitor—Mr. Davis—tracked down your mother, found out your name and gave her a copy of all the completed documentation for your trust as well as her certificate of marriage to prove you as the rightful heir. The title is currently held by a distant cousin in America who has no interest in the peerage. Mr. Davis remembered seeing you during his visit, a child of three. Your mother was visibly sick at the time, living in a small room let in Covent Garden. No one knows what happened after she died, but she pinned all the information you might need to your clothes. Blaidd found you, lied about your given name, invented a new surname, and kept all the information to himself. To be revealed at the time of his choosing. You're set to inherit a substantial sum, Alexander. Enough to support you for the remainder of your life."

I was still staring at Alexander's back as Quinton concluded his tale. At some point I'd raised my fingers to my lips and could feel them trembling against my skin. Alexander's chest rose evenly while he gazed out the window. He said nothing.

"But how did you know?" I turned back to Quinton, not explaining myself very well—too shocked to fully express the entirety of the question.

The Earl of Sullivan seemed to understand what I meant regardless. "I was not aware of your…association with Mr. Hill until the Duchess of Compton brought it to my attention. I believe you referenced Blaidd in a recent conversation with her. And I had the name of Robert Greene's heir—Alexander—in my correspondence with Mr. Davis. The duchess and I pieced it together and decided to speak with you as soon as possible."

Fiona stepped forward to stand beside me. Her warm hand squeezed my arm as she spoke gently to Alexander's still-turned back. "You could petition the Court with your claim of legitimacy. With all the information Mr. Davis has, there are not likely to be any complications. The petition will be reviewed, and since proof of marriage and your birth predates that of the current baron, it will be approved. No need for the Committee of Privileges. You would be free to use the title during the short review process. And the anniversary of your birth is nearly upon us. Your new status would change many things, Alexander." Fiona's eyes met my own as she continued to speak. "You could distance yourself from Blaidd once and for all. As a member of the aristocracy, you'd be untouchable for someone like him, not to mention your knowledge of his crimes. You could live a life of your choosing…marry whomever you pleased."

The pieces clicked into place with a horrible sensation in the pit of my stomach. It wasn't supposed to happen this way.

I could not imagine what Alexander was going through. The very idea that this might be true—that he could be a baron and heir to a fortune—would be overwhelming. He'd spent his whole life stealing and serving and hating the peerage. This would be too much for him to take.

Despite what Fiona seemed to think, this was not a tidy solution laid at our feet and tied with a lovely bow. There were layers to this deception and painful realizations to sort through.

The duchess finally spoke softly to me alone. "We'll give you a moment. He'll need time." Her smile was small and sad.

Our three guests moved to quit the room.

Fiona paused, and advised, "Don't linger too long. You'll be missed by your family in the ballroom. Your exit was not discreet."

There was so much more to the duchess than what I knew, and the realization was staggering. Somehow her life intersected with Quinton's. I wondered if Jane knew about all this. But with everything I'd learned in the last quarter hour, I was too distracted to care that my friend apparently had a secret life I knew nothing about.

The trio left, closing the door to the study with a quiet snick. I turned to Alexander who was still staring out the window and far, far beyond this study. "Alexander?"

His attention snapped to mine at the same time I heard voices in the hallway. I didn't want to hear what Fiona and Quinton and Daniel had to say, so I focused only on the man before me.

Stepping close, I pressed my body to his in a comforting embrace. "Are you…" It was foolish to ask if he was all right. He was not all right. "What can I do? How can I help you?"

"Do you trust them?" came his question instead.

He didn't elaborate but I knew to whom he was referring. "I do," I said vehemently, tilting my chin up to meet his gaze. "My recent ignorance notwithstanding. I would trust Fiona with my life. And Sullivan loves Jane. He would never do anything to hurt us. They would not lie to us about this." I cupped his cheeks, pressing my lips delicately to his—offering comfort and reassurance. "I believe that with my whole heart, Alexander."

The voices in the corridor were still muffled but growing steadily in volume. That was odd.

Alexander stiffened as the sound of footsteps approached and shouts reached our ears.

And then the doorknob was turning.

Perhaps something had happened. Maybe Fiona was coming back to speak to me.

But it wasn't Fiona in the doorway. Rather, it wasn't *just* Fiona.

My mother and father burst through the entry amid voices from the hallway beyond. Fiona was attempting to intercede as well as Quinton and Daniel, but it was no use.

"What is the meaning of this?" my father bellowed.

Belatedly, Alexander and I sprang apart from our intimate embrace.

Everyone was talking over one another. It was utter chaos. My mother was crying, and then more people were there as Alexander and I stood frozen. Mary and Jane and Ashleigh and Eliza and Nicolas all pushed through the open doorway. They were all trying to calm my father who was red-faced and demanding to know why I was being attacked by a footman in Sullivan's home.

And then more faces filled the corridor—faces I hardly knew. The Duke and Duchess of Benton and others still. The men and women I'd chatted with in the ballroom not more than an hour ago.

My panic was rising.

We were caught…again.

Forcing a deep breath, I attempted to calm my racing heart. I needed to gain my footing, gain my voice, and gain control of this situation.

So, I stood next to Alexander, straightened my spine, and yelled, "Stop this!" with as much authority as I could muster. The voices ceased and everyone froze.

Wide eyes in all shades and colors met my own, but I looked to my parents and said, "I love him, and I'm marrying him."

Someone in the corridor swooned and the talking erupted again after that— loud and overwhelming. I could feel Alexander's incredulous stare searing the side of my face, but I didn't look. I couldn't. This was not how this was supposed to happen. I had a plan. I was going to work this all out once Blaidd was firmly part of the past and Alexander had a future, free and clear. One in which he could decide for himself if it included me or not. I was going to approach my family and seek support from my friends.

Being caught and ruined was not a part of the plan, dammit.

Fiona stepped forward and guided my parents toward a seating arrangement on the far side of the room.

"That is quite enough excitement for today. Let's return to the ballroom. Everything is well in hand here." Quinton's authoritative voice brooked no argument as he herded everyone else from the room.

Ashleigh's wide blue eyes met mine, and that was the last thing I saw before Sullivan guided her out and closed the door behind them.

I hadn't moved and neither had Alexander. I reached over and snagged his hand, certain that he'd bolt through the second-floor window without my firm hold on him.

Finally, I peered over. Alexander's expression was wild—equal parts disbelieving and cornered animal. He looked young and vulnerable in a way I'd never seen him before. "Cassandra," he breathed.

I squeezed his hand firmly. "It will be all right." I nodded. "I have a plan."

~

THE PLAN INVOLVED an hour-long meeting in the Earl of Sullivan's study with my parents, Fiona, Alexander, and myself.

After extremely awkward introductions were made, Alexander sat rigidly by my side as Fiona proposed a private and intimate wedding in her home the following week in order to salvage my reputation.

My mother was tearful, and then angry that she was tearful. My father was incredulous and cross.

Once the details had been arranged and decided upon, Fiona turned to Alexander and asked if he would accompany her to speak with Quinton. Her brown eyes met mine and I saw the moment for what it was. An opportunity to speak to my mother and father and assuage their fears and explain my behavior and my relationship with Alexander—to some extent.

I was so desperate for time alone with Alexander. We needed to discuss what had happened in this study—so very many things. I needed to tell him I loved him and would support whatever future he wanted. He needn't marry me if he didn't wish to. And he shouldn't claim a title and a fortune if he'd hate himself for doing so.

But I knew there would be no more private moments for Alexander and myself right now. I needed to speak to my family.

Fiona eventually led a silent Alexander from the room. Panic flared suddenly when I thought I might never see him again. That all of this would be too much. All the theatrics and drama of the afternoon would be more than he could bear. The outcome was admittedly not what he intended in forming an arrangement with me. I reckoned that men seldom expected to marry their mistresses. And, in the most simplistic of ways, that was exactly who I was. A dalliance. A passing fancy. If there was any chance to save my family's reputation after today, I would need to be married, and quickly.

Alexander had said he loved me, but in his eyes there were too many complications for any lasting future between us. A final goodbye had been poised and waiting on his lips as long as I'd known him. And then the truth of his parentage had been revealed without any chance to process what that meant.

But I needed Alexander to see the possibilities rather than all the challenges. If only I'd had more time. I regretted that I hadn't confessed my love or my ideas for the future—for *our* future. I'd thought I could fix our problems and manifest the life I wanted. And in doing so, I'd failed to share my plans, leaving Alexander ignorant and unaware.

Now everything seemed like an afterthought, a reaction to an impossible situation. Would Alexander ever truly believe that I'd wanted to marry him before the mess of this day? Before he'd learned the truth of his past?

I hoped he would. I prayed he'd give me the chance to explain and to be honest. Showing someone your heart under duress couldn't really compare to baring yourself freely.

Deep down, I believed that Alexander had a tender, romantic soul. I never wanted him to question my love, but he would after all this. He'd see my admission as contrived and forced. A part of him would always wonder. Alexander was suspicious at the best of times and openly distrustful all the rest.

Perhaps he would put the time he spent with the unluckiest woman in London behind him and disappear from my life forever. In typical Cassandra fashion, disaster had struck. I wouldn't blame Alexander if he needed to get as far away from me as possible. It was practically standard operating procedure at this point. Every other man of my acquaintance hadn't seen fit to stay. But this was the first time that the possibility might very well break my heart.

I pushed my doubts and my fears away for the time being and faced my family. With heartfelt remorse and contrition, I said, "Mama. Papa. I am terribly sorry for my disgraceful behavior today. I never meant to damage my reputation and, by extension, our family's good name. I love you both very much." I took in my father's stubborn profile as he refused to look at me, and my mother's suppressed emotion. "Alexander Hill did not attack me or coerce me or seduce me or any other terrible thing you're imagining. His presence here this evening was an anomaly. He lives and works on Baker Street in North London. We were acquainted from the restaurant where he has been employed for several years. We became friendly this season, and…I fell in love with him."

While the recent revelations of Alexander's parentage would have simplified certain aspects of this conversation, it was not my truth to tell. I didn't know if he would even claim his title or his inheritance. There hadn't been time to work any of that out.

"But, Cassandra, he is not a proper match. You know he isn't right for you." My mother's words were beseeching, her blue eyes earnest.

"Alexander would agree with you, Mama. He has reminded me of that fact at every turn," I admitted around a bitter smile. "But it is I who ignored what was proper and expected. He believes himself unworthy, while I have pursued him. I know our match is unorthodox. But he is devoted and loyal, and he *loves* me. Alexander makes me happy, and that—more than anything—is what I wish to be."

"So you orchestrated this, then? Forced the issue to get your way? Ruined your reputation in such a public spectacle that we'd have to allow a farce of a wedding?" My father's accusation had me wincing.

"I did not plan this," I insisted to my father's stern profile. "What I had planned on doing was talking to you both about the future I wanted— the one I hoped to have with Alexander. You arrived home so recently...I hadn't the opportunity. I realize it's unconventional and improper and will undoubtedly impact my place in society. But I have always tried to be honest with you about who I am. I've always been too loud, too animated, too...much for my peers. Yet you've loved me in spite of all that." I took a breath as my father finally turned to look at me. "I realized I was allowing my expectations for making a sound match supersede any happiness I was likely to find. I was resolved to accept my due simply because it was expected. But Alexander loves me for who I am—not for a dowry or for a connection with our family. Actually, he loves me in spite of those things."

My mother peered at me thoughtfully. "Do you think you and he will be accepted after this? That Mr. Hill can simply escort you to an event amongst your peers and no one will whisper, no one will gossip?"

"They did that anyway, Mama. Even when I did everything right, they tried to tell me I was wrong."

"I don't like the idea of my daughter being demeaned or described as anything less than," Papa said fiercely in that way that only good fathers could manage. It made my nose sting and my chin tremble. "And I won't tolerate it when she thinks it of herself either."

I lost the battle with my tears but kept my gaze steady on my father as he continued.

"You're not too much, Cassandra. You're made of sterner stuff than most, but with an open and joyful heart. That is not something to apologize for. If those idiot gentlemen can't appreciate you, and run scared because of silly accidents, then they bloody well don't deserve you."

"Thank you, Papa," I murmured as Mama handed me a handkerchief for my damp cheeks.

My father looked over to my mother and took her hand. At her soft nod, they both turned their attention to me.

Mama cleared her throat. "I suppose we have a wedding to plan."

Twenty

Nearly a week had passed with no word from Alexander.

The wedding was scheduled for tomorrow morning and yet I had no idea if there would be a bridegroom. I'd left my balcony doors unlocked every night this week, hopeful and despairing in equal measure.

When last I spoke to Quinton, he had not heard from him either. Alexander had excused himself from the garden party after leaving with Fiona. He'd never made it to a meeting with Sullivan.

As a result, Fiona and I had gone to the Baker Street Coffee House to inquire after him earlier in the week. Mr. Patel informed us that Alexander had requested a leave from his position and would be away for a short time. I didn't know what to make of that, but I wrote him a letter and slipped it under the door of his third-floor apartment. He would show up to the Compton home and marry me tomorrow or he wouldn't. There was nothing more I could do.

I regretted a great many things. I wished I'd told him of my true feelings prior to the events at Randolph House. I wished we'd had the opportunity to discuss the revelations of his past. There was so much I wanted to say. Mostly that I didn't care if he was a baron or a footman or a thief. I wanted to marry him for the simplest of reasons—I loved him and wanted to be his wife.

"Cassandra, you've hardly touched your meal." My mother's concerned voice interrupted the fruitless turn my thoughts had taken.

Shaking away my regrets, I removed my hand from the pocket of my dress, relinquishing my hold on the handkerchief within.

The strain between myself and my family was easing slightly. My father had spent the prior week meeting with his solicitor and preparing the marriage contracts. I hadn't the heart to admit that there might not actually be a wedding. Fiona had advised me to ignore the gossip surrounding my hasty betrothal, proceed as normal, and we would all hope that Alexander came to the correct conclusion. I appreciated that my friend considered the appropriate option being married to me.

"Sorry, Mama. I was woolgathering," I finally responded and collected my cup for a sip of tea.

The awkward silence was interrupted by Jansen entering with *The London Post* and a gossip paper, the *Ton Tattler*.

My father gathered the newspaper for himself and I reached for the *Tattler* as a distraction more than anything. However, the headline on the front page had me nearly dropping my teacup in my lap.

Forgotten Heir to Barony Reclaims Title and Announces Upcoming Marriage

My eyes widened and I skimmed the article. In my desperate effort to consume the information therein, I could not manage to slow my heart nor my frantic scanning. My eyes caught on *Alexander Greene, Baron of Hackstone* before alighting briefly on *betrothal to Lady Cassandra Fields, daughter of the Earl of Crait.*

"Cassandra, darling? Are you unwell?"

I forced my eyes from the ink and met my mother's worried gaze. Papa lowered his newspaper and looked on in concern as well.

"I am...to be married."

My father frowned. "We know that, Cassandra. We were there."

"Alexander—" I cleared my throat and tried again. "Alexander claimed his title and announced our betrothal."

Mama's eyes widened comically and I fought the urge to laugh. In fact, the sudden lightness in my chest made nearly everything inappropriately humorous. But I swallowed it down and read the article aloud. I didn't know a better way to explain. I didn't know how the *Tattler* had come by this information, and I didn't know what it meant for Alexander and all parties involved. But I felt increasing surety that there would be someone standing opposite me on my wedding day.

"Have you known that Mr. Hill—Alexander—was actually a baron this whole time, Cassandra? Why would you hide the truth? Why was he working at a restaurant in Marylebone?" My mother was more confused than upset.

"No, Mama," I explained. "Alexander himself didn't know until the gathering at Randolph House last week. It was a surprise to everyone. His mother died before she could tell him of his origins, and he was raised by a horrible man who kept the truth from him."

My mother gasped. "That's terrible. Alexander has no living relatives?"

I shook my head sadly. "He's lived a very solitary existence." Then my voice firmed with the promise of a future. "But no more."

"No more," Mama agreed.

My father gave a decisive nod and went back to his newspaper.

I was grateful for their reactions. I knew most mothers would have shown relief that their daughter would be marrying a baron rather than a working citizen. If either of my parents felt that way, they hadn't expressed it. Mama had asked after his relations and that had been that.

Moments later Jansen returned, announcing an unexpected early morning visitor…for me. He'd refused to wait in the foyer or in the parlor. My stubborn Alexander was on our front steps.

Of course he was.

My mother told me to take a few minutes to speak with him in the blue receiving room and then to please escort him to the breakfast table so that she might share a meal with her future son-in-law.

Still clutching the gossip paper in my hands, I strode determinedly to the entryway of Dameron Hall. My breathing quickened along with my steps. I felt relief that Alexander had indeed turned up, while irritation rose swiftly to the surface. How dare he hide from me? We were getting married, dammit. I wanted a partnership with communication and understanding. I wanted Alexander to lean on me when he needed to. And I wanted to lean on him in return. We would figure this marriage out *together*.

With impatience guiding my movements, I flung the door wide. And there he was.

Alexander, holding a large bouquet of flowers, looked very unsure of his reception. His elegant dark suit, fashionable navy waistcoat, and dapper top hat announced that a fine gentleman had come to call—someone who entered through the front door, not the servants' entrance.

How could he believe that truly mattered to me?

"My lady," Alexander murmured, spine straightening.

"You're impossible." I rolled my eyes, took his gloved hand in mine and dragged him through the open door before closing it behind us and leading him to the front receiving room.

Alexander appeared shocked by my reaction.

"You can't just disappear like that, Alexander. I thought you'd left for good. Mr. Patel didn't know your whereabouts. You didn't return my letter. And then this!" I shook my copy of the *Ton Tattler* in my fist. "You did all of this on your own. You didn't talk to me or consult me, and worse than all of that—you didn't *need* me. I want to be there for you. I wished you'd talked to me about your title and your decision to claim it. Everything happened so fast, what with being caught and then betrothed. I needed your comfort as well. Can't you see you kept us apart when we needed one another?"

Alexander's gaze was intent and focused. I could see him turning over the events of the past week. "I wanted to do right by you, Cassandra. There was a way forward for us. I had to seize it. It was the right decision."

I could feel my features softening. He was so earnestly misguided. "Sometimes the right decision is the one you make together."

He opened his mouth but then closed it just as quickly.

I continued softly. "I know how hard it must have been for you to hear the truth from Sullivan. I'm so sorry for what you've had to endure. But, Alexander, I never would have asked you to turn yourself into someone you never wanted to be."

He frowned. "Even if it meant we could marry?"

"We were already going to marry. Perhaps you weren't paying attention when half of Jane's guest list caught us in the study."

"You know what I mean. If I had a title and a yearly income, we could marry without your family or your reputation suffering. I was willing to claim that title because it meant we'd have the smoothest path forward—together."

I smiled. "It did not matter. I wanted you any way I could get you."

His face twisted. "At what cost? You would lose everything. I was no one. The daughter of an earl cannot marry a footman."

"You are not a footman," I argued.

"Are the alternatives any better? A thief? A street urchin? An orphan? Take your pick. None are equal. None measure up. But in this—claiming the barony I was left—I could do something finally to make things right. Make us fit."

Hearing him describe himself thus made me immeasurably sad. But I risked approach and slid my arms around his waist. A simple embrace that felt like coming home. "*This* daughter of an earl can marry anyone she chooses. And she has chosen the man who makes her happy." My cheek pressed firmly to his chest. The steady beat I heard grounded something wild inside me, an answering touchstone for my reckless heart. "I chose you long ago, Alexander. I'm sorry everything got so twisted up. Our discovery altered our timeline, but I was already trying to figure out a way to marry you."

"Be serious," he begged. And it was truly a plea—to explain further or to put him out of his misery, I didn't know.

Raising my head and meeting his powerful gaze, I confessed, "I should have told you after the Crestleigh ball. I knew it then, but I wanted everything to be sorted. I wanted to speak to my parents and get you free of Blaidd so you had a choice for once in your life. But I should have realized there was never going to be a perfect time. I didn't need the stars to align to tell you I love you."

Alexander stiffened beneath my hold.

"I love you," I repeated.

The disbelief was pronounced in the crease of his brow and the incredulousness of his stare. So I kissed him.

And in between the press of my lips, I murmured my devotion. "I love your strength." I caressed his full bottom lip. "I love your loyalty." A gentle graze to his cupid's bow. "I love your ceaseless, brilliant mind." My tongue touched the corner of his wide mouth. "I love how you fight and argue with me and never treat me as a weakness."

He surged forward, meeting my kiss. *Finally.*

But it was over as quickly as it had begun. Alexander's hot tongue invaded and then retreated before he pulled back to look at me, depositing the bouquet on a side table.

"Oh, but you are a weakness, Cassandra. You are *my* weakness. We wouldn't be here—in this mess—if I had been strong enough to resist you. It is my failure that has ruined your life."

I'd been pushed too far, beyond the boundaries of what I could accept. The hopelessness in Alexander's voice was one step too far.

Grasping the lapels of his coat, the newsprint of the *Tattler* crumbling around my hold, I allowed my anger to fill me up. "My life is not ruined! My life is *yours*! How can you not see that? Do you want me to find some higher-ranking gentleman to marry just so I can meet your ridiculous expectations for how my future was supposed to be? You want me to be miserable for the rest of my life, just so I can prove you right? Well, that is just too damn bad. I want to be happy,

Alexander. And the only way that's going to happen is if you marry me tomorrow."

I stepped back and took the gossip column still clutched in my fist. I ripped it right down the middle and continued as the pieces grew smaller and smaller and littered the patterned rug beneath our feet.

"I don't care if you're a baron or a thief or a footman—as long as you are mine. And as long as you confide in me and bloody *talk* to me, and allow me to comfort you when you need it."

My breathing was ragged and my color was high. I could feel the heat blooming beneath my cheeks as my frustration tainted the speech I'd planned to declare my love.

"What if I am not enough?" His quiet worry pierced my heart.

The conversation with my father at Randolph House flashed through my mind. I thought myself *too much* and this beautiful man thought he wasn't enough. What a pair we made. "I cannot determine your self-worth, Alexander. But I won't stand for you diminishing the man I love."

His eyes were bright and the frown lines bracketing his mouth had dissipated, I noticed. He asked softly, "What if no one accepts us?"

"Impossible. I am quite beloved. You may recall."

His lips twitched. "I don't want to jeopardize your work with the Home."

"You won't. I appointed myself, and Thomas isn't going to oust me."

"What if I still can't manage to get free from Blaidd?"

I stroked a hand over the stern line of his dark brows. "I have faith. I have enough for both of us." When no more questions or objections were forthcoming, I asked very gently, "Will you please marry me tomorrow, Alexander?"

For the first time, he didn't look ready to argue. "Are you certain?" he whispered instead.

"I am." Seriousness tightened my features but it was honesty that I hoped shone through. "But if you are not, if you don't wish to spend your life with me, I will not force you into something you don't—"

My statement was cut off by Alexander's arms squeezing me to him, erasing the distance between us and bringing his mouth firmly over mine.

"This is a dream." The words formed against my tender lips as he spoke. "I fear I will awake tomorrow and it will have all been a figment of my imagination. That is the only explanation for the future laid out before me."

"This is real," I countered, nuzzling his nose with mine. "If it was a dream, things would have gone much more smoothly."

Alexander's soft huff of laughter warmed my cheek. "Perhaps you are right. Fantasy Cassandra would likely see reason and do as she was told."

I grinned against the dark stubble beneath my lips. "Doubtful. Even Dream Cassandra is willful and stubborn."

He pressed a smiling kiss to my mouth before I recalled suddenly.

"Oh! I made something for you." I reached into the hidden pocket of my pale yellow dress and retrieved the handkerchief I'd kept with me this week as a talisman. Tugging Alexander to the settee beneath the front window, I indicated he should sit beside me. "Let's call it a wedding gift." I held out the linen to him.

Alexander tentatively took the folded fabric from my hand before smoothing it gently across his thigh. His callused fingertip traced the intricate border before stopping over the tiny princess tiara in the corner. He looked at me with an amused quirk to his mouth.

"You know what this means, don't you?" I asked innocently.

"What's that, Your Highness?"

My smile was all devil. "You're my prince."

Alexander's eyes closed and his shoulders shook with suppressed laughter before he hauled me close in a tight embrace, the handkerchief held safely in his grasp. "Thank you," he whispered against the shell of my ear. "It's perfect."

"It's just a handkerchief," I murmured.

"It is not *just* anything, Cassandra. It is your time threaded into the fabric. Your care and your attention stitched by your own hand. And the fact that you focused your thoughts on me…means it's the most precious thing I own."

"More precious than your books," I teased so I wouldn't cry.

He grinned knowingly, and confirmed, "More precious than my books." Slowly and reverently his lips pressed his gratitude into my skin.

"Do you accept my wedding gift?" He knew what I was really asking. Would he set aside his doubts and self-recrimination? Would he marry me tomorrow?

For once, his gaze was neither covetous nor intent. He didn't watch me as if he was so desperately wanting. Alexander's stare was soft and accepting, as if he'd finally acknowledged that I was already his.

"Well, what do you have to say for yourself?" I prompted as his smile turned into a lovely grin.

"I'm not exactly a one-eyed duke but perhaps you'll still have me?"

I laughed and hugged him to me. "We'll join forces and have adventures."

"And fight French spies," he finished for me.

After a moment we leaned back, smiles still firmly in place.

"I should go," he whispered. "It isn't proper."

"Oh, yes. We wouldn't want to be caught in a compromising position," I deadpanned.

He pinched my side in retaliation but my involuntary smile belied my artificial gasp.

"You can't leave. Mama bid me to bring you to the breakfast table following our conversation."

"What?" came Alexander's strangled response. "Why?"

I widened my eyes comically. "Well, for breakfast, of course." When he continued to stare incredulously, I elaborated. "She wants to spend time with you and get to know you. You'll be family soon, Alexander. You'll have a family." I squeezed his hand as my voice nearly faltered at the end.

I didn't wait for a reply. I got to my feet and tugged him along with me, content when he followed and tucked his handkerchief carefully into his interior pocket.

"It will be all right. She and my father want to know you. That is all. And I'll be there to distract and take over the conversation."

"All right," he breathed, and I didn't know if the utterance was for me or for himself.

I reached for his arm and pulled him in the direction of the corridor. Just before we rounded the corner, I whispered, "I love you."

His head turned and he could not hide his surprise—joyful and slightly overwhelmed—before he whispered back, "I love you too, Princess."

Twenty-One

The following morning broke gray and foggy—as so many November days in London often did.

I was eager and impatient as my maid helped me dress. It was the feeling of knowing that the rest of my life was just on the other side of a door, and being withheld the key.

My family and I arrived at the Compton home amid bustling preparations. Candles were lit and flowers were everywhere. While the wedding would be quite small with few guests, it seemed my thoughtful friend had ensured a glorious celebration nonetheless. A traditional breakfast in the formal dining room would follow the ceremony. I found suddenly that my earlier enthusiasm had flared into vicious nervousness at the sight of my friends all gathered in their pale dresses. They'd forgone bonnets since the wedding was taking place in Fiona's home. We'd congregated in the duchess's quarters per her instructions. My mother and father awaited us below stairs and I was told by Fiona upon my arrival that Alexander was here and all was well. He was being entertained by Compton, Sullivan, and Nicolas.

That knowledge caused the fluttering in my stomach to ease a bit.

I stood among my chattering friends and felt the urge to speak. So I cleared my throat and began. "Thank you all for being here. Your support means more to me than you will ever know. I realize that the path I've chosen is not the traditional one."

"Well, we wouldn't expect anything less from you, Cassandra," Eliza said with a smile, her blue eyes shining with warmth.

We'd discussed the article in the *Ton Tattler* earlier upon my arrival. The ladies knew of Alexander's reclaimed title, wealth, and newly acquired property—which would be our London home in Belgrave Square. I didn't feel the need to reveal Fiona's prior knowledge regarding Alexander. I merely explained the recent developments and how he'd come to claim the Hackstone title.

"Nevertheless, I— I— Just…thank you. I love you all dearly. That is all I wanted to say." Shaking my head, I mused aloud, "You know, I shall undoubtedly become much less entertaining now that I am to be a married woman. No more Cassandra disaster stories and courting mishaps to report at our weekly gatherings."

"Somehow I think you will still garner attention and inspire amusement," Fiona countered, brown eyes sparkling.

"I didn't find that marriage altered my personality overmuch," Jane offered. "Admittedly, my relationship with Quinton is rather unconventional and I'm odd all on my own. Perhaps other matrons see a dramatic shift in their personalities following nuptials. That would be an interesting study. Although the results would likely be skewed by the subjective nature of the recorded data."

"Very true," Eliza agreed. "And you'd have to examine the changes over the life of a marriage. A lengthy study in most cases."

Jane focused her shrewd attention on the duchess, a target for her hypothesis. "Do you feel very different, Fiona? You've been married for some time. Have you changed drastically since meeting Compton?"

Fiona looked thoughtful. "I suppose in some ways I am still the person I've always been. Motherhood and marriage to Gregory have surely changed my priorities." She paused for a moment and her eyes lost focus. "Shifting roles requires certain personality traits to dominate others. I think life is a constant battle between losing and finding oneself. Jane, you may discover strengths you never knew you had as your marriage grows and matures. And, Cassandra, you'll uncover both the wonders and challenges of cohabitating. Those early days are a magical time."

I considered Fiona's advice. And then I recalled the upheaval Alexander had been through—claiming an identity so very foreign to him. "Do you think that one individual has to change in order to meet the needs of their husband or wife?"

Fiona smiled at my question. "I don't think change is a requirement, but it happens nonetheless. You're changing right now, Cassandra. Growing and accommodating to allow Alexander in your life. Building a marriage together requires sacrifice and compromise. That doesn't mean change is a bad thing. Don't look so morose."

Kathleen's soft voice drifted into our circle. "I think you'll create new spaces in your heart. Alexander is within. You'll grow around him." Her dark eyes were warm and perhaps slightly uncomfortable. She was being so brave to speak up when I knew it was difficult for her. I appreciated her efforts and her thoughtful reflection on the situation. "Your separate roots twisting and twining, becoming even stronger together as a result."

Jane piped up unexpectedly. "Like a weed! Alexander is a flower and you're like a weed growing around him."

"Thank you, Jane," I said flatly, but amusement claimed my features. "And what about Sullivan? What would he be?"

Jane brought a finger to her chin and tapped thoughtfully. "He's rather too stoic and masculine to be a flower. But I am most definitely a weed." We all laughed, before inspiration struck her. "Oh, I know! Quinton would be a stump!"

Our laughter continued, and in the midst, Fiona leaned forward and said through gasping giggles, "Gregory would be an old plow that got stuck in a field."

The hilarity of the situation combined with my heightened stress from the day culminated in a fit of amusement that had tears leaking from the corners of my eyes. Kathleen's smile was wide as she and the other ladies joined me in fresh peals of laughter at the image Fiona had conjured.

I was so very fortunate to have these women in my life.

When our amusement slowly ebbed, Ashleigh turned to me with a solemn expression. "And yer sure this is what ye want? Because it is not too late."

Before I could answer, Fiona's gentle touch turned my attention to her. "Ash is right. If you want a different path, we could—"

"No." I cut her off before she could put forth well-meaning alternatives to today's events. "This is what I want." Turning back to Ashleigh, I confirmed, "Alexander is who I want—baron or not."

My friend nodded, blue gaze still scrutinizing. I smiled at her obvious suspicion. She and Alexander were so very much alike. They would get along quite well if given the chance. I could feel it.

When it was time for the ceremony, my lace veil was pinned into place. Jane, Eliza, Mary, Ashleigh, Fiona, and Kathleen all took their seats with their respective spouses and families. Mama and Papa sat quietly up front. Eliza's father, Dr. Finley, was in attendance, as was my good friend Thomas Burke. Daniel O'Connor joined the assembled guests as well. Candles lit the space in a warm glow and suddenly Alexander and I were facing the rest of our lives…together.

He looked both nervous and stoic, but when our eyes met I watched him swallow with some difficulty behind his cravat. Pearl-colored gloves with black embroidery elegantly covered his hands, and I wondered briefly where he'd acquired them. I'd wager it was the duchess and her talent for mothering those in her care. And today she was a flawless hostess. I could feel her guiding hand in all things. From the brevity of the ceremony to the intimacy of the guest list. Fiona made sure we started our journey in marriage surrounded by love and support.

The day proceeded as important events often do…in the stillness of moments and then in the racing of them. I would always remember the sound of Alexander's deep voice as he spoke his promises to uphold, and the way his hand shook when he reached for me afterward.

The breakfast was loud and energetic. Despite the circumstances of our betrothal and the gossip surrounding Alexander's new title, there was nothing uncomfortable about the gathering. I credited my friends for their positive attitudes and ability to turn what could have been a very awkward day into one of celebration and merriment. I was grateful for that. I was thankful for all of them.

Alexander was quiet by my side—not in an angry or morose way. He simply observed the interactions around him. No doubt my odd female friendships were confusing his world view.

Nicolas sat on Alexander's other side and drew him into conversation about all manner of things. I watched their exchange with a warm feeling in my chest. What would it mean for someone like Alexander—so solitary and self-contained —to have a male friend? Someone to consult for advice. A resource for engaging conversation. Or just a friend to jest and laugh with. Alexander's life had been devoid of so many things that I took for granted. I wanted to give him everything, to make up for a lifetime of hardship.

I began to regret the friendly relationship I saw forming between Alexander and the others when Sullivan, Compton, and Nicolas absconded with my husband—*my husband!*—shortly after midday.

While they disappeared within Fiona's home, I chatted with my circle as they kindly included my mother.

I was distracted from the conversation and craning my neck to look for my husband amongst everyone gathered when Thomas approached. I moved to join him and offered a happy greeting. I was so very glad he was here.

"Well, not to put too fine a point on it, but I do believe I am owed some small measure of gratitude, Lady Hackstone."

The use of my newly married name gave me quite the jolt.

"I am partially responsible for your current matrimonial bliss." His expression remained solemn throughout his teasing.

I laughed. "You are correct, Thomas. If we had been successful in our scheme, Alexander would have given up his quest in the face of such obvious devotion. I am in your debt. Truly." Thomas allowed a small smile at this. "Thank you for coming. I know you are not given to such displays, but your friendship is important to me and I value your support."

Thomas looked resolved suddenly and guided me to the other side of the receiving room where we wouldn't be overheard. "Your friendship is important to me as well, Cassandra. I realize I am not particularly demonstrative, nor am I emotional. But I have always wanted your happiness. There are not many people who are so trustworthy or accepting."

His eye contact faltered for a moment at the reference to his very personal preferences, but then he regarded me once more. I smiled softly as Thomas recovered his voice.

"I encouraged you early on with Alexander—when everything about your situation seemed hopeless—which was undoubtedly inappropriate of me. But I could see that something was different. It was the first time I saw you react to a man beyond platitudes and niceties. I thought…this could be your chance for something true. Not settling for any suitable aristocrat because that's what you've been trained for. And not settling for a convenient marriage with me."

I opened my mouth to object—to tell him that anyone who chose him could never merely be settling.

But he shook his head, claiming my attention and forestalling my efforts to speak. "If all you truly wanted was a household and marriage, you could have accepted our arrangement at any time. That's why I asked you every month if you were betrothed. I wanted you to realize that, deep down, you wanted more. That with every 'no, not yet' you uttered, you deserved more. And you could have it, if you wished. It wasn't just the accidents and disasters. You could have found someone to marry. They would have been glad for it. Or you could have accepted my hand and given up your seemingly desperate search. But something in your heart wouldn't allow that."

I watched my friend in wonder, marveling at his perceptiveness.

"You possess a romantic soul, Cassandra. You wanted a love match. You simply didn't know how to ask for it. Or perhaps you didn't believe you deserved it. Mayhap that's why you remained unmarried for over four seasons. I don't really know. But now that you've actively chosen this for yourself, I think you're exactly where you're meant to be."

Silence followed in the wake of Thomas's pronouncement—the longest speech I'd ever heard him make.

"Thomas," I breathed.

He nodded as if that response explained everything and said quite earnestly, "I am incredibly astute."

A bubble of laughter burst out of me then. His answering smile was slight and satisfied.

I grabbed his hands on a rush of affection, wishing I could embrace him and squeeze him tight. "Thank you, Thomas. Thank you for believing in me when I apparently did not believe in myself."

"Of course," he replied easily. "And please know I will do whatever I can for you and Hackstone. I'm headed to the Home later today actually to see Paul. I look forward to telling him of your recent nuptials."

"Oh, do take your brother some cake," I encouraged, allowing the swift change of subject to avoid Thomas becoming uncomfortable with my emotions. "And do send my regrets that I will not be able to marry you and improve your overall mood as your brother had so fervently hoped."

Thomas grinned once more before nodding his farewell.

I thought about the claims my friend had made. I *had* actively chosen to pursue a future with Alexander—before the grand reveal of his parentage. He was the first man of my acquaintance to stir something within. I'd been curious about him from the very first. And then everything about him had drawn me in until I could no longer go back to the Cassandra I had once been —the one who'd accepted her due and followed the mandates of society. My future was too important. That life I'd always wanted—marriage, household, and family—was happening on my terms. On *our* terms, mine and Alexander's.

Before seeking out my friends, I took a moment to center myself amidst my realization. I scanned the space again to see if Alexander had been returned to me.

Fiona caught my eye and bustled over. "Come," she said, tucking her arm firmly through my own. "Let's go rescue your husband. I feel certain he is in need of escape."

I fell into step with Fiona as she led me out into the corridor toward, I assumed, Compton's study. "Are we ever going to discuss your secret life?"

Fiona cast me a wary glance. "It's not a secret life, merely one that runs parallel to my own. It's probably better if you don't know the specifics currently. I'm not ready to be exposed, and I do not want to put you into a difficult situation of keeping secrets from those you care about."

I nodded. "I can respect that." I paused, considering. "It seems quite unsafe, your involvement with criminals and dangerous individuals. Are you taking care, Fiona? I don't want anything to happen to you."

The duchess gave me a sly little smile—one I hadn't seen on her delicate face before. "I assure you, my dear, I am quite capable of taking care of myself. You needn't worry."

"All right, then. But if you ever need to confide in someone or you need anything at all, I am here for you. It is the very least I can do after all you've done for me. Truly, I don't know how to adequately thank you for rescuing Alexander and I from—"

"Cassandra, you owe me nothing," she said, interrupting what was destined to be an emotional outpouring of gratitude. Fiona halted our progress and turned to me, our full skirts brushing together. "Friendship does not come with a scorecard. I am so relieved that I could assist you in your future with Alexander. We spoke a bit…this morning upon his arrival. He loves you. That is evident. And that is good enough for me. I want nothing more than your happiness, and it seems as if you shall have it. Don't worry over the gossip and the whispers. After everyone retreats to the country to celebrate the yuletide, your hasty marriage will be mostly forgotten. Something new will have certainly come along to replace it by then."

She was minimizing the fallout, and I loved her for it. Because to her the scandal of my new marriage was a fair trade for my happiness. And I found I quite agreed with her.

I pulled her in for a quick embrace, squeezing her soundly with all my affection.

The duchess pulled back with a smile and tugged me toward the sound of male voices. We slowed our steps outside an open doorway as Gregory Bowen, the Duke of Compton, proclaimed in a superior tone, "Alexander, I am going to bestow upon you—generously, I might add—the truth about marriage. Sullivan, it would behoove you and Morgan to pay attention as well. I have wisdom to impart." A pause. "Listen up and stop rolling your eyes."

Fiona pressed a hand to her smiling mouth to muffle a laugh before it escaped and announced our presence.

It was unbelievably rude to eavesdrop, but you could not have driven me away from that doorway with a wild boar.

"Here it is," Compton said loudly. "The way you're feeling right now—unworthy and utterly inadequate in the face of your new bride—is the truth."

The room was silent following the duke's pronouncement, and I looked in alarm to Fiona. She put her finger to her lips and smiled knowingly.

Finally, Alexander said quietly, "Is it so obvious?"

"It's written all over your face," Compton confirmed. "But, Hackstone, we are all similarly afflicted. It's one of the universal truths of good marriages—of love matches. The women we love are superior to us in every conceivable way. You are in excellent company because we are all undeserving scoundrels who were at least smart enough to know a good thing when it came crashing into our lives. Accept it. Accept it and happiness with it, my good man. Fiona is stronger, wiser, cleverer, everything…far greater than I. But do you know what?" Compton paused dramatically before saying at last, "I am the lucky bastard who married her."

A moment passed before the sound of glasses clinked in a toast. "He's not wrong," Quinton murmured at the same time Nicolas said, "Hear! Hear!"

"Drink up," Compton advised. "You're going to need it with this lot."

Fiona's watery smile met one of my own before she reached for my hand and pulled me toward the room, calling a cheery, "There you all are! It's bad form to kidnap the groom."

"Apologies, darling," Compton said dryly when he spotted us entering his large and well-appointed study. The duke wore an exquisitely cut gray wool suit and a permanently unaffected expression—as was his way—but his dark eyes glittered with intensity as they moved over his wife of nearly a decade.

I found my husband with a mostly full crystal glass in hand seated beside Nicolas on a large tufted sofa. I smiled widely. *My husband.* "You're meant to run away from the bride before you marry, not after."

It seemed the word *bride* had a similar effect on Alexander, because his own grin stretched his lips wide.

"We've kept you too long," Nicolas said with a clap on Alexander's shoulder and a wink for me. "Go see to your wife. There will be other opportunities for Compton to impart his wisdom, I'm sure."

"You should well hope so," the duke chimed in.

Laughing, Nicolas relieved Alexander of his glass as he stood and quit the room. Quinton followed soon after with a quiet farewell.

I sat down next to Alexander with my smile still firmly in place.

"Come, dearest," Compton called as he slid an arm around Fiona's slender waist. "I'm feeling peckish. Let's see if there are any more of those puddings I enjoy so much."

"Take your time, Cassandra," Fiona said as they made their way toward the hallway.

"But not too much time," Compton called without looking back. "It's rude to hide from your guests. And I am partial to that sofa."

Fiona shot her husband an exasperated look before they disappeared from view.

Alexander looked positively scandalized with his incredulous expression and pink cheeks. I laughed out loud.

"I didn't know that dukes could behave in such a way," Alexander said when my amusement finally faded.

"Compton is…his own sort of duke. He wasn't born with a title and perhaps that makes all the difference. He's a good sort, all told." With a cheeky grin, I asked, "So, how are you feeling, husband?"

"I don't know," he answered around a dazed expression. "I don't know how to be a husband."

"Well, neither have I been a wife before. So I think we shall trudge along together until we figure it out."

Alexander's gaze touched every part of my face as he looked at me. His soft expression kissed the red curls at my temple, then skated along the curve of my cheek before settling on my mouth briefly. Suddenly he reached for my hands and held them on the sofa, in the space between us. His eyes stayed fixed on our entwined fingers as he spoke. "But you do know how to be a wife. You've been educated and preparing for this role for most of your life. I am…scared, Cassandra. I feel out of my depth. I've been merely surviving for so long that I don't know how to truly live. And I assuredly don't know how to navigate high society."

Swallowing around the lump taking up the majority of my throat, I managed,

"Do you regret marrying me, Alexander? Regret claiming your title? I wouldn't blame you. I know how much you hate—"

He startled, tightening his grip. "No, of course not. I could never regret you. I'm just trying to prepare you for how woefully unprepared I am to be your…husband."

He stumbled over the word, and I knew the feeling. It had weight behind it now—after today—and it was a clumsy thing that required getting used to.

"You won't be able to dress me up and pass me off as anything other than what I am. I don't know if I can change to be who you need me to be, who the title demands I be. To complement your good nature, smooth my rough edges. Learn to dance. Accompany you to events. If we'll even be accepted anywhere. If I haven't ruined you, just by breathing."

I recalled the conversation I'd had with my friends about marriage and change.

It was my turn to tighten my hold. I scooted closer until our bodies touched all along our sides. I placed our clasped hands in my lap and forced him to look me in the eye. "You have ruined nothing, Alexander. I don't expect you to change. I don't *want* you to change. I love the person you are. But I hope you'll grow in our love. Learn to trust. I want you to rely on me. Yes, I was taught to be a gentleman's wife and manage a household and plan events. But what I want is to be *your* partner in all things. I need your happiness as deeply as my own. The good Lord knows I am not perfect. We will fight and argue and bicker and disagree. But as long as we love and respect each other through it all, we will find our way. Together."

"And the rest of it?" he wondered. "You're not worried about the scandal of our marriage, and the gossip and the mess of becoming Hackstone?"

I smiled softly. "That is the thing about London. There will be a new scandal bubbling to the surface any day now. But you'll see. You're a bright, shiny new thing. Because of the Hackstone title, we'll have a comfortable home and security. There will be invitations as well. But we needn't accept. I would never put you in the situation of feeling like a novelty. Even if our social interactions are limited to my family and our friends, I would be happy."

"Your friends," he corrected.

"No, *our* friends," I insisted. "That is not how my relationship works with these women. They are your friends now too, God help you. And you can count a renowned stage performer, a duke, and a powerful earl among them. They will use their influence and connections to smooth our entry into society. But that is nothing compared to their thoughtful natures and generous hearts. Jane will regale you with facts about the migratory patterns of the humble pigeon. Ashleigh will challenge your preference for English poetry, Mary will dance with you at every event and make it look effortless, Eliza will force upon you herbal teas for improved circulation, Fiona will mother you the way she mothers us all, and Kathleen will convey unparalleled wisdom when you least expect it. You have been welcomed with open arms. They are good people who want the best for us."

The crease between his brows was thoughtful rather than angry. "Accept it and happiness with it." He quietly repeated the words I'd overheard Compton impart.

"Indeed." I nodded, warmth filling my chest.

It wouldn't happen overnight. Self-preservation, learned mistrust, and a lifetime of cautionary habits likely wouldn't allow instant acceptance of friendships, much less happiness. But I would be there every step of the way to remind him he was loved and valued beyond measure.

"You're right. Compton and Morgan were kind to me today as well. They all were."

The wonder and confusion reflected in his voice tightened a sharp band across my ribs. I would need to fight my natural inclination to weep over Alexander's heartbreaking realizations.

"And Sullivan—he came with me yesterday to meet with Blaidd."

I straightened suddenly with concern. We hadn't had a chance to speak yet of these recent developments.

"It's all right." As if sensing my unease, Alexander came close and pulled me into his embrace.

I could feel him touching every part of me, from his strong arms—so secure in their hold—to the steady beat of his heart beneath my palm, to his chin resting atop my head. I felt comforted and surrounded. I breathed in his warm, earthy scent and tried to let go of the fear and the uncertainty plaguing me.

Alexander had wanted to settle things once and for all with Blaidd. And while I could see the benefit of facing your problems head-on, to me Blaidd was a mysterious danger lurking around every corner. It was the unknown element that made me so fearful. And perhaps the fact that Alexander was the target. Fear for one's loved one far outweighed fear for oneself. That was a fact.

I'd expressed my concerns yesterday during our conversation on the topic at

Dameron Hall following breakfast with my parents, but Alexander had assured me.

"It will be all right. I have a plan," he had said, repeating my own words back to me after we were caught in Sullivan's study.

My lips had curved involuntarily. "Using my own claims against me, are you?"

"I learned from the best." I could recall the smile in his voice. He'd pecked a brief kiss on the top of my head before pulling back to look at me. "Now you're the one confounded and out of your element."

"And you're attempting to reassure me?" I'd questioned.

"Isn't that what partners do?" he'd asked, his answering smile both sweet and proud. "You took control when I was completely out of my depth, and managed a situation I was helpless to cope with."

Isn't that what partners do?

Now, I was seeking comfort from my partner and hoping the news from Covent Garden was manageable.

My husband had spent half his life working for Elias Blaidd. I was sure the man had some expectation that he could keep Alexander under his thumb for as long as he pleased. But marrying the daughter of an earl was likely not a path Blaidd could have foreseen for Alexander. Nor could he imagine Alexander would find out the truth of his parentage on his own. Blaidd undoubtedly thought their partnership would endure. Even though Alexander had kept his distance and pulled away in the last few years, his new title as Hackstone was sure to complicate things for Blaidd's illegal organization. Blaidd lacked the funds he'd planned to receive through Alexander's inheritance, and his subsequent control. Desperate men did desperate things.

Alexander had assured me that his former master prized himself on being a gentleman criminal. That it was Alexander himself who had done the required dirty work. Mr. Blaidd took meetings and made connections in order to secure buyers for stolen, smuggled, and counterfeit property. No one seemed to be worried that a meeting might turn dangerous. No one save for me.

And, worse still, I worried that Blaidd would see Alexander's new position in society as an opportunity. I didn't want the man to turn the tables and impact our future by threatening to disclose the various illegal acts Alexander had committed over the years. I hoped whatever backing Quinton could provide would be enough to pose a significant warning, should Blaidd be reckless enough to retaliate.

I cleared my throat, and said simply, "What happened?"

"Sullivan agreed to wipe away Blaidd's debt to Piker House."

I gasped at Alexander's words. Quinton hadn't promised us that.

Alexander nodded. "I couldn't believe it. He said it so easily, as if it was nothing. In exchange, Blaidd will leave us alone. For good. The information Sullivan has gathered in addition was damning. He threatened to expose him, not to the authorities, but to his known associates. I wasn't even privy to that information. Nor Ember, as far as I know. The fact that Sullivan seemed familiar with these men made Blaidd willing to cooperate. He said he'd gotten more out of me than he ever expected and so the decade I spent thieving for him was nothing but a bonus."

"That was cruel, Alexander. I am so sorry," I said, cupping his cheeks.

"He's right though. I should have been dead in a gutter long ago."

"No, it's wrong. I know you've never minced words about Blaidd, but he raised you. And for him to toss you aside so callously is unbearably cruel."

Alexander covered my hands with his own and stroked over my knuckles. "I never thought of him as my father, Cassandra. I didn't…love him or seek his approval. That was something he snuffed out in me early on. I knew why he kept me—for what I could do for him. I should have known there was more to my past. Blaidd was always secretive about finding me. He never spoke of that time nor allowed me to ask about my mother. I never even thought to search out the letter she'd left with me before she died. I should have suspected something. For a man like Blaidd, raising a child would require a worthy reward. He'd been waiting for me to come into my inheritance and to manipulate me to claim it for himself. Nevertheless, you needn't worry about my feelings, Princess. His disregard is good news for me—for us."

My heart still clenched painfully for the boy who'd been denied a family in the face of a predator. "Did Blaidd seem to know of our plans to marry today? Did he indicate anything?" I'd been worried that Blaidd would use this knowledge to attempt to manipulate Alexander, but he put my worries to rest with a shake of his head.

"No, he was too focused on my change in circumstance. Seemed to realize that my title made me nearly untouchable. He didn't mention you or our wedding. And Ember stayed quiet."

I frowned. "She kept our secret. Is there anything we can do to help her?"

"No, Cassandra. She's in too deep. He'll never let his daughter and his payday go. And besides, she doesn't want to be free of him. That was always the difference between us. She sought his approval and I was disgusted by it. It will take a force of nature to change Ember Bellamy."

I thought about the young woman with so much potential and intelligence, forced into a life of crime. Ember didn't seem evil, just misguided. I prayed the day would come when she could be free of her father and his hold on her.

I let out a breath I felt like I'd been holding all day. "I'm so grateful you're all right and that you're free to make your own decisions now. A future of your own."

Alexander's blue eyes sparkled. "Well, not all my own. I believe our future is quite entwined."

"Like a weed," I added helpfully around a large smile.

He looked at me like I was odd but his smile never wavered. "If that is the metaphor you most associate with, then I suppose." And then he pressed a quick kiss to my nose as if he just couldn't help himself. "The point is, for the first time I feel like I could be happy. There isn't a sword over my head. And that is because of you."

"It's not," I insisted.

"It is. Without you, I never would have tried to escape. I never would have asked for more. I didn't know how to choose myself, until you chose me first."

My chin wobbled determinedly. "I will always choose you."

His thumb swiped a rebellious tear beneath my eye. "And I will spend the rest of our lives making you happy. I swear it. I love you, Cassandra."

"I love you too," I managed as more tears escaped.

Alexander leaned forward, bringing his soft lips to mine. He kissed away the salt from my tears, and the sweetness of the gesture only made more fall.

I could feel our future taking shape. My daydreams were given room to grow. And I would make sure Alexander never regretted choosing the unconventional life we were destined to lead.

The path to happiness wasn't always the smoothest. Ours had barely started but it had been unexpected nevertheless. There would be twists and turns, fallen logs and brambles blocking our way. Under the very best of circumstances it would be a long and winding road into the future. The trail would split, forking off in ways we could never anticipate. But as long as we chose to walk the path together, we'd find our way.

Epilogue

"I cannae believe you think the ending was contrived."

"It was," Alexander argued. "The resolution was ridiculously improbable. And the imagery was flat and emotionless."

"The imagery was the best part!" Ashleigh's voice rose in exasperation.

She and my husband had a two-person book club and had chosen today's embroidery salon at Eliza's home to facilitate their regular discussion. They had tried to include others in their monthly reading, but the rest of us didn't care nearly as much as they did. Their debates were more entertaining when I had no idea what they were talking about. I'd failed to complete the reading for our first selection and was summarily ejected from the club when I didn't know any of the characters' names and simply said whatever rubbish I could think of to further the discussion.

As their literary bickering continued, I asked Jane to pass me the biscuit tray. Quinton insisted and handed the platter across to where I was seated.

The men were in attendance today for our weekly meeting because we all planned to leave from Eliza and Nicolas's home to see his play this evening. They retained a box at the Collins, and we were excited to support his creative endeavors.

"Thank you, my lord."

"Do you think we'll have an uneventful trip to the theater, Lady Cassandra?" Quinton wasn't smiling, but his ice-blue eyes held a mischievous glint.

Jane laughed from his side. "I don't know if Cassandra can make that sort of promise, Q. It's far too early to tell."

"Christ, let's not have a repeat of the fire incident," Mr. O'Connor chimed in helpfully.

I smiled innocently. "I have no idea to what you're referring." I proceeded to ignore the laughter and teasing of my friends and focus on my shortbread. *That* was a story for another day.

Alexander and I had actually taken in a matinee viewing several months ago, just after our wedding. The theater made a rather adequate introductory event into society following our gossip-worthy union. We had some measure of anonymity at the playhouse and Alexander could scowl in the dark to his heart's content. Strangely enough, he was able to ignore the whispers and immerse himself in Nicolas's show. Alexander wore a smile for the majority of the comedy performance, and I was so overwhelmingly happy to share that experience with him that I didn't care who saw me hold the hand of my new husband.

We were settling into married life—learning how to coexist and share the same space. Society events were not frequent, and we generally only attended those of our friends and close acquaintances—ladies and gentlemen who were genuine in their regard. We didn't entertain those seeking our novelty.

Alexander was navigating his new title and responsibilities rather well. He was even developing a comfortable friendship with Sullivan and the other husbands, which made me immeasurably happy. I couldn't be Alexander's only connection to the wide world. He needed a circle…just as I did.

My eyes snagged on Daniel across the drawing room. Bless the man, he was attempting to draw Kathleen into conversation. She was staring with wide eyes at a charmingly exuberant Daniel. But, wonder of wonders, a small, shy smile claimed her features as his tale reached its conclusion and he chuckled happily.

When I was done spectating, I turned back to see if Alexander and Ashleigh were nearly finished.

"I think we should read *Twenty Thousand Leagues Under the Seas* by Jules Verne next," Ashleigh was saying.

Why they continued to torture each other, I would never guess. But I was thankful they'd established this…relationship, as contrary as it was. Initially, I'd been afraid that Ash would never accept Alexander and his place in my life, but this was their fourth such book club meeting, and they seemed pleased with the results.

Alexander nodded. "I'm amendable to that selection. I did enjoy *Around the*

World in Eighty Days…for the most part. Phileas was an adequate main character.”

“Aye. Agreed,” Ashleigh said.

And then I laughed. “You finally agree on something! I feel I should alert the press.”

Ashleigh looked disappointed in me. “Cassandra, proper discourse is the only path to true enlightenment. Of course we disagree. That is the whole point.”

Alexander nodded somberly, and I felt properly chastened.

Well, then.

“I’ll prepare my notes for next month,” Ashleigh announced. “I think I’ll join Eliza now. I want her opinion on this pattern.”

My friend gathered her sewing and went to sit next to Eliza and Fiona on the arrangement nearest the fire.

“I’m glad you’re enjoying yourself,” I said with a smile.

Alexander returned it. “I am. Miss Winstead is a worthy adversary.”

I laughed. “I knew you would be fast friends. You’re both obscenely stubborn and pigheaded.”

“Is that so, wife? *I* am the stubborn and pigheaded one?” His dark blue eyes glinted dangerously. And still, nearly four months later, the word *wife* caused a swoop in my middle.

“Well, you *and* Ash,” I corrected sweetly.

Lowering his voice, Alexander said, “I seem to recall you refusing to get out of bed this morning until you’d received fourteen kisses exactly.”

“I simply value my time abed,” I said primly.

He snorted. The truth was that I took every opportunity to be my true self with Alexander. Outrageous. Absurd. Silly. His life had been devoid of those things for so very long. No more, I’d decided.

Raising one superior brow, I accused, “And I did not hear you complaining, I might add, when you found very creative ways to deliver those required kisses.”

His grin was utterly wicked. It spoke of tongue and teeth beneath my nightgown, and it promised more where that came from.

“No looking at me like that, husband,” I chided. “I’ve heard Nicolas is rather fond of this sofa.”

Alexander’s bark of laughter surprised nearly everyone in the room—Alexander included. He wasn’t quite so open with his emotions even amongst our close friends. I felt ridiculously pleased that I’d prompted his joy for all to hear.

"I've always known you were trouble." Now his smile was fond. This one spoke of remembered battles in ballrooms and merry adventures across London —past, present, and future.

Uncaring of our audience, I grasped the lapels of his black jacket and hauled him close. Sliding one hand to Alexander's jaw, I stroked the jagged line of his scar tenderly before leaning in to whisper teasingly against his lips, "And don't you forget it."

Our smiles connected in a playful kiss. It was short and sweet. But later, in our home—in our bed—I would take my time. I'd spend hours showing Alexander my love and devotion. I'd give him everything.

After all, he'd given me more than I'd ever expected. More of himself. More of a future. More than I'd ever dreamed.

About the Author

Laney Hatcher is a firm believer that there is a spreadsheet for every occasion and pie is always the answer. She is an author of stories that have a past, in a language of love that's universal. Often too practical for her own good, Laney enjoys her life in the southern United States with her husband, children, and incredibly entitled cat.

Find Laney Hatcher online:
Facebook: https://bit.ly/3s6KnuY
Newsletter: https://bit.ly/3sUGwAk
Amazon: https://amzn.to/3IaOwU7
Instagram: https://bit.ly/3s4IRcS
Website: https://laneyhatcher.com/
Goodreads: https://bit.ly/3BD0Gme
TikTok: https://www.tiktok.com/@laneyhatcherauthor

Find Smartypants Romance online:
Website: www.smartypantsromance.com
Facebook: https://www.facebook.com/smartypantsromance
Twitter: @smartypantsrom
Instagram: @smartypantsromance
Newsletter: https://smartypantsromance.com/newsletter/

Also by Laney Hatcher

Bartholomew Series

First to Fall: A Friends to Lovers Historical Romance

Second Chance Dance: An Enemies to Lovers Historical Romance

Third Degree Yearn: A Second Chance Historical Romance

Last on the List: A Grumpy Sunshine Historical Romance

Smartypants Romance

London Ladies Embroidery Series

Neanderthal Seeks Duchess: A Smartypants Romance Out of this World Title

Well Acquainted: A Smartypants Romance Out of this World Title

Love Matched: A Smartypants Romance Out of this World Title

Checking You Out by Ann Whynot (#10)

Architecture and Artistry by Nora Everly (#11)

Scorned Women's Society Series

My Bare Lady by Piper Sheldon (#1)

The Treble with Men by Piper Sheldon (#2)

The One That I Want by Piper Sheldon (#3)

Hopelessly Devoted by Piper Sheldon (#3.5)

It Takes a Woman by Piper Sheldon (#4)

Park Ranger Series

Happy Trail by Daisy Prescott (#1)

Stranger Ranger by Daisy Prescott (#2)

The Leffersbee Series

Been There Done That by Hope Ellis (#1)

Before and After You by Hope Ellis (#2)

The Higher Learning Series

Upsy Daisy by Chelsie Edwards (#1)

Green Valley Heroes Series

Forrest for the Trees by Kilby Blades (#1)

Parks and Provocation by Juliette Cross (#2)

Letter Late Than Never by Lauren Connolly (#3)

Story of Us Collection

My Story of Us: Zach by Chris Brinkley (#1)

My Story of Us: Thomas by Chris Brinkley (#2)

Seduction in the City

Cipher Security Series

Code of Conduct by April White (#1)

Code of Honor by April White (#2)